---- ★ ----

She didn't scream or struggle, feeling her husband's presence growing stronger and stronger. She said to him, "I can't breathe," and he responded, from a distance, with "Darling...darling...come to me."

When her life ended, her assailant gently removed the pillow from Meg's face and slipped it back under her head. Standing back to look at the fragile, lifeless form, pride rose like sap in the killer's veins, filled with an equally unmistakable sense of pleasure: The job was well done, the task had grown easier, the power of life and death was in the killer's hands. There was an incomparable thrill in performing the deed, and in being clever enough to remain undetectable. Easy.

---- ★ ----

"...cleverly plotted; Ransom and Charters make a great team."

—*Booklist*

"Hunter achieves a certain freshness with his material..."

—*Publishers Weekly*

Previously published Worldwide Mystery titles by
FRED HUNTER

RANSOM FOR AN ANGEL
RANSOM FOR OUR SINS

Forthcoming from Worldwide Mystery by

FRED HUNTER

RANSOM FOR A HOLIDAY
(in 'TIS THE SEASON FOR MURDER: Christmas Crimes)

FRED HUNTER
PRESENCE OF MIND

WORLDWIDE.

TORONTO • NEW YORK • LONDON
AMSTERDAM • PARIS • SYDNEY • HAMBURG
STOCKHOLM • ATHENS • TOKYO • MILAN
MADRID • WARSAW • BUDAPEST • AUCKLAND

If you purchased this book without a cover you should be aware that this book is stolen property. It was reported as "unsold and destroyed" to the publisher, and neither the author nor the publisher has received any payment for this "stripped book."

PRESENCE OF MIND

A Worldwide Mystery/August 1998

This edition published by arrangement with
Walker and Company.

ISBN 0-373-26282-5

Copyright © 1994 by Fred Hunter.
All rights reserved. No part of this book may be reproduced or transmitted in any form or by any means, electronic or mechanical, including photocopying, recording or by any information storage and retrieval system, without permission in writing from the publisher. For information, contact: Walker and Company, 435 Hudson Street, New York, NY 10014 U.S.A.

All characters in this book are fictitious, and any resemblance to actual persons, living or dead, is purely coincidental.

® and TM are trademarks of Harlequin Enterprises Limited. Trademarks indicated with ® are registered in the United States Patent and Trademark Office, the Canadian Trade Marks Office and in other countries.

Printed in U.S.A.

For Stann

ONE

HE KNEW HE was dead. That was the one thing he *did* know. In the brief moment of confusion that followed the sound of the shot, he tried to make sense of what had happened. But unlike all the stories he'd read in which the victim's life passes before his eyes, his reeling mind could find no point in his life that would have led him to this end. It didn't scan. He was nobody. He didn't see how you could link his name with *victim*. But the word kept ringing in his ears.

If in the moments before he died he could make no sense of his life, he could make even less sense of the incident itself. He had seen people shot a million times on television and in the movies, and it was always the same: The killer steps out of the darkness, the victim recognizes him, the shot rings out, the victim recoils, and then it's over. But there was no natural progression in this event. He couldn't separate the sight from the sound from the pain. He seemed to have felt the searing pain in his chest before he heard anything—practically before he saw his assailant. A smile flickered on his face through the pain—chicken or egg, chicken or egg—which came first?

He was on his knees now. It was cold. The cold seemed to be pouring into his chest, replacing the burning that had forced its way in there. Cold pouring in, heat pouring out. Heat. That was it. It was almost as if his life was heat, and it was draining out of his body. Another faint smile darted across his contorted features. How odd, he thought, to become a philosopher and humorist at the point of death.

His mind shifted again. Point of death. Did everyone know when they were at the point of death? Perhaps this is the one thing all humanity would have in common: No matter how they died they would know when they were at the point of death. But not like this.

Whatever strength was left in his legs gave way, and he slumped backward, his head hitting the pavement hard. He was sure it wouldn't be like this. He was sure that at the point of death, the rest of humanity would wonder why they'd lived, not why they'd died.

His head swam—thoughts—words—swimming—pools—pools of blood—a pool of blood was beside him. His blood. Through his filmy eyes, he could see a fly flitting over the pool of blood, then fly away, as if it could smell the death that had created this sticky mass of fluid. Thoughts—words came faster—jumble—like the incident: What was it? Sound—sight—recoil—recognition—sight—recoil—sound—recognition—recognition. No natural progression. There was no sight, no sound, and no recognition. That was it! That was the missing link! There was no recognition. He knew he was dead, and he didn't know his killer.

EMILY CHARTERS peeked out through the faded lace curtains that covered the window of her front door. It wasn't that she was timid, as one might expect in a woman exceeding seventy years; it was more from a dislike of wasted motion. At her time of life, she felt she should jealously guard her movements, as if she were saving them for the things she loved the most. Her movements were all small, but graceful, and her economy of motion lent to her appearance a certain aura of self-containment.

It had escaped her, however, that the daily ritual of peeking through the curtains was a wasted move: The newspaper was always laid on the porch long before she was ready for it—after she put on the teakettle and before it started to boil—but she hated the thought of going through the bother of opening the door for no reason at all. So she peeked. The paper was there, on schedule, as always. She opened the door and reached down to retrieve it. Oh dear, she thought. Even though he always placed the newspaper carefully on her tiny porch, the delivery boy never failed to spill parts of it here and there.

As she scooped up the paper, Emily couldn't help but think, as she did every morning, that the world would never be the same as it was when she was young—that the standard of excellence all over the world had slowly deteriorated as her life had dwindled, and that the paperboy was simply indicative of the deeper problem: Nobody cares about what they do. And she was sure that the standard for excellence was as irretrievable as the years that she had already lived.

Emily was fortunate, though, in that she was possessed of a gentle enough spirit that she could forgive the world its shortcomings. If the inhabitants of this world might fall short of perfect, they were infinitely preferable to those of the next, where she wasn't sure she would know anybody. Of course, many of her friends had gone before, but most of them had died long ago, and much as she loved them, the memory fades fast, at least for faces. She wasn't sure she'd recognize them if she saw them.

She closed the door behind her, tucked the newspaper under her frail arm, and headed for the kitchen, where the teakettle was just beginning to whistle. She laid the newspaper on her small wooden table and busied herself preparing her tea.

The kitchen itself was quite pleasant and sunny, despite the fact that the walls, once white, were now fading to a soft gray. No amount of paint could change the subtle dinginess of the walls. It was as if the tiny wood-frame house in which she'd lived for so many years was determined to fade out of this life right along with her. Emily didn't mind. She felt that at her age, walls that were too white and curtains that were too bright required too much work for her dusty blue eyes. And besides, it was rather comforting to feel her house growing old along with her. The house, like Emily, was neat and clean despite the graying and wrinkling.

Emily poured some tea into the blue china cup she had already placed on the table and emptied the used tea leaves into the dustbin. She settled down in the padded vinyl chair at the side of the table and slowly separated the food circulars from the rest of the newspaper. She carefully sipped her tea as she turned the pages of Section One, scanning the heading for anything that might interest her. On page five, there was a picture of a man beside the heading: *LAWYER FOUND DEAD*.

How odd, she thought. She recognized the man in the picture, although she was sure she didn't know him. She sat back in her chair, perplexed. The horrible trick of memory, she thought, was once more holding sway. She was sure she knew the man, and yet sure she didn't. She picked up the paper again and scanned the brief column, looking for his name. Lawrence Watson. She said it aloud, savoring the tones as the words left her and entered the empty kitchen. No, it didn't sound or feel like a name she had ever spoken before.

She turned and looked out the window. A cardinal had landed on the feeder that her husband had nailed up on the crooked tree in their backyard. The tree had been a healthy, strong, Y-shaped oak when he had placed the feeder there, but about twelve years ago, not even two whole years after he died, the tree was struck by lightning and the right branch of the Y was completely severed. The feeder remained unscathed, though slightly crooked, and no amount of effort seemed to be able to straighten it. The birds didn't seem to mind, though. A local boy stopped by once a week to pour a little seed into it for her.

But Emily didn't see the cardinal, or the feeder, or even the tree. She was traveling back through her memory. Lawrence Watson...Lawrence Watson. It rang no bells. Still, she could swear she'd seen him before.

Although it was common for her now to see notices of the deaths of those she knew, she felt she would never become completely accustomed to it. And the man in the picture, if she knew him, looked as if he were in his forties. Unless, of course, they had printed an old picture of him. They often do that, Emily told herself. It's as if the newspaper editors would occasionally find a little kindness hidden somewhere in their hearts and print a picture of the deceased that didn't make him look like he was dead when it was taken.

Emily read more carefully through the article. No, it wasn't kindness that accounted for the picture. Lawrence Watson was forty-five years old and had been found shot once through the heart, lying on the sidewalk a mere two hundred feet from the front door of his house on the northwest side of Chicago.

Emily clucked her tongue and said to herself, "So young, so young." She turned the page, dismissing the whole matter from her mind. She was fairly certain that once she was thinking of something else, she would remember exactly how she knew Lawrence Watson.

She glanced down at one of the food circulars she had set aside. Eggs were on sale, sixty-seven cents a dozen at the market down the street. She smiled, remembering all she'd read about how eggs would clog the veins in your heart and cause you to die. Sixty-seven cents! Death comes cheap, she thought.

DAMIEN LIDDLE had chosen his name with great care. He had wanted something that sounded British but could be easily pronounced by most Americans. It was memorable, eminently lyrical, and the few lowly people who would not be able to pronounce it at first glance were not worth his attention.

This affectation (though he would be loathe to call it that) was indicative of the lofty ideals he held for himself. There would be no movie stardom for Damien Liddle. He would confine his career to the stage, and at that, only the classics. And if one day he did get lured onto the screen, where was the shame in that? Olivier had done it. If he were to inherit the mantle of Olivier, could he in good conscience toss it aside? He thought not. Besides, he could always use his inflated salary to fund a Shakespearean theater. That was his dream, to bring the classics to the masses. His status as a movie star—not that he wanted to be one—would draw people to the theater who had never before experienced Shakespeare, Shaw, or Molière—and his command of the language would open their minds to even the most difficult passages.

At the moment, he didn't need to worry about how stardom would affect his standing as a serious actor. His main worry was how to keep his storefront theatre afloat. He had joined with some of his friends from acting class to form the Pennington Players (another name he found vaguely British, and therefore dignified). They had longed to prove that you didn't need large budgets and glamorous buildings to present exceptional theater. The great playwrights and great actors could stand on their own merit, without elaborate sets and costumes. They firmly believed that they should rely on fine acting, raw talent. And *that* they had. There were enough angry young men and women in Chicago to make up a hundred acting companies, and all of them wanted to form theaters. The Pennington Players felt they were unique in that they were not only talented but had the guts to band together to do something about it. They would prove themselves before audiences and critics alike.

Unfortunately, all they had proven so far was that the theater is a dying art. Their storefront was sadly located on the far north side of Chicago, miles and miles away from anything that could be called a theater district, and there was no parking once you got there. In a city with movie theaters on every corner and a VCR in every home, most of the locals shrank from doing anything bordering on inconvenient. And compounding the problems of their location was the little building itself. Since it was literally a store and not a theater, it had only one bathroom, and the Pennington Players had seen to it that it was strategically located backstage for the convenience of the actors—to the consternation of the audience. The bathroom facilities probably cost them more audience members than any other factor.

Also unfortunately for their eager band of players, the world simply had not been waiting for them. In the two years of their struggling existence, the Pennington Players had failed to become the media darlings they had hoped to be, and so had failed to set the world on fire. Even friends and families of the actors, the usual source of support of a newborn theater, had tired of the whole project.

"You know you are losing," Damien had often said, "when even your mother won't come to see your play."

But as with most other smaller theater companies, the biggest problem was the actors themselves. Although all of them had been gung-ho on the project at first, many lost interest as they realized that there was more to running a theater than appearing on the stage. All of them were interested in starring in the plays, but few were interested in doing the tedious backstage work, or cleaning the solitary bathroom, or even helping in the box office. "Box office" was, of course, a term they used very loosely. It was little more than a painted plywood booth they had set up in the lobby. A booth, phone, answering machine, and the proverbial cigar box in which their non-existent proceeds were kept. All of the work had fallen to Damien, and to Gail Shelly. Gail was a rather dowdy young woman who became involved with the company not through any interest in great drama but because she basically had nothing else to do.

It was because of the poverty of their company that Damien was so surprised when he received the call that it had been broken into...at least, he seemed surprised on his way there. He wasn't exactly sure yet if, under the circumstances, his response should be one of shock or simply resignation. It was Gail who called him with the news, and Damien was not unamused by how upset she'd sounded: as if the fate of their theater mattered anymore.

"This is all we need," she had said. "I mean, we don't have anything! It must have been pure vandalism! Why would vandals have anything against us?"

"They probably didn't," he had said, trying to calm her down, "they probably just hit us at random."

He realized even as he said it how hollow the words sounded. It wasn't the personal angle that was so frightening about being vandalized; it was the idea of being violated at all.

Damien chuckled to himself at the thought of Gail walking into the theater, alone, to find it broken into. He could hear the quick intake of breath as she realized everything was not as it should be. He could imagine the shocked look on her plain face as the full weight of the act sank in. She was such an idiotic creature, he thought, albeit under the circumstances, a necessary one. With so much work to be done around the place and so few people willing to help, it was a great aid to have someone who would do any form of work just to be around people. He wondered at what an untapped asset lonely people are. Gail was less than nothing to look at, she talked a bit too much, and she spent a great deal of her time apologizing for things when you didn't know what she was talking about. But she didn't have anything else to do, so she worked. She did a lot of work.

Although Damien hated to admit it, Gail was a necessary evil. He didn't think their theater would have lasted this long if it hadn't been for Gail doing the sweeping and cleaning, finding props, and tracking down costumes, usually bartering to get them for free in return for a terse acknowledgment in the program. With nothing but time on her hands, Gail was the perfect lackey for him. In fact, it was because of her officiousness that they had found out about the break-in so soon. The last performance of their latest travesty, a rather unhappy production of *Love's Labor's Lost*, had been on Saturday. Ordinarily they would have had a performance on Sunday afternoon, but it had been canceled, as so many others before, due to a lack of interest on the part of the public. Usually their next performance would be the following Thursday, but in this case even that was denied them. With only six tickets sold for their last performance, and no calls for tickets to any other performances, they had decided to cancel the rest of their run.

They really had no reason to ever return to the theater, an idea to which Damien had given some serious consideration. Perhaps the rigors of trying to run the thing for so long were finally getting to him. Seeing his dream for the theater slowly eaten away by reality had caused a decided lowering of his standards. He had taken to flying out to Los Angeles when he would scrape enough money together to audition for films and—he choked when he thought of it—television. And producers seemed to be finally taking an interest in him, especially for television. There was a very real possibility that he was about to be hired for a prospective series. Perhaps the break-in was an omen. Perhaps the gods were trying to tell him that creature comforts might be more important than lofty ideals, which do not pay rent or put food on the table. Whatever it was, each night when he left the theater, he had to fight harder and harder the feeling that it would be a relief—a tremendous relief—to keep going—out to the airport, onto the plane, out farther and farther to a new world. A new life. Indeed, there was no reason to return to their little theater at all.

But then, of course, there was Gail, who like clockwork showed up at their storefront headquarters immediately after work at her day job on Tuesday, Monday being the only day she would take off, to find the place ransacked. As Damien hopped off the bus and walked the half-block back to the theater, he felt almost sorry for Gail. Pity was an emotion he usually reserved for himself. He half wished he had been the one to discover the break-in, or at least that he had been with her when she did. But it was probably better that he hadn't. He wasn't unaware that Gail had something of a crush on him. She was the type of lonely person who found it impossible to hide that sort of thing. It was manageable under the best of circumstances but would probably be harder to deal with if he was in the position of having her cry on his shoulder. He was not at all that comfortable about being alone with her at all, a situation in which he found himself often enough, without a scene.

He reached the door of the storefront, twisted the rusted handle, and walked in. There was Gail, her face red from crying, quietly setting chairs straight. The folding chairs they used for the audience were thrown everywhere, the bits of scenery—what little there was of it—torn down, and the makeshift box office totally demolished.

"Damien! There you are! Thank God you're here!" cried Gail as she reached for his hand.

He took her hand carefully, applying just the right amount of pressure to express sympathy but not to imply anything personal.

"You shouldn't take it so hard," he said. "So somebody trashed the place. It's not like we had anything!"

"But the idea of someone being in our theater," she whimpered, placing careful stress on the word *our*. "And they—whoever they were—they did take something."

"What? We don't have anything."

"They took the answering machine!"

She gestured to the wreck of the box office, and Damien bent down and carefully moved some of the bigger pieces. She was right. The phone was still there, but the answering machine that acted as their box office help was gone. The machine was old and had been donated by a former company member who had moved to the coast. But it still worked and was vital to the life of their theater. Since all of the members had to work during the day, it functioned as their reservations clerk. The loss of the machine meant their box office staff was gone.

"I mean, it's like things aren't bad enough, now people won't even be able to make reservations!"

"It'll be all right," said Damien, halfheartedly.

"Why did this have to happen?"

Damien stood up slowly, his eyes fixed on the remains of the booth.

"Damn."

TWO

JEREMY RANSOM'S DEVOTION to detection could be called a matter of mind over money. He had come to prefer exercising his mind to the higher wages that a promotion to sergeant, lieutenant, or captain would bring. He firmly believed that the only real fun in police work was finding out who the bad guys were, and the only place you got to do that was as a detective. Oh yes, he might grumble on occasion about not being able to afford new shoes, or an extra suit, or a week in the Bahamas (like some people he knew), but he knew it beat the hell out of walking a beat or being an overpaid desk clerk.

There were some other advantages as well. He was able to work pretty much on his own, save for Gerald, his latest partner, and Gerald was basically harmless, as well as being very helpful with legwork and all of the attendant difficulties in any case that Ransom didn't particularly like to deal with. Gerald was, in fact, the best partner that Ransom had ever had: there when needed, but just as content to sit back and leave Ransom to the workings of his mind. He was much better than the usual sort with whom Ransom was teamed. Ransom had come to dread the prospect of each new partner, as the last invariably took the test for sergeant and moved up. Most were overanxious twits who inevitably got in his way rather than helped.

But for Ransom the biggest advantage to remaining a detective was that over the ten years he had been in the department he had built up something of a reputation. He was known to be able to solve cases that might be called unsolvable, as when somebody died who shouldn't have. So, many of the more interesting cases came his way. Ransom himself was fond of saying, "Those in authority know that if they put me on a case, they may be fairly certain it will be solved."

Of course, like any other loner, especially one with his sometimes startling straightforwardness, he had also earned the reputation of being something of an egotist. Gerald had asked him more than once why he was always so sure he'd be able to track down a killer, and his answer was always the same:

"Because I have presence of mind, and they don't. I retain my presence of mind because I tell the truth. Murder you see, is like lying. Once you've done it, you're stuck with it. Obviously, unless you want to get caught, you can't tell the truth about it, you have to lie. And you have to remember the lie—the first one, and then all the attendant lies. After a while, it's like you're trying to hold on to a dozen strands of cord that've all been greased. Pretty soon, something's got to slip. I don't have to hold on to anything. I tell the truth. Anybody could see that gives me a definite edge."

Gerald wasn't sure that he agreed, but he was pragmatic. You simply cannot argue with success, and Ransom was, if nothing else, successful. He knew that Ransom had solved cases that had been lost causes, presumably through a combination of dexterity and luck. So Gerald and everyone else in the department would allow him to occasionally pat himself on the back.

It was because of his propensity for solving hopeless cases that the Lawrence Watson killing was sent his way.

"I've got the preliminary report here," said Gerald, pulling a chair up beside Ransom's desk.

"Let's have it."

"Lawrence Watson," Gerald read, trying to decipher the words amid the typos, "forty-five, married, no children. Partner in the law firm of Danners, Herald and Watson."

"What are the circumstances?"

"He was on his way home from work, supposedly."

"Supposedly?"

"He worked late last night."

"Ahhhh."

"He was shot once, through the heart, on the sidewalk just outside his house."

"Any witnesses?"

"Of course not."

"Any enemies?"

"Not according to the wife."

"Any friends?"

"Perhaps—according to the wife."

Ransom smiled and tapped the ashes off the end of his plastic-tipped cigar. "The wife sounds like a font of information. Perhaps we should start with her."

"Right."

ALTHOUGH HE KNEW it was detrimental to his work, Ransom could not keep himself from forming instant likes and dislikes for people he was forced to interview. He excused it by telling himself that it was a human frailty to which we are all subject, but he still wished he could be more like the detectives in the novels who could stay cool and objective, no matter what first impression a suspect gave. He could also excuse this tendency by reminding himself that his first impressions were seldom wrong.

He formed his impression of Marian Watson the moment she opened the door. She was a tight woman. Everything about her was tight. Her painfully pulled-back hair, her sallow cheeks, and the pointedness of her features all lent to the impression that if she were pulled any tighter, a hidden seam in her skin would rip. Ransom didn't like her.

"I talked to the police already," she said sharply as she led them into her living room.

"We understand that, ma'am," said Ransom as he took a seat, "but I thought I'd like to talk to you myself."

"Why?"

"Well, because your husband doesn't seem to be the sort of man who would go around getting himself killed."

"Is anyone that type of person?" Marian asked, crossing her legs as if to close herself up even tighter.

"Frankly, yes," said Ransom. "Generally they're people who are doing something they shouldn't."

"Really."

"That's why we detectives are…fairly good…at tracking down the murderers. We find out what the victim was up to, who he was up to it with, and generally that leads us to the killer." He paused for a moment to see if she would respond. She didn't.

"Was your husband doing anything he shouldn't?"

Marian smiled disdainfully. "Not that he'd get killed for."

"Hmmm?"

"I think murder is a rather excessive response to just about any situation, don't you?"

Ransom finally smiled at her and shot a brief glance at Gerald, who was quietly taking notes.

"Was yours a happy marriage, Mrs. Watson?"

The smile remained frozen on Marian's face, and she exhaled sharply before speaking. "It depends on what you mean by happy, doesn't it? For my husband and me, happiness could probably be defined as the absence of unhappiness. We were comfortable together, and we always made ourselves available for each other's business dinners. There was never any open tension. Never any arguments. Never much of anything, really."

"Well," he said after a brief pause, surprised that this tight woman would release so much information so quickly, "I suppose the next question I should ask is, do you know of anybody who would want to kill him?"

"Lawrence? Mr. Ransom, my husband was innocuous at best. I can't think of anybody that would care enough to kill him."

Ransom considered her quietly for a moment. Gerald paused in his note taking and shifted his glance from Marian to Ransom. Despite his dislike for her, Ransom couldn't help a small bit of admiration. Surely she must realize, he thought, that such open hostility toward her husband would mark her as a prime suspect.

"Mrs. Watson," he said, breaking the silence, "was your husband doing anything that he shouldn't have been doing...that *wasn't* worth killing him for?"

"He was having an affair, if that's what you mean." Ransom wondered how she perpetually sounded as if she was exhaling when he could not detect her inhaling at all.

"Really?" he said, not changing his expression. "And would you happen to know who the woman was?"

"I really don't know."

"Then how do you know it was happening?"

"I suppose I had to read all the classic signs, Mr. Ransom. He was always either working late, or staying out late, or whatever. Whatever he was doing, he wasn't here, that's all I know. It was very unusual to find him at home."

"What did he tell you he was doing?"

Marian shot him an angry glance. Then, trying unsuccessfully to keep her voice level, she spat back at him: "He told me he went to the movies!"

"WELL GERALD," said Ransom as they climbed back into the car, "what do you think of our Mrs. Watson?"

"I should think Mr. Watson is much happier now."

"Perhaps."

"What did you think of her?"

"I think she's entirely too honest for her own good. The anger she's so obviously displaying toward her husband may just be the usual anger that so many people feel for a loved one who's just died—but I don't think so. She seems quite hostile toward him."

"But do you think she killed her husband?"

Ransom fingered the window control absently as he considered the question, his mind playing back his impressions of Marian Watson. Despite himself, he focused on the moves and gestures she had made, the tightness of her features, and the tone of her voice: all things that, taken together, reinforced his first impression of her. He sighed, in slight disgust at the woman herself and with even more profound disgust at his inability to shake his first idea of her and give her the benefit of the doubt.

"No," he said finally, "I think she would get more pleasure out of keeping him alive and torturing him."

Gerald smiled at this, as he turned the key in the ignition. He knew better than to point out to his partner that perhaps he had not been able to size up the whole woman in the brief space of time they had been together.

"Where to next?"

"Well...if he was really having an affair, who would it be with?"

"If he was as boring as his wife seems to think, his secretary."

"Righto, Gerald—off to the office!"

THE LAW FIRM of Danners, Herald and Watson was located in a building not more than two years old in the middle of downtown Chicago. As they pulled into a space near the building, Ransom once again thought to himself that one of the things he liked most about being on the police force was the privilege of parking anywhere he liked.

The offices were of the sort that Ransom found particularly offensive. The entire building was austere to the point that it was difficult to imagine any living organism surviving within it. They took one of the silent glass elevators up to the fifth floor. The elevator door opened onto a hallway that Ransom imagined was like all the others in the building: cream-colored walls and light maroon pseudo-Oriental carpeting. Directly to the right of the bank of elevators was the glass wall that fronted the law firm, with Danners, Herald and Watson embossed in gold letters just to the left of the door.

Through the door they could see the receptionist, a carbon copy of receptionists throughout the building, possibly the world. She was blue-eyed, slender, and impeccably dressed. Even Gerald could not help noticing that her hair was perfect, not a strand out of place. She looked as if instead of stopping at a coffee shop on her way to work she had a daily appointment with her hairdresser for a touch-up. On her immaculate desk was a medium-sized wooden plaque that read "Sarah Bower."

Gerald, slightly intimidated by the person and the place, paused after they passed through the door to make sure it would close noiselessly, as if the slightest sound from human movement would upset the balance of this environment.

"Miss...uh, Bower," said Ransom with a glance at the plaque, "Detective Ransom."

"Ah, yes," she said, without blinking. Miss Bower picked up the receiver on her phone and pressed a button. "Mr. Danners? A Detective Ransom to see you."

Ransom stifled a laugh at being referred to as "a Detective Ransom," as if he were a specimen of some sort. Miss Bower smiled and returned the receiver to its cradle without saying another word to the party on the other end.

"Go right in, Mr. Ransom. To the right, the door at the end of the hall."

"Yes, thank you."

Gerald moved to follow him, but Ransom stopped him, as if in afterthought. "No, Gerald—I think I'd better talk to him alone. Why don't you wait out here?" He glanced at Miss Bower over his shoulder. "That would be all right, wouldn't it?"

"Of course," she said, motioning to a chair.

Gerald watched Ransom walk away, hoping for some indication of what he was to do. As he passed the reception desk, Ransom glanced briefly at Miss Bower.

Right, thought Gerald.

Ransom followed the directions to a heavy wooden door at the end of the hallway. The door bore Virgil Danners's name in raised metal letters. Ransom plunged into the room without knocking. He knew that Danners had been told he was there, but he still liked to keep his interviewees slightly on the defensive.

Virgil Danners sat behind an enormous, heavy oak desk that couldn't disguise the size of the man himself. Though he tried to hide it Ransom was taken aback by the overwhelming girth of the man sitting before him. Danners's face gave the impression of being random features floating in pudding, and Ransom couldn't help but notice that when the lawyer rose to greet him, his body seemed to ooze instead of move in a particular direction. He was almost surprised that Danners could successfully navigate his hand to reach Ransom's on the first try. He wondered if trial juries could overcome the faint repulsion that he felt at the sight of this amorphous lawyer. He gripped with reluctance the huge hand with its stumplike fingers and shook it. It seemed as if ripples went through Danners's body like shock waves from the simple handshake.

"Shocking business, eh?" said Danners, motioning Ransom to the overstuffed chair at the side of the desk. "People get shot down in the streets all the time, don't they? But you don't expect it to happen to someone you know."

"Tell me, Mr. Danners, what kind of law do you practice here?"

"Corporate law."

"Ah. You never handle any criminal cases?"

"It all depends on what you mean by criminal, doesn't it?" Like an obscene Claymation figure, Danners's mouth molded itself into an unpleasant smile. At least Ransom supposed it was a smile. It was a sorry thing that looked as if the corners of his mouth were straining under the pressure to push up his fleshy cheeks. Ransom imagined that this joke and this smile had been repeated endlessly in the bar at the base of the building. "Why do you ask?"

"Well..."

"Oh, yes, of course, I see. You wondered if any of our clients would be prime suspects, eh? Want to know if anyone has an ax to grind?"

"Well, given your profession, if you were involved in criminal cases at all, there is the likelihood that someone you've put away might be unhappy."

"Yes, well, no—we only handle mergers and things

like that. The corporate world, Mr. Ransom, is sort of like countless little kingdoms, all going after parcels, small or large, of each other's land. They don't generally kill if they lose anything, they just go away with what's left of their troops, regroup, and live to fight another day. There's always another kingdom to conquer."

The phone on Danners's desk buzzed, and he answered it after a brief pause. While Danners held his conversation, Ransom used the time to consider him. A large unpleasant man with a small unpleasant mind, he thought. Although he had to admit that the idea of the kingdoms at war was not an inaccurate one. Ransom could imagine the battle taking place while this vulgar potentate sat behind his desk, happily manipulating the players, most likely with little concern about who won, only concerned with the game.

"Thank you," said Danners, hanging up the phone. He turned back to Ransom. "Sorry for the interruption. Now, where were we?"

Ransom was unruffled, since the interruption had given him a little time to think.

"So, you don't know of anyone who would want to kill Mr. Watson."

"Larry? No. So you think he was actually murdered?"

"He's dead," replied Ransom, not quite understanding Danners's statement.

"Well, I know that. It's just, I took it for granted that it was—what do you call it—he was an innocent bystander."

"A street killing."

"Right, a street killing. I can't imagine anyone wanting to kill Larry. I figured he was just in the wrong place at the wrong time."

"It's possible," said Ransom, without changing expression, "but we do have to take into account all possibilities."

"I understand," said Danners, once again forming his unpleasant smile. Ransom got the uncomfortable feeling that Danners meant this smile to imply that there was some sort of understanding between them.

"Tell me," said Ransom, "do you know much about Mr. Watson's personal life?"

The smile almost immediately left Danners's bloated face. "Oh, no, not really. Things here aren't like they are on TV, you know. We usually, I should say *I* usually make it a point to stay out of the lives of the others here."

No doubt, thought Ransom, it was easy for him to do so. He couldn't imagine anyone particularly wanting this man prying into their lives.

"But surely, you've been working together for quite some time. You would be bound to know something of his private life."

"Of course, one does pick up the odd bit of information here and there."

Like an old lady, thought Ransom. He had in his mind an amusing picture of Danners lurking about a watercooler, voraciously picking up the office gossip from the secretaries. He purposely shook his head, ridding himself of the thoughts that were keeping him from concentrating on what Danners was saying.

"I got the impression that he wasn't happy at home, or at least that his home was not happy, if you know what I mean."

"I think I have some idea."

"Ah, good. I hate to spread idle chatter, especially under the circumstances."

"I understand that."

"Of course, Larry didn't really hang around after hours,

or anything of that sort. He rarely stopped for a drink after work."

"He didn't?" said Ransom curiously. "I was under the impression that he often worked late."

"He didn't do it here."

Something like a leer managed to spread across Danners's pudgy face. Ransom was finding it increasingly hard to control his repulsion for this mass of a man and decided to draw this interview to a close as quickly as possible.

"You have no idea what he might have been doing?"

"Hmmm. I'm a lawyer, Mr. Ransom, I wouldn't speculate on that type of thing without evidence." But the attempted sparkle in his eye told Ransom that Danners clearly thought there was another woman, and probably was quite jealous about it, and he wanted Ransom to know it. Ransom gave him a nod, indicating that he understood, and with a great deal of relief rose to leave. On his way out the door, he paused and said, "Did Mr. Watson have a secretary?"

"We share a secretary," said Danners, his leer becoming more pronounced. "Miss Bower can introduce you to her."

"Thank you," he said. As he passed through the door, he glanced back at Danners, who was oozing back into his seat behind the desk.

"GLORIA DIDN'T COME in today, Mr. Ransom."

"Really? Is that unusual for her?"

"I would say so," replied Miss Bower, her professional smile still frozen into place. "She is quite reliable and she rarely misses a day."

"Did she call in?"

"Of course. She said she was ill."

"*Said* she was ill? Didn't you believe her?"

For the first time, Miss Bower's face registered surprise, and Ransom silently congratulated himself for this achievement.

"Of course I believed her. What a strange question."

"I'm very sorry," said Ransom, trying to mask his pleasure. "I assure you I didn't mean anything by it."

"That's all right." She looked him over for a moment, almost as if now that her defenses had been momentarily let down, she was as free to size him up as he was her. Like Ransom, she was quick to form impressions. She took Ransom for a man who could be trusted, and a man with a sense of irony.

"To be quite honest," she said, leaning toward him with an air of uncharacteristic confidentiality, "I think she was more shaken up by Mr. Watson's death than the rest of us."

"For a particular reason?"

"Yes, Mr. Ransom. She has a heart!"

"DID YOU GET anything out of her?"

Gerald heaved a heavy sigh. "All attempts to engage her in polite conversation netted me no more than a cup of coffee. You got more out of her in two minutes than I did in all the time you were gone."

Ransom smiled at his partner. "Don't worry about it. She seems like a pretty shrewd young woman. I imagine the only reason I was able to catch her off guard was because her guard was up for you."

"I guess it worked out, one way or the other."

"Yes," said Ransom, slipping the piece of paper on which Miss Bower had written Gloria Forsyth's address into his coat pocket. He pushed the car lighter into the dashboard and pulled another plastic-tipped cigar out of his pocket.

"The only thing I *did* find out was that the third partner, Mr. Herald, is vacationing with his wife in the Bahamas."

"The Bahamas," said Ransom with an envious sigh.

"Yes. He is, therefore, unavailable for comment. He was also unavailable for murder."

"I really dislike people with alibis like that," Ransom said, drumming his fingers on the armrest.

"What was Danners like?"

"A truly grotesque person. I'm hoping he had nothing to do with the murder so I don't have to see him again."

"He have any ideas?"

"He thinks Watson was just in the wrong place at the wrong time."

"A reasonable assumption."

"I hate to disagree with you, Gerald, but I think it's an entirely unreasonable assumption." The lighter popped out, and Ransom lit the cigar.

Gerald smiled to himself at this statement. He knew all too well that Ransom didn't at all mind disagreeing with him or with anyone else, for that matter. "Why do you say that?"

"Because he was shot not more than two hundred feet from his house as he arrived home. What does that suggest to you?"

"That someone was waiting for him."

"Quite right. I would say he was in exactly the right place at the right time."

"What did you think of Miss Bower?"

"Too efficient. A bit too streamlined to be real."

"It looks like his wife might have been right about him having an affair, though."

Ransom smiled. "You mean you were right, eh, Gerald? If it was an affair, it was with his secretary."

"So it would seem. Do you find something wrong with the boss-secretary scenario?"

"Yes," said Ransom, exhaling a steady stream of smoke through the open car window. "From what I've heard of him so far, I think that Watson was too boring even for that."

"So where to now? You want to question the Forsyth woman?"

Ransom thought for a moment and took another puff of his cigar. "No, I think we'll leave her for tomorrow. Why don't you drop me off back near Watson's house. I think I'll start questioning a few of the neighbors—see if maybe they know or heard anything."

"Drop you off? You don't want me to go with you?"

"No, I have something else I'd like you to do." He sighed and looked out the window. "I don't like it, not at all."

"What?" Although Gerald was used to his partner's tendency to wander off on his own track, he still found it frustrating when it happened in the middle of being given instructions.

"What *if* Watson was having an affair with her? What does it matter? Who would have killed him? The jealous wife, the jealous mistress? Do people really kill over something like that anymore? I don't really think they do, at least not as often as the possibility would allow. But if that's the obvious motive and I don't believe it, then we have to look for a less obvious motive. That's what I want you to do."

"Financial statement time," said Gerald, rolling his eyes.

"Yes. The law firm, Watson's personal finances, everything. Perhaps a look into their finances will put the gun in someone's hand!"

JEREMY RANSOM was older than he ought to be. At least, that was the way he felt. As he inserted the key into the lock on the door of his studio apartment, he thought with a smile that he knew he was getting older the first time he found he could no longer juggle packages and open the door at the same time. To him, having to set things down to get his keys out was a sign of age.

He went into his darkened apartment, flipping the light switch next to the door with his left elbow. He slipped his keys back into his right-hand pants pocket, reminding himself, as he did every time he came home, that if he put his keys anywhere besides his pocket, he'd forget where they were.

He wearily removed his jacket and tie, tossed them over the back of a chair where his ties from the last two days still hung, and went into the bathroom. He switched on the overhead light and looked at himself in the mirror. He sighed with displeasure at his unruly dark blond hair. He greatly disliked anything that could be termed "fussing with himself" but equally disliked the fact that his hair was consistently out of place. He was content to shower and shave quickly in the morning and run a comb through his hair, but it was a constant source of irritation that his hair was blown out of place every day the moment he went out into the world, and was irreparable after that. He found it vaguely annoying that the precision that he brought to his work could not be applied to his personal appearance.

He splashed some warm water on his face and rubbed his eyes. After patting his face dry with a cloth, he scrutinized himself more closely. Although he was only thirty-seven years old, he felt he was aging faster then he should be. The area under his eyes was softer and puffier than it once was, and his blue-gray eyes now had a tendency to be streaked with red. To add to the picture, crow's-feet seemed to be growing steadily back all the way to his ears. Excessive smiling, he'd been told. Ah well, there was no way to stop the passage of time, but all the same, he was conscious of passing through a particularly difficult period of life, seeing the signs of age while retaining the appearance of youth. It was the first time he actually began to realize that his countenance would alter as time went on, and although he was by no means old, the days of his youth were over.

Oh well, he thought, it was always like this when he started a new case: He transferred the insecurity he felt over his ability to solve a case to his person as a whole. He really had no reason for insecurity about his ability, given his record, but whenever he was set on a new case, he instantly felt like a child encountering a puzzle in which all information was square pegs and round holes.

He sighed heavily and turned on the water in the bathtub. He stripped off his clothes, letting them drop to the floor, and went into his living room to retrieve a copy of *Bleak House* that he had left on the floor by his bed. The bathtub was now full, and he shut off the faucet, climbed into the tub, and lowered himself gently into the water. Before opening the book, he reached down into the pocket of his shirt that had fallen beside the tub and pulled out a cigar and book of matches. He lit the cigar and carelessly tossed the matches on the floor.

This, he thought, was the meaning of life: calm, serene, enveloped in the deliciously hot water. He slid farther down into the tub, took a long drag from the cigar, and exhaled slowly, the cares of the day dissolving away into the air along with the smoke. He opened the book to the page at which his bookmark was inserted and began to read, content for the evening.

THREE

IT IS DIFFICULT to understand the complexity of the human mind, which is so attuned to its environment as to notice any minute disturbance, and will, at the same time, dismiss the disturbance as pure imagination. Barbara Landis had such a mind. She had rented the same apartment for five years, and in her mind she could trace every line and angle of floor and wall, which boards would creak when stepped on and which would not, and the precise sound the door made when it closed and latched behind her. It was probably true, she thought, that anyone who had lived in a particular place long enough could almost tell by sound if something needed to be repaired. So it was that night when, struggling with her groceries and her keys, she put the key in the door and it felt slightly different. It seemed to open with more ease than usual. As it closed behind her, she noted the barest additional sound of metal against metal, signaling to her that the lock, indeed, must be wearing away and would bear some looking into.

But it was when she was actually inside her apartment that the real change overcame her. Perhaps it is simply through the Power of Place that a home, whether an apartment or a house, will become so familiar that any change is noticeable to its inhabitants. Perhaps it is tiny ripples in the air, or heat that wasn't there before, or perhaps it's just that a home, being at one with its owner, cannot help but betray the presence of an intruder. Barbara knew there was someone in her apartment.

And yet, she dismissed the thought as mere fancy.

Nothing was out of place, nothing had been stolen, and nobody confronted her. Her eyes darted furtively around the room, as if she half expected the lines and angles of the floors and walls to somehow not meet as neatly as they always had, but all was as it should be.

She continued into her apartment and went through to the kitchen, trying to shake the feeling of insecurity. She placed the grocery bags on the kitchen table along with her purse and with some difficulty slipped her jacket off, draping it temporarily over the back of one of the kitchen chairs. She smiled to herself when she realized that she had difficulty in removing her jacket because she was still clutching her keys tightly in her hand, as if having them there would aid her in making a hasty departure if necessary. She put the keys in her purse and snapped it shut.

She paused for a moment and felt the air around the room, wondering if the shimmering vibrations were from the presence of an intruder or from the accelerated beating of her heart. She shook her head, as if making her own vibrations would dispel any that were foreign to the place, and smiled to herself. She knew she would have to go around the apartment as soon as she finished putting the groceries away and check her bedroom (under the bed, of course), the closets, and the bathroom. She almost laughed out loud at the thought of this, knowing that she actually would do it and believing wholeheartedly that it was a foolish gesture at the same time.

But she refrained from laughing out loud. She had the feeling that even her own laugh would be out of place in the oddly vibrating air of her apartment at this moment. She shook her head again, dismissing the dismal thought, and brushed the stray strands of her long brown hair out of her face. It was time, she thought, to quit imagining things and get to the business at hand.

She pulled a half-gallon carton of skimmed milk and two small packages of cheese from one of the bags, and with her hands full, awkwardly pulled open the refrigerator door. As she leaned forward to place them on one of the shelves, a strange, muscular hand slipped over her mouth. She gasped, but there was no sound. Her mind raced. The hand pulled her back into an upright position, and she felt something cold and very sharp against her neck.

Thoughts sped through her mind as if her ability to think had been severed from her ability to control thought. She closed her eyes, hoping that shutting out light might imprison her thoughts, but all she could see was a cyclone of disconnected words whirling through a blank void. Then one word flung itself out of the tumult, emblazoning itself across her as if it were the title on a movie screen: *startled*. That was it, she thought, her mind beginning to slow. She had been startled, but not surprised. She knew—her home itself had tried to tell her—that there was an intruder. Taking this for fact, she had known someone was there. The hand over her mouth, therefore, had startled her, much as she would have been if a child had playfully jumped out from behind the bushes and yelled "boo!" Being able to put this word to her reaction somehow lessened her increasing panic.

The hand over her mouth, then, should have been expected. Barbara felt herself beginning to relax, still frightened but somehow feeling that the muscular hand and the warmth of the body pressed up against her back somehow belonged there, since the presence had been announced. Had she been capable of rational thought, she would have realized that this sensation of relaxing and familiarity were the result of the blood rushing from her head to her toes, leaving her only semi-conscious.

The hand, the body, didn't say a word. The cold sharpness she felt at her neck sank into her flesh, her blood flowing over the tiny gold chain she had so carefully selected early that morning. As she sank to the floor, she could feel her mind being released from her body, mingling with the vibrations that had been the sound of her voice and the movement of her hair when she shook her head. She wondered if some time in the future someone else would come into this apartment and notice that she was vibrating in the air around them.

The assailant stood over the now lifeless form of Barbara Landis, experiencing a surprising sense of uncertainty. Though unaware of the vibrations in the air, the killer *was* aware of an emotion not usually associated with the handiwork lying on the kitchen floor: It was pride.

"STOP! STOP! Go away from there!" Emily called out the back door of her little house. Cyril, the bronze tabby, paid little attention to her, pausing only briefly to give her a displeased glance, and then going back to the matter at hand, dancing around the bottom of the twisted oak, trying to get a poor sparrow who had stopped to feed. Cyril was a harmless animal, though. Emily had had him declawed years ago in deference to the brocaded upholstery on her furniture, so there was no chance of him climbing the tree to get at the birds. But she saw no reason why he should be allowed to worry the poor creatures.

Worried. That is what Emily was at the moment. That is why she had called so crossly to her little cat. She had been worried since seeing this morning's paper and the picture of a young woman who had been killed in her own apartment. Emily was not worried about the girl or about her own safety. She was not even worried about the state of a world in which people are killed so easily, although one might expect a woman of her character to do so. No, Emily was beginning to worry about her mind, in particular, her memory.

The girl in the picture was another supposed stranger who looked all too familiar to Emily, and the fact that, like the man of a couple of days earlier, this woman looked familiar and unfamiliar at the same time was causing Emily to seriously doubt her faculties. She was beginning to believe there was one thing or another wrong with her mind: Either she was losing her memory—perhaps she had one of those diseases she had read so much about and seen in television movies—and she was beginning to lose people much as one might lose a stray sock in the laundry, or her thinking was scrambling in an even more insidious way, and she would no longer be able to distinguish those she knew from those she didn't. Soon, she feared, everyone would look vaguely familiar. She couldn't even find comfort by reminding herself that having lived so long and seen so many people, everyone *was* bound to look alike. Whatever might be happening to her memory, Emily was worried.

Cyril had now lost interest in the sparrow and was darting back and forth across the lawn, trying to capture a particularly elusive butterfly. Butterflies, thought Emily, must have very sharp minds. They seem to play with cats, dipping down low enough to interest them, the flitting just slightly out of reach of them, as if their intent was to frustrate the felines, playing with cats much in the same way that cats will, in turn, play with cornered mice. The game goes on until one day, Emily thought ruefully, the poor butterfly starts to lose its faculties and can't get out of the way as quickly as it used to. "Can't get out of the way as quickly...as it used to," she mumbled to herself.

Emily smiled to herself a little sadly. All she seemed

to be able to think about these days was aging and dimming faculties. She hadn't been like that in the past; now, it seemed, she couldn't be any other way. She closed the screen door of the kitchen behind her and left the inner door open to admit the midmorning sun. She glanced down at the dustbin by the door and remembered that she hadn't yet disposed of the bundle of newspapers from the past week. Then she glanced over at the kitchen table, where today's paper was still lying open to the picture of the murdered girl.

At that point Emily made a decision: It was time to take her failing memory in hand, so to speak. She went to the small desk in the hallway and fished a pair of scissors out of the top left-hand drawer. She came back to the paper on the kitchen table and slowly, carefully, cut out the picture of the murdered girl. When she had finished, she neatly folded up the remainder of the newspaper and placed it beside the pile by the dustbin. She then began going through the piles of newspaper, looking for the one that contained the picture of the murdered man, Lawrence Watson. Fortunately, it was on top of the pile. Oh yes, she thought, it was yesterday, just yesterday.

"I will keep these pictures," she said aloud, "until I remember just where I've seen them before."

Pleased to have made this resolution, she smiled to herself as she leafed through the pages looking for Watson's picture. Suddenly, a sound at the door made her jump. She turned cautiously, finding that Cyril had thrown himself against the screen in an attempt to latch onto it, forgetting that he no longer had his claws, and had fallen in a lump on the porch. He slapped angrily at the door.

"Silly cat," she said as she let him in, "you scared me!"

THE THEATER WAS, indeed, dead. At least for Damien Liddle. The Pennington Players gasped their last breath of life at a meeting of the membership, which was attended by a total of five of the twenty-seven people in the company. The meeting took place at their storefront space a mere five days after the break-in, was adjourned after exactly twenty-three minutes, and was followed by a period of mourning observed for the remainder of the evening at the Ridge Bar, a small neighborhood establishment within walking distance of the theater. The atmosphere at this ersatz Irish wake was jubilant for all except Gail, who was stunned into silence by the decision to dissolve the company. She sat to the right of Damien, not crying, but not speaking either, trying to decide how she would now spend her nights.

However, Gail seemed to be the only one at the table at a loss for what to do. The four actors with her seemed to have so many plans for the future that one would have thought they had been anxious for the Players to dissolve so they could get on to more important matters.

"It's all the same, you know," said Lorrie Reed, an actress who had been far too young and far too inexperienced to play Rosaline in the Players' most recent production. One critic had pointed out that she had played the aging heroine with all the charm of a gum-twanging cashier, a remark that Lorrie discounted, believing that critics would only give you good reviews if you slept with them, and sometimes not even then. As she spoke in between sips of her beer, she chewed a strand of her long blond hair, trying to make it look like an absent gesture that would give her character. "It's probably a good thing we stopped now."

"Why do you say that?" asked Danny Leming, her equally inexperienced Berowne.

"Well—" she smiled in an attempt at coquettishness "—I've got a part!"

"Where?"

"I'm gonna be playing Sandy in *Grease* at the Celestial. I found out a week ago!"

"Why didn't you say something?" asked Damien, a trifle miffed that he had not been informed he would be losing a cast member.

"I thought I'd wait till after this weekend. You know, till I found out if there was any reason to worry...about our company, I mean. I mean, I'm not blind, you know! I could see nobody was coming to see us, and so I thought this last weekend would probably be it." She reached under the table and gently stroked Damien's leg. "And, I didn't see any reason to send you scrambling around looking for a replacement when you didn't need one, you know what I mean?" Her hand traveled up his inner thigh, and he pushed it away firmly.

"So, you kept it from me to spare me trouble, huh?" he said, trying to hide his irritation.

"All right, all right—I just didn't want to have another fight," she said with an overly heavy sigh. "You know how you get. And I didn't see any point in going through all that shit for nothing. I mean, you always act like it's something personal if someone has to leave one of the shows."

"Probably because I have trouble understanding how someone would prefer musical comedy to Shakespeare."

"Come on, Damien, you're not in charge anymore. Lighten up!" Danny grabbed Damien's shoulder and shook him playfully, smiling broadly.

Damien smiled too, not because he recognized the irony of being angry about a problem he no longer had to deal with, but at the thought of these two ridiculous people together. Lorrie, he thought, played valiantly at being a fresh-scrubbed innocent, with her blond hair, blue eyes, and slight figure. But she didn't fool him for a minute. At times when she would arrive late for rehearsal, he would yell at her, and she would turn demure and kittenish, purring for forgiveness, not satisfied until she had quelled his anger. But often he would catch her glance, only for a second, at the end of her apologies: rolling her eyes under her blue shaded eyelids to see if her act had worked. It was the same effect that marred her performance onstage: She played her role and appeared to be asking if she were doing it right all at the same time. Damien also knew that her insistence that she would have told him of her impending departure from his production was another game, and that she would have thought nothing of walking out on a moment's notice.

Danny, thought Damien, was another story altogether. Danny had all the grace of a football player wounded in the game (a line from another review), and his main interest in the Pennington Players had been Lorrie. He kept close to her heels like a tiny dog, a most unsuitable role given that he was over six feet tall, but he quickly responded to her every request: fetching her costumes, bringing her car around, paying for her meals, and servicing her when she did him the great honor of allowing him entry. Although it had often been remarked by the company members less charitable than Damien that they didn't know what she saw in Danny, Damien felt it was quite clear: Lorrie felt that she had every right to expect the adulation of adoring fans, and at the moment, the club consisted of Danny.

Of the two, Damien had the most contempt for Danny. Lorrie might be conniving, irresponsible, and self-centered, but at least she had a brain. Danny was merely a fool. He seemed to be the only member of the company who didn't know that if Lorrie, God forbid, "made it," Danny would be quickly forgotten. Damien wasn't quite so sure on that point, though. Whatever his faults might be, Danny was pretty handsome, in a rather parochial way, and Damien occasionally had fantasized Lorrie as a star, clad in very white furs and very dark glasses, meeting the paparazzi with this hulking thing on her arm. Lorrie would probably like giving the world the impression that she could lead this strapping young man around by the nose.

"Did you hear me?" said Lorrie, a little irritated.

"What?" asked Damien, bringing his mind back to the table.

"I asked you what you were gonna do next."

"Oh. Well...believe it or not, I think I'm going to be doing television. I'm waiting to hear about a television series."

"You're kidding!"

"Not the great Damien Liddle! Not Bill Shakespeare's little boy!"

Damien blushed visibly and smiled. "Yeah—the last time I was out in L.A. I auditioned for a pilot, and I think they were really interested. I haven't heard from them yet, but—" he crossed his fingers "—it looks pretty good."

"Don't worry, you'll get it," said Danny, giving him a playful slap on the shoulder. Damien shot him an annoyed glance, which went unnoticed.

Alice, the fifth member of the mourning party, set down her beer and chimed in. "I can't believe *you're* going to L.A. Television, for God's sake!"

Damien flushed. "I know, I know."

"I didn't think you'd be caught dead in a television studio."

"Well, I thought it might be nice to actually make some

money for a change," Damien said, beginning to get defensive. "I have this secret desire to go grocery shopping without worrying about how much everything costs."

"Hear, hear!"

"I'd like to reach the end of the week with enough quarters to do my laundry."

"I take mine home to my folks' house," said Danny. Lorrie rolled her eyes.

"I could never do television," said Alice, with an air of superiority that was all too familiar to her colleagues.

"I didn't think I could either, but if I get this pilot, it might free me up to do the rest of the stuff I want to do. I'd make a lot of money. And when I'm big enough, people will come to see me in anything—including Shakespeare." This last was added with a note of condescension that served to imply his awareness that the surrounding company was less aware of the glories of the classics than he was.

At this point a small but distinct voice was heard from around the area just to the right of Damien's view. It had the effect of calling out into the air and standing still there, poised in a sudden silence.

"Does that mean you'll be leaving Chicago?"

Damien lifted the corner of his mouth in a half-smile, all he could spare for Gail. Lorrie and Danny exchanged glances, barely trying to hide their smirks, and Alice was silent.

"Yeah," said Damien, "if I get it."

For the first time since the death of the theater, somebody cried.

FOUR

"I DON'T KNOW who would want to kill him," said Gloria Forsyth, gently dabbing her nose with a wadded-up tissue.

As she spoke, Ransom considered her appearance carefully. He thought that outside of her grief she was probably a very attractive young woman. She was about thirty years old with long, tawny hair that fell softly on her shoulders. She was slender and pale, well-dressed even in her everyday clothes, but at the moment, her eyes and cheeks were reddened with crying, and Ransom noticed a slight trembling in her hands indicating that although she was openly grieving for her former boss, she was still struggling to hold herself together, a fact that he felt lent strongly to the idea that the love affair might be more than mere conjecture.

"I suppose you think I'm awfully stupid, I mean, he was my boss, and I probably shouldn't be...carrying on like this."

"Not at all," said Ransom quietly. Gerald sat with his pencil poised on his small spiral notebook, patiently waiting for her to continue.

"I'm not like this all the time. I'm sad...but when I actually think of him lying dead...I try not to, but sometimes I can't help it—when I think of him I can't stop crying."

"Take your time."

Gloria pressed the tissue to her eyes for a moment, blotting her tears, then continued. "It's just that Mr. Watson was such a kind man. I don't know why anyone would want to kill him."

"He didn't have any enemies?"

"No."

"Not among any of his clients? None of them had any reason to bear a grudge against him?"

Gloria thought for a moment. "Not that I know of. No. I don't think so."

"Tell me about his relationship with his partners."

Gloria looked slightly confused, as if her three employers together was an idea she had never considered. Her hands slowly fell into her lap and she spoke. "Well...all of them...all three of them...get along pretty well together, I guess. Mr. Watson and Mr. Herald especially."

"What about Mr. Danners?"

"That pig!" she answered with a vehemence that surprised both Ransom and Gerald. "Have you met him?"

"Yes," said Ransom, his right hand going up to his mouth as if to muffle a cough, trying to stifle the laugh that he felt at the directness of her description of the gluttonous lawyer.

"He's a pig!" she repeated, a scowl marring her fair features. "Whenever I'm in his office, he looks at me as if he's picturing me roasted with an apple in my mouth."

"He does have a rather hungry look about him."

"He drools."

"Be that as it may, what was his relationship with Mr. Watson?"

"Nobody has any sort of relationship with Mr. Danners. He's an onerous man. If I were going to kill anyone, it would be him!"

"Indeed?"

Gloria, realizing to whom she was talking, blushed. "I

suppose I shouldn't have said that. I guess it makes me sound like a suspect."

Ransom smiled at her warmly. "Not in Mr. Watson's murder. And I can assure you that if Mr. Danners is ever killed, just about everyone who has ever met him will be suspect."

Gloria almost laughed, and Ransom carefully placed his hand on hers. The tension he had sensed earlier in her hands drained away. "Now, if you think you could go on, I have a couple of more questions to ask you."

"I'm okay."

"So...Mr. Watson got along well with Mr. Herald, and nobody got along with Mr. Danners." Ransom released her hand and sat back in his chair. "What about his relationship with you?"

"What do you mean?" she said, surprised.

"What was Mr. Watson's relationship with you?"

"He was my boss. I was his secretary."

"And that's all?"

For the first time, Gloria's features hardened. "Why do you ask that?"

"There was some talk that he might have been having an affair."

"I suppose that must have come from his wife."

"Is there any truth to it?"

Gloria looked down at her hands. With her slender fingers, she unrolled the damp tissue and started to pull it into little pieces. "I don't believe it."

"What?"

"I don't believe that Mr. Watson was having an affair with anyone."

"And if he was, that person would not have been you."

She absently brushed at some of the flecks of torn tissue on her skirt, which did not move. She didn't speak.

"Miss Forsyth?"

Gloria looked up after a moment and spoke over Ransom's right shoulder, as if she felt she should be speaking in his direction but didn't want to look in his eyes. "Larry Watson was a kind and gentle man and I loved him. He was the type of man I guess they used to call unassuming. A lot of people thought he was nothing special, but a lot of people probably think the same about me."

Ransom could have argued this point, but he felt he was about to receive important information, so he restrained himself, and prompted her to continue.

"I did not have an affair with him. He was not the type of man who would have approached me about something like that, and...well...he was married, so I really wouldn't have approached him about it, either...even if I wanted to. We shared..." Her voice trailed off, as if she didn't think it was quite possible to describe what she was thinking. Ransom waited a moment before prompting her again.

"Yes?"

"We *shared*," she said with more emphasis. "I know it's going to sound idiotic, but we *shared*. I wasn't having an affair with him, you must believe that."

"I must?"

"Well, I suppose you don't *have* to believe it," she said stiffly, "but it's true. We weren't having an affair, but we had...a very special relationship."

"How so?"

"Every now and then he would ask me to bring him a cup of coffee in his office, and tell me to bring one along for myself. And then, we'd just sit in his office and talk."

"About what?"

"About anything—everything—our lives. He told me about things he wanted to do, and things he *had* wanted to do when he was younger. And..." She paused and looked up at Ransom, not sure whether or not she should go on. Ransom sensed that she wanted to talk about it, and although she might be perfectly straightforward about her own feelings, she belonged to that rare breed of people, all too few and far between these days, who did not feel it necessary or seemly to pass on information she had heard in private. He also believed that Gloria was a woman with scruples and would be keenly aware of saying anything that might implicate someone in the matter of murder. This intelligent woman understood the importance of any information she might be able to give. He decided to prompt her once again, hoping that directly asking her questions would help ease any guilt she might feel in giving out information.

"Did he ever speak to you of his marriage?"

"Yes. Yes, he did."

"Was he happily married?"

"Didn't you talk to his wife?"

"Yes."

"Oh," she said sadly, "then that *is* where you got the idea of the affair. I knew it. She is the type of woman who would jump to a sordid conclusion." Gloria stopped for a moment and straightened her shoulders, drawing up a store of indignation on behalf of her late employer. "He was not having an affair."

"It seems that he was spending a goodly amount of time...away from home. Would you have any idea what he did with his time?"

"He went out."

"I beg your pardon?"

"He went out, Mr. Ransom. His wife—I've never actually met her but I've spoken to her on the phone—she's a shrew. Larry never said that—he would never say anything unkind about anybody. But I could tell, in the little he did say of his situation at home, and in the brief moments I talked to her on the phone when she called. She was a bitch, poking at him and picking at him until she drove him out of the house. He went out.'' She stopped, looking dissatisfied with her own description of Watson's actions. Then she had an idea. "Like Tom, you know, the son in *The Glass Menagerie*. You've seen it, haven't you? He couldn't stand being at home so he went to the movies all the time.''

"Is that what Mr. Watson did?"

"He went anywhere and everywhere, I guess, as long as it wasn't home."

"But you never went with him."

"No."

Ransom paused for a moment, more for effect than anything else. "Did he ever say anything to you about getting a divorce?"

"A divorce?" she said, genuinely surprised. "No, he never said anything about that. I don't think he would have."

"Why not?"

"He never asked me for advice, and I never offered him any. I don't think he ever would have mentioned getting a divorce to me unless his plans were already made. But I don't believe he would ever get a divorce, either. It's probably hard to believe but he was really a very old-fashioned man. He believed in the sanctity of marriage—even a bad one—and I'm not all that sure that wife of his would have wanted a divorce, anyway. She seemed to like the idea of having a lawyer for a husband. Good for business. Made her look good. That sort of thing. And…"

"Yes?" said Ransom, prompting her one last time.

Gloria smiled a bit sheepishly. "Well, I hate to be nasty, but I have a feeling that she—his wife, I mean—wouldn't have wanted a divorce...not if *he* wanted one."

"WELL, THERE we have it," said Gerald, once again climbing behind the wheel of the car. "The man was a saint, everybody liked him—almost everybody—nobody had any reason to want to kill him—if we're to take the word of the Forsyth woman, he wasn't having an affair with her or anybody else. Did you believe her, by the way?"

"Yes, I did, as a matter of fact. I thought she was quite honest. Although I think her own feelings for him might have gone beyond the soul-searching coffee breaks in his office, I'm perfectly willing to believe that there was never anything physical between them."

"Funny, though," said Gerald, "she switched from 'Mr. Watson' to 'Larry' awfully fast when she started talking about their personal relationship."

Ransom shot him an amused glance. "Do you sleep with everyone who calls you by your first name, Gerald?"

Gerald laughed and blushed a deep red. "A point well taken."

A light rain started, and Ransom rolled up the window on the passenger side of the front seat.

"I'd have to agree with you, I guess," said Gerald, "all across the board. She seems honest—I can't imagine her being able to successfully handle the sneaking around required in sleeping with a married man—and at her worst I can't imagine her having any reason to kill him, let alone doing it."

"That's the trouble with this case. We have this gentle idiot who's dead and apparently never offended anyone in his life. Then we have these people who are still alive and by rights any number of people could want to kill."

"So?"

"As far as suspects go, we've got only two possibilities that I can see so far: the wife, and Danners."

"Why Danners?"

"Because I don't like him."

"Ah."

"And for God's sake, I *hope* it's Danners. I would think society as a whole would be better off if he were put away, if they could find a cell big enough."

"You're running away with yourself there, Jer."

"Sorry," said Ransom a little curtly, and then fell into contemplative silence. All the while he had been talking his mind had been going over the interview with Gloria Forsyth, her actions more than her words. He liked the fact that she was grieving for her boss, a man who didn't seem to bring any kind of emotion out in anyone else. He also liked the way her hair moved when she shook her head, and the way her back stiffened when the memory of Watson was called into question. Yes, he thought, she was the type of woman that would inspire the confidence of others, one with whom you would feel safe talking about private matters. In fact, the type of woman in whom he himself would be interested.

Ransom was fully able to admit to himself, though, that part of his admiration for the girl was in the fact that her assessment of the other people involved in the case so well agreed with his. He might, he thought, be interested in a growing acquaintance with this Miss Forsyth once this murder was cleared up. Ransom held a strict teacher-pupil relationship with suspects during a case. Whatever other faults he might admit, he would not become involved with an interested party during an investigation. In addition to the unprofessionalism of it, he always liked to be sure whether a person was going to jail for life before getting involved with her. But he sighed rather heavily to himself, remembering that the case itself would remain a problem in that respect even after it had been solved. In the few attempts he had made to strike up relationships with former suspects, he found much to his discouragement that he tended to serve only as a reminder to the poor women of the painful ordeals through which they had just passed.

Ransom smiled, a gesture that did not go unnoticed by Gerald, although he said nothing. I must, thought Ransom, resign myself to remaining a bachelor. Ah, well.

FIVE

MEG FERGUSON WAS a tiny old lady, made even tinier by the osteoporosis that had left her stooped so that when sitting she looked poised to read a book, and when standing or walking she looked as if she were searching the sidewalk for something she'd lost. Like many old people, she slept only fitfully, waking often during the night and spending much time in the dreamy state one finds halfway between being fully awake and fully asleep. And like many people given to such night waking, especially the elderly, her nights were somewhat haunted by shapes and figures, some remembered from the past and wandering through her mind as she woke in the night, some moving, shadowy figures that darted across the wall in the moonlight just as she woke or just as she slid into a full dream state.

Meg would occasionally wake with a slight start, calling to her late husband to come to bed, only realizing with time that there was silence, that she was alone, and that her husband would never come to her again. Other times, as she drifted off to sleep, the walls of the room would hear her quiet voice groggily admonishing her husband to make sure the doors were locked and the lights turned off, or to close the windows against the rain. The walls stood silently around her on these occasions, as if their very silence would bring Meg back to herself and make her realize that if there were windows to be closed, she must rouse herself, and that nobody would lock the doors for her.

On this particular night, the wind was slightly higher than usual and rustled through her sheer curtains as if it would waken her if it could to put her on the alert. The moon was full, providing a beacon over her as if to light her room and guard her against intruders. Meg had already been awake twice that night, once when she found herself thirsty and had a sip from the water glass she kept at her bedside, and the second time when she imagined a quick snapping sound that happened once, she thought, and then not again, so she had drifted off back to sleep.

Now, an hour or so after the last time she had awoken, she woke again. Through her tired, half-opened eyes, the world seemed a fog. Her head lolled to the side and she saw the shadows of the curtains flapping across the wall in the bright moonlight and the strong branches of the tree outside her window waving slowly, offering much more resistance to the insistent winds than the flimsy curtains. While she looked on groggily, one branch of the tree moved slowly over to the other, as if performing sleight-of-hand for her personal enjoyment. It had looked, she thought wearily, as if one branch had split and sent half its bulk to the other branch. Then slowly, cautiously, the other branch split, and there were three branches.

The show made Meg even more wary, and she closed her eyes to it, when she suddenly became aware of the presence of her husband once again in the room. Her face tensed slightly as it always did on these occasions; she felt comfort in his presence, and yet she knew something was not right in his being there, although it always took her some time to remember that he was dead. As she so often did, she called out absently to him, "Darling, darling...come to bed." The third branch of the tree, the new branch, paused in its movement. Then it performed a different trick that would even have surprised Meg had she been fully awake or had she kept her eyes open: The third branch split off from the trunk of the tree entirely and moved toward her.

"Darling...darling..."

The branch reached out to her with the smaller branches that sprang from its side and gently lifted up Meg's head with its twigs, sliding out one of the pillows on which she rested.

"Darling...darling..."

The branch took hold of each side of the pillow and gently pressed it down on Meg's face. She didn't scream or struggle, feeling her husband's presence growing stronger and stronger. She said to him, "I can't breathe," and he responded, from a distance, with "Darling... darling...come to me."

When her life ended, her assailant gently removed the pillow from Meg's face and slipped it back under her head. Standing back to look at the fragile lifeless form, pride rose like sap in the killer's veins, mixed with an equally unmistakable sense of pleasure: The job was well done, the task had grown easier, the power of life and death was in the killer's hands. There was an incomparable thrill in performing the deed, and in being clever enough to remain undetectable. Easy.

The walls stood silently and watched.

EMILY DIDN'T HAVE to wait for the newspaper to learn of the death of Meg Ferguson, and she greeted the news both with a sense of grief, which was to be expected, and with a slight sense of relief that for once she could be sure that she knew the victim. There was none of the vague uneasiness, none of the wondering and questioning of her own faculties that had accompanied the news of the two murders. When she received the call, she almost said aloud, "Meg! Oh yes, thank God, I *know* Meg." She could see Meg. There was a name to go with the face.

If there was a sense of relief and consolation in having her faculties reaffirmed, it was a very small one. Emily and Meg had been friends for more years than Emily was able to remember. When their husbands were alive, the quartet had vacationed together both in the United States and abroad, they had played bridge on Friday evenings as long as they were able, and they spoke together almost every day by telephone. When Emily's husband died, Meg cried along with her, helped with the funeral plans and all attendant arrangements, and even made dinner for Emily every night for a week. When Meg's husband died, Emily stayed with her at her house for over two weeks, giving up her personal comfort and familiar surroundings so that Meg would not have to face the empty house alone right away. In the decade that followed their losses, Emily and Meg had continued as best of friends and confidants, and rarely would one make plans for the evening without taking the other into account. Emily was sure that the young and middle-aged housewives in the neighborhood all smiled at the sight of the two old neighborhood ladies going around together arm in arm.

It hardly seemed possible to Emily. Her one link to the past was now gone. Emily had outlived both her brother and sister, her husband, and now Meg. The voice on the phone, the one that had called to tell her about the tragedy, had been the minister from their church. She recognized the voice the minute she heard it. But, after breaking the terrible news, as he continued to speak, the voice became more and more unfamiliar. She tried through her tears to remember when this new minister, who was in his forties, had come to their church. It was when Reverend Daniels had retired, she thought, but she couldn't exactly remember when that was. It had been so long ago, though, that it was hardly fitting to think of this minister as being new. As the voice droned on, suddenly unfamiliar and with a tone of sympathy that Emily was beginning to find insipid, her mind raced through the people she knew. In light of this news, all of the people who passed through her mind seemed like mere acquaintances. Almost all of them were considerably younger than she, not that that was bad, but it didn't add to her feeling of security. Everyone seemed separated from her, somehow—either by age or because she hadn't known them very long or very closely. It is odd, she thought, that as one gets older, the attachments to the world seem to fall away, almost as if the earth would prepare you to be given up when the time comes. The earth, she thought, conspires against us, loosing one by one the ties that bind us to it until...until...you float away. Until there's nothing left to keep you in this life. Maybe that was the secret to dying. Maybe you drift away when there's no reason left to be here.

The Reverend Herman's voice was now saying something else to her, something about being there for her—and she immediately thought of those faceless, voiceless help lines you hear about that try to keep you from committing suicide—and then said good-bye in an embarrassed tone, as if now that he had said his piece, he sincerely hoped that she wouldn't be needing anything. He signed off assuring her that he would be praying for her.

The next day a sparsely attended wake was held in the church chapel, followed by an even more poorly attended funeral. Emily was chauffeured through the day's sad events by a woman from her church with whom she had a nodding acquaintance. Mildred Peck was a plump woman of about fifty years who, despite her frame, had a surprisingly angular face. Mildred could always be counted on to do the endless little tasks about the church that nobody else wanted (or had time) to do. She twittered rather than talked, and most of her twittering concerned her many responsibilities, so that one was always given the impression, in the nicest way, of course, that Mildred was making quite a sacrifice by helping.

As she drove Emily to the chapel, she chattered endlessly about flowers she had to deliver, cleaning she had promised to pick up, dinner she had to cook, and nieces and nephews she had to take care of. Nobody else could be relied upon. The chatter didn't bother Emily, though, who was far too absorbed in her own thoughts.

The chapel had been chosen for Meg since with no remaining family and few friends or acquaintances left to speak of, it was felt that using the church would be wasteful and would accentuate the small size of the turnout. Emily was assisted up to the casket by Mildred, who kept her twittering to an unhushed whisper during the journey. Much to Emily's surprise, Mildred had the good grace to leave her side once they reached the casket so that she could spend a few moments alone with her dear old friend. Too much makeup, she thought automatically when she first saw the body. Why do they always do that? She looked down at her friend with a great sense of emptiness, but she had spent all her tears when she first received the news and could find no more within herself. Death was not something to be feared, but something inevitable to be accepted when it came. And as she had gotten older she had come more and more to believe that death was the end of tribulation and that there was indeed something better lying beyond the veil. What was that quotation, she asked herself—she had heard it so many times—about dying a thousand deaths? Despite the lack of tears, her sense of loss was palpable. She could only find comfort by reminding herself that even if Meg was gone, she would surely be joining her soon.

Mildred appeared at her side as if on cue and ushered her back to a pew. Reverend Herman gave a brief sermon, and then the few in attendance retired to their cars to follow the hearse to the cemetery. Mildred twittered about how bad traffic was and how late she would be getting home and how they could have hoped that the weather would be a little better for the funeral but perhaps the weather was supposed to be gloomy on the more solemn occasions. Emily chimed in with an occasional "hmmm" when she thought to speak at all.

At the gravesite, the minister said a few more words over the casket, and the company was disbanded for the day.

"Well, that's that!" said Mildred, shuffling Emily back into the car and making no secret of her relief that her chores were now over and she could get back to her more important duties—although, admittedly, it was difficult to tell exactly which duties were important for her, since it always seemed something else was more important than whatever she was doing at the moment.

"Funerals are so sad," she twittered. "I just hate going to them. They always remind you, you know, that we're none of us getting any younger. And we never need any reminding, do we? At least, I don't! God, I just hate the thought of it. I wish we didn't ever have to go to funerals. Who needs to be reminded of death?"

"It seems to me most strange," Emily quoted absently, "that men should fear, seeing that death, a necessary end, will come when it will come."

"Well, yes...I suppose," said Mildred, flustered for the first time, partly because of the quotation itself and partly because it had been the most Emily had said all day.

After Emily was unceremoniously dropped off at her house, she made straight for the kitchen to fix her obligatory cup of tea. She was unaware of her own movements, her mind still entertaining the quotation she had repeated to Mildred. She turned to the refrigerator to retrieve the small cream pitcher, and her eyes fell on the pictures of the murdered man and woman she had taped to the refrigerator door.

"See that...death will come when it will come," she said to herself. "Oh my God!"

ON THE SAME DAY that Emily received the call that brought her the sad news of Meg's death, Damien Liddle received much happier news by phone from Los Angeles. Warren Brown, a television producer for whom Damien had auditioned several times, called to say that he had gotten the go-ahead to film a pilot for a half-hour series and that Damien was wanted for one of the leads. Brown was sure the series would be picked up by one of the networks.

Now, Damien had been in the business far too long to get his hopes up, even over such seemingly positive news, but it was all he could do to keep from cheering when he hung up the phone. In a mere two week's time preproduction would be started, and he would soon be needed to begin rehearsals. He tried to remain calm, reminding himself that a pilot was not a series, and even if a network picked up the pilot and ordered five of thirteen episodes, there was no guarantee they would all be shown, or even that they'd be made at all. The rational part of his mind kept telling him these things, while the rest of his mind was in a whirl, envisioning himself in Brown's office, standing over the desk smiling calmly and professionally as he signed a five-year contract, making up acceptance speeches for the Emmy Awards, and picturing himself on the cover of People magazine. How would it be, he wondered, to be recognized in restaurants and on the street—to have to send someone out to pick up your groceries, or better yet, have your groceries delivered because you couldn't dare show you face in public! These were the prices of fame with which Damien was confident he could deal. If nothing else, it would mean money.

No, no, he thought, shaking his head to clear it, I mustn't get all worked up over nothing. It's not really happening until the cameras are rolling, and even then there are no guarantees. But even as he thought, the smile spread even wider across his face, lending him an expression he was sure would be inappropriate for Hamlet but was inescapable now. Damien was happy. There was only a momentary pang as he thought of the Bard, which he dissolved quickly with a shrug, telling himself that later...later he could dazzle the world with his classical expertise. Later, when he was a star. Now was the time to make money.

If there was one slightly off-color cloud to darken the morning's news, it was that he could not reach anyone by phone to tell them. The members of the now-defunct Pennington Players all worked during the day. He was the only one, he thought with a rather unpleasant sneer, who was serious about acting and devoted all his time to pursuing his career. When the times came, and there had been many, that he needed to work in order to pay the rent, he would work only long enough to qualify for unemployment, then draw on all his acting abilities to play the incompetent and get fired. The only problem with this was that at times he played the part so well that some of his employers had felt sorry for him and tried to help him become competent. But in the end, they all fired him. This pattern had served him well throughout the life of the Players.

He tried to think of someone to call to tell his good news. He tried Danny first, mainly because Danny was a lug and was bound to be happy for him. Damien felt that after a cheery pat on the back from Danny by way of telephone, he could move on to the people to whom he most wanted to give the good news: Lorrie, for example, who would gush and slobber over him with congratulations while turning green with envy. She wouldn't be able to be openly hostile, though, because she was far too shrewd to burn any bridges that might come in handy in the future. Then there was Alice. He might tell Alice, but he knew she would be inclined to look down on the project and accuse him of "prostituting himself," therefore negating any good feelings he might have about it. All the others would probably fall into the Lorrie category, and Damien was far too pleased with himself to be considerate in the face of thinly veiled hostility. He sighed as he considered, however briefly, the hazards of pursuing a career in a business in which nobody ever seemed to be truly happy with your success except you.

Unfortunately for Damien, Danny was out making deliveries for his father's company when he tried to reach him and wasn't expected back for hours. But Damien's news couldn't wait. He figured he would go on to Lorrie, braving it on his own but she had called in sick at work, and when he tried to reach her at home he got her answering machine. This, he knew, meant that she had an audition for something and had called in sick for the time off. He cursed her and hung up the phone before her overly perky message was finished because his news was simply too good to waste on a machine. And besides, he wanted her there in person, at least by phone, to enjoy her reaction. His success would be her bane. Irrationally, he became angry at her for this latest proof of her irresponsibility, believing she should have been *somewhere* to receive his call.

Alice! He would call Alice. He hadn't wanted to tackle her until later, but in the face of his last two attempts, he felt Alice might at least provide minor compensation. But Alice was unavailable, or so he was told by a silky-voiced secretary. She was attending an insurance seminar.

"Damn," he said, slamming down the receiver. It was just like the gods to pull this sort of joke on him—to give him this great news and not give him anyone with whom he could gloat about it.

He got up from the desk and went into the kitchen for a can of Coke. He closed the refrigerator door and rested his back against it, calming himself by taking a long drink and letting the fluid slide down his throat. His mind was full of wild expectations for the future that, at the moment they came to mind, he would automatically and unsuccessfully try to tame. At the same time he was nagged by the irritation of nobody being around to hear about it. After work, he thought, I can get them to all go to the bar and celebrate. But what about now? I want to tell somebody now!

Suddenly, his thoughts solidified into one name: Gail! Of course, good old reliable Gail, who was always where she was supposed to be with such boring regularity. *She* would be there to tell.

He went back to the phone and flipped open his address book. He had dialed Gail's number a thousand times, but he still looked it up each time, subconsciously trying to keep from admitting that he was that familiar with her. He found the number, dialed it, and tapped his right foot impatiently while the phone rang.

"Service Department," said Gail mechanically when she picked up the phone.

"Gail? Gail? This is Damien."

"Hi," she said, her tone warming noticeably in the one syllable.

"You won't believe it! I've got great news!"

SIX

"Perhaps you were expecting a confession. I'm afraid I don't have one for you."

"What *do* you have?"

Ransom glanced down at the old, cheap, shopworn desk of Sergeant Newman and smiled to himself, remembering the beautifully polished solid oak desk of Danners's office. The man sitting behind the desk, Mike Newman, was in no better shape than the furniture. Although he was a mere ten years older than Ransom, he looked almost twice that much older. The pepper in his hair had long since lost a losing battle to the salt and had a rather unpleasant, dusty look rather than the silver shine one might have expected. His skin was ashen and maintained a moist glimmer that gave him the appearance of being perpetually overheated. His wardrobe, although nice when it was purchased, had all been worn a bit too long, so that his shirts were all faded and stained and his suit coat was almost worn through at the elbows.

"Well?" he said, drumming his cigarette-stained fingers on the desk.

"Nobody killed Mr. Watson," said Ransom with a smile.

"It's been a week."

Ransom heaved a heavy sigh and spoke monotonously. "None of the neighbors heard or saw anything. On further examination, the ones that heard something either thought it was a car or some such nonsense and didn't think anything of it or thought it was a gun but didn't investigate.

That is, of course, the way of the world. As far as the suspects go, if you can call them that, so far we have discovered nothing—except that the victim was a singularly undistinguished person. Nobody in the world seemed to have a reason for killing him. I suppose, like everything else, it will boil down to either money or passion. Gerald is checking out the money angle right now, but the passion side is a bit stickier."

"Why?"

"Well, the wife seems to think he was having an affair, which I suppose might be a motive for her killing him, but she didn't seem to think the affair worth bothering herself about. Seems she was only using her husband for an arm ornament at dinners. Now the other woman—if that's what she was—seems to have been loved primarily for her mind."

"Did she now?" said Newman wryly. "You've definitely settled on who the 'other woman' was?"

"I should think so."

"Hmmm. Where was the wife when he was shot?"

"She was in the house; he was shot just outside."

"She sounds like the obvious suspect."

"That's just it. It's awfully hard to believe she'd kill him in a way that would make her the prime, if not only, suspect. Not only that, but she doesn't make any secret of her contempt for her husband. Very stupid."

"Or very clever."

"I don't think so," said Ransom, tapping his unlit cigar on the arm of the faded chair in which he sat facing Newman. There was a silence, the type to which Newman was well accustomed. Ransom had an annoying habit, thought Newman, of falling silent—at times in midsentence—and seeming to process information on the spot. It was almost as if Ransom's random thoughts would choose their own time to gel, and he had to stop whatever he was doing or saying to listen.

"I don't think any of them did it," said Ransom, finally breaking the silence. "I don't like them—at least, not all of them—but I don't think any of them actually *did* it. They might be foolish people, even downright unpleasant, but I didn't get the impression that any of them were liars."

Newman smiled. "You still don't think it was random?"

Ransom's eyes narrowed, and he considered Newman. "No," he said. "It feels wrong. There's something weird about all this. I don't like it."

"That will look great on your report," said Newman, sitting up straight and assuming an air of authority before continuing. "Ransom, in case you don't read the papers, we're up to our privates in murder. You've got to close this one and get on with it. Do whatever it takes, but get on with it."

Ransom stifled a laugh as he rose from his chair. "Yes sir," he said, and as he left the office, he shot a salute back to Newman, who was already busying himself with the papers on his desk.

Outside Newman's office, he was immediately cornered by his sympathetic partner.

"On the carpet?"

"No," Ransom answered wryly, "just Newman's regular boot up the butt." They continued to Ransom's office as their talk progressed. "He must think we're working too slowly—he was trying to fire me up with an appeal to my ego."

"Did it work?"

Ransom smiled coyly. "Of course it did. It always does."

Gerald almost laughed out loud.

Ransom continued: "I've always prided myself on knowing myself. I'm afraid I'm a big enough fool to fall for dime-store psychology, even when I know it's being used on me. It's a dance we do at least once during each case."

"I've been going over everyone's finances. Everyone concerned, that is," said Gerald smoothly, changing the subject drastically but making it sound as if it were a natural progression in the proceedings.

"And?"

"You're not going to like it."

"Let me guess—nothing."

"That's right. There's nothing amiss in the Watsons' accounts. They're not rich, but they're pretty well off. They have considerable savings. They didn't have any kids, so the missus is the sole heir, but she has a pretty good income of her own, and fairly substantial savings—also her own."

"So we can rule out murder for money if Mrs. Watson is our man—excuse me, woman."

"I'm not as ready to rule out murder for passion as you are," said Gerald, sliding into the chair next to Ransom's desk. Ransom, in turn, took his place behind his desk and lit up the cigar he had been fingering through the past half hour.

"Perhaps."

"I mean, she looked to me like the type who wouldn't take kindly to her husband taking up with another woman. It's the oldest story in the world."

"Not *the* oldest, but one of the oldest." He paused for a moment and puffed thoughtfully. "Passion. Perhaps, but I don't think so. There's a special type of woman—a special type of person—that dislikes change so much they can stay on in a situation long after everything that made it work is dead. There's others who would rather die than admit to the world that they've made a mistake, especially in marriage, and that's what you do when you divorce. The Watsons come from a world where keeping up appearances is more important than being happy. The funny part is, they never fool anyone. Everybody we talked to seems to have known the Watsons were unhappily married, so if they were staying together to keep up appearances, they were a dismal failure."

"Of course...if he died, she'd be rid of him without admitting to being wrong."

"Why Gerald," said Ransom, trying not to smirk, "I believe you disliked Mrs. Watson more than I did."

Gerald flushed. "I wouldn't want my son to marry her." Ransom agreed with him on this point. "Well, so much for Mrs. Watson committing the murder. What about the law firm?"

"Danners, Herald and Watson is flush. It's like the old saying, the only one that makes money out of the lawsuits are lawyers."

"Christ, Gerald, we're never going to get a break in this, are we?"

"I wish that presence of mind you're so famous for would manifest itself."

They fell silent. Ransom sat back in his chair and took a long drag on the cigar. It was as frustrating as always to not be able to figure out a solution immediately from a simple look at the problem. To a certain extent, he felt that solving crimes should be like finding the solution to a math problem where you're given a set of numbers and they all add up. In reality, solving crimes seemed to be a bit more mystical—more like a logic problem on an IQ test where you've given several seemingly unrelated words and you have to figure out the relation among them. You stare at the words for ages, and suddenly—almost without explanation—they make sense. It was in this way that Gerald studied his notes while Ransom thought: as if he expected the words in his notebook to suddenly rearrange themselves and say "So-and-so killed Lawrence Watson." This silence might have gone on forever had it not been interrupted by something that was to change the course of their investigation.

"Excuse me. Can you help me?" said a voice that Ransom didn't recognize. He looked up and with a slight sense of dread saw a little old lady. He didn't speak for a moment as he appraised her. She had a very healthy head of thick gray hair, far more hair than he was used to seeing on a woman her age. It was swept back and tied tightly in a small bun. She wore a faded blue skirt with a matching jacket and tan blouse with a ruffled front that was meant to look like silk but was obviously synthetic. Tucked in her sleeve was a crisp white handkerchief that Ransom imagined had been given to her as a gift by someone who didn't know what else to give an old lady. She struck him immediately as the type of woman who would retain the gift because it *was* a gift, whether or not she particularly liked it. All in all, she gave a soft and favorable impression, and if Ransom still experienced that slight sense of dread, it was from fearing that the old lady's visit would be time-consuming.

"Excuse me?" she said again, a bit nonplussed at the lengthy pause.

"I'm sorry," said Ransom, "can I help you?"

"Yes. I think so. I hope so. I talked to a gentleman downstairs, and he told me you were the one I should talk to," she said, taking a couple of hesitant steps into the office.

"Gerald?"

The partner took the hint and rose, blushing slightly at not having thought of it sooner, and proffered his seat to the lady. "Here you go, ma'am."

The old lady took the chair with a grateful "thank you," laying down her purse and folding her hands neatly in her lap.

"I'm Detective Ransom and this is my partner, Detective White."

"Oh. I'm very pleased to meet you."

"Now, what can I do for you?" asked Ransom, realizing that she was waiting for him to give her the go-ahead.

"Well...I'm afraid you're going to think I'm crazy, or at least foolish," the lady said, a bit flustered, realizing that now that she was here she would have to tell her story.

"Not at all."

"My name is Emily Charters, and I want you to look into the death of my friend Meg—I mean Margaret, Margaret Ferguson."

"Why?" said Ransom, not altering his expression.

"Why?" she repeated, quite confused. This was certainly the last question she expected to be asked. "I don't understand."

"Well, I'm assuming that this..."

"Meg."

"...Meg died, and that if there was anything unusual about her death, the police would have looked into it already. Did they?"

"No, of course not."

Ransom glanced at Gerald, who was now leaning against the doorjamb. Ransom could read nothing in his partner's face, and he himself didn't know how to take the lady's statement. Did "of course not" mean that she thought the police irresponsible, or that she felt this had simply been a stupid question? He folded his hands, unconsciously mirroring Emily, and waited.

"They didn't look into her death at all, Mr. Ransom."

"They must have in some way."

She sighed, realizing that Ransom was dreadfully uninformed. "When an older woman dies, believe me Mr. Ransom, people simply don't ask very many questions."

"Miss Charters, was this Meg around your age?"

"Meg was two years older than me," she answered stiffly.

"And what was the given cause of death?"

"Heart failure. Her heart stopped."

Ransom inhaled deeply, attempting to modulate his voice so that it sounded neither sarcastic nor condescending. If anything, he actually felt sympathy for the old woman.

"Miss Charters, it occurs to me that in a person of your...your friend's age, heart failure is entirely possible."

"The ravages of age are no secret to me, young man," she said calmly, almost wistfully. "I have seen age take many of my friends and loved ones. Most of them, in fact. And it's easy for me to believe at my time of life that one day the heart can grow tired enough that it slows to a stop. It isn't something I fear, mind you. It's something that I would almost welcome. After all, it would be a rather peaceful way to die, don't you think?"

Neither of the detectives answered, feeling that no answer was called for. There was a pause during which Emily seemed to be contemplating something beyond the ken of Jeremy Ransom or Gerald White.

"Miss Charters," said Ransom quietly, almost as if it

would be disrespectful to speak too loudly in her presence, "do you have any reason to believe that your friend died of something other than heart failure?"

Emily frowned, the creases of concern mingling with the lines of age. If she feared seeming foolish before, she feared it even more now.

"Mr. Ransom, I'm terribly afraid you're going to think me a silly old woman. I may be, I don't know. But I'm not fanciful. I've never been that."

"Go on."

"I'm quite used to my friends dying. At my age, that happens at very regular intervals. And I've never before thought there was anything suspicious or unusual about their deaths."

Ransom's right hand automatically swept up to his mouth to cover the smile he could feel growing. There was something that could only be described as cute in hearing this delicate old woman approach the subject of murder. Gerald's expression was unchanged.

"Then what's different about this one?" asked Ransom, recovering himself.

Emily stopped and looked at him. It was her turn to appraise him. What she saw was what she called a young man, as she would any many under sixty. He was dressed respectably but not expensively, as she might expect of a man in his position. It was his face that interested her. It was not the type of face she would have expected of a homicide detective. Although he looked ordinary for the most part, and hurried, as might also be expected, there was something about his face that Emily felt drawn to. Kindness, she thought, relieved that she had been able to put a name to it. Whatever else this Detective Ransom might be, and whatever he might think of her, Emily was sure that he was a kind man. She decided that foolish or not, she could risk telling her story to him.

"I've been so muddled lately, I don't know if I'm just imagining things. If it had been at any other time...or anyone other than Meg, I would have taken her death as quite natural. But...lately I've been seeing people that look familiar."

"Familiar?"

"Yes."

"That's also quite natural," said Ransom gently.

"Oh, I realize that, but it's not exactly what I mean. What I mean is, I've been seeing people...in the papers...people who I think I know, but that I don't know. Do you know what I mean? I'm afraid I'm not explaining myself at all well."

Stifling a laugh, Ransom straightened in his chair. "I'm afraid I don't."

"Oh, of course you wouldn't. You're still young."

Ransom cringed a bit at this, remembering his thoughts of the evening before, but said nothing.

"When you get to be as old as I am, it becomes a way of life. You have met so many people and seen so many faces that they all seem to look alike. Everyone starts to look a bit familiar. But this was a little different. I saw a picture in the paper earlier this week of a man who'd been murdered, and he looked familiar. Not in the usual sense, in a way that made me feel...well, for lack of a better term, in a way that made me feel somewhat haunted."

Ransom furnished himself with a punch line to this, something to the effect of being somewhat pregnant, while Emily continued.

"The exact same thing happened a day later, except this time it was a young woman. She was murdered, and her picture looked familiar. I set it down to what I was just saying—to everyone looking familiar. But then Meg died, and I realized that it wasn't a trick of the memory. I *did* know these people."

"Yes?"

"It was when Meg and I were last together. That's when I saw the other two. It just seems too coincidental."

"Now wait," said Ransom, stopping her for fear she was about to wander again, wanting to sort out her thoughts. "Who exactly were these other two people?"

"You see," said Emily, primly opening her purse and withdrawing the two newspaper clippings, "I didn't really *know* them, I only saw them when I was last with Meg—that would be last Saturday night."

Emily laid down the pictures one at a time. The first, the young Barbara Landis, meant nothing to Ransom, but when he saw the second picture he fairly shot out of his chair. It was Lawrence Watson.

"Miss Charters! Where did you see these people?"

"At the theater, Mr. Ransom. I saw them when Meg and I went to the theater."

RANSOM CAUGHT HIMSELF instantly and settled back in his chair, tempering his initial reaction by reminding himself that the "witness" before him could be faulty at best, given her age and state of mind. Age must be a very sad thing, he thought, and he could imagine that she, out of the sadness of losing her friend or purely out of age, was willing to believe there was more to Meg Ferguson's death than there really was. Perhaps coming in to question her friend's death was an expression of questioning death in general. But if Ransom's perceptiveness was still intact, he couldn't support this looking at the old lady seated before him. Emily might believe herself to be muddled, but he wasn't quite so sure, even if he wasn't immediately ready to accept the idea that the three deaths were connected. In his eyes, it had taken a fair amount of mental acumen to link the deaths, even if it had taken her slightly longer than it might have taken a younger person with the same information, and Emily herself, while her tendency to flutter undoubtedly gave people the wrong impression, still had an air of one who is able to keep her wits about her, even in the worst of circumstances. Yes, thought Ransom, she had said it all herself: She is not fanciful.

But he still found the idea that the deaths were connected a bit farfetched. With an uncharacteristic lack of cynicism, he looked at the deaths themselves. Surely if studies were done on audiences all over America, it wouldn't be unusual to find that, given the size of the downtown theaters, three of the audience members had died within a week of any particular performance. This would be especially true given that though two of the victims had been murdered, according to the newspaper clippings they were murdered in two completely different manners and in wildly differing circumstances. The last death, he was sure, had been from natural causes. But still there was the earnest lady before him, and a vague, growing sensation that his job was about to take a turn for the worse.

"Miss Charters," he said calmly, "how can you be so sure that you actually saw these other two people when you were at the theater with your friend? I mean, there must have been hundreds—thousands of people, maybe, at the theater. What made you notice these two in particular."

"Oh no," she answered, blushing slightly, "Meg and I are—were—both on fixed incomes. We could seldom afford to go to the downtown theaters to see the big productions that come to town. You know, the big touring companies, the musicals. Of course, sometimes we were given tickets by friends or acquaintances that, I'm embarrassed to say, I think felt sorry for us, and then we'd go to the big shows—isn't it amazing how so many people these days seem to have so much money and it seems to mean so little to them that they can give away expensive tickets like that? But mainly we went to little theaters. Actually, if the truth be known, I find the big shows to be a bit too presupposing for me anymore, and getting in and out of the theater can be difficult, everybody pushing and shoving and nobody giving any mind to you no matter what age you might be."

"So this was at a small theater where you saw these people?"

"Oh yes, so often in these small local theaters you see much more interesting things than you can see downtown, and the actors are young and so much more eager. Although, I'm afraid this simply wasn't the case with this particular play. It was a rather unfortunate version of *Love's Labor's Lost*."

"But how can you be sure that it was these two people you saw in the audience?"

"I can be sure, young man, because there were only a handful—literally a handful—of people in the audience. I certainly was able to see them all in full view during the intermission. That's why these people looked so familiar to me, you know. You must have had that happen before—you stand around in a group of people during an intermission and you look at each one very intently, but you don't really see them, if you know what I mean. For whatever reason you look at their faces but they don't really register—perhaps because you're having a glass of punch or because you're chatting with a friend. I'm sure that Meg and I chatted all the way through the intermission."

This made all the difference to Ransom. For three out of a thousand in the same audience to die within a week was plausible, for three out of a dozen or less was downright provoking.

"Miss Charters, I'd like you to tell me everything you remember about last Saturday night. Where was this play you saw?"

"It was the Perry...no, that's not it...the Pennington, that's it, the Pennington Players. They're a little theater company way up on Clark Street." Emily was rather flustered. Although she did have her suspicions about the three deaths, she was quite willing to believe she was mistaken. She hadn't been quite so willing to believe she was correct. "We had to take the bus there."

"Was anyone there familiar? Did you see anybody you knew?"

"Oh no, Meg was the only one there I knew, and we had never before been to that particular theater, I don't think. As I said, they were doing *Love's Labor's Lost*, so there were ten—or maybe twelve—people in the play. It's hard to tell. They all play more than one role, so you end up not knowing who is what or how many of them there really are. Anyway, there were at least ten in the play."

"You didn't know anyone in the play or in the audience?"

"Only Meg."

"And you didn't know anyone in the cast," he said, more ruminating to himself than speaking to her. "Hmmm. I wonder just who was in the cast."

"Well, I still have my program," she said, interrupting his reverie.

"You do?"

"Yes. I always save all the programs. It's a bother, and it takes up room, but I like to keep memories of things I've seen and done. I mean, I keep albums of snapshots of all the places I visited with my husband when he was still alive. This is just more of the same thing, saving programs. Who knows? One day I might see one of those young people on the television, and then I can look back in my programs and see if it really was someone that I saw in person a long time ago. It's happened, you know."

He smiled at her warmly. "Would you mind if I came around tomorrow and looked at this program of yours?"

"No, of course I wouldn't mind."

"And in the meantime, you think about that night, and see if you can remember anything that might be helpful. I'll keep these," he said, picking up the clippings, "and give the matter some thought. See if I can come up with anything. You just relax. I promise you I'll do some looking into your friend's death."

"Oh, I'd really appreciate that," she said as she rose to go. Ransom rose at the same time. "Meg was a dear friend, Mr. Ransom, and I should like you to catch her murderer."

He smiled at this. She sounded like a schoolteacher who had set him to a task that she expected to be completed in the allotted time.

"I'm not saying there's anything to it, but it always pays to be thorough. Did you come by bus? Detective White can give you a ride home, can't you, Gerald?"

"Thank you, that would be most kind!"

Emily passed through the door to Ransom's office, and Gerald started to follow, but Ransom took hold of his arm gently, tapping the clipping of Barbara Landis.

"Drop her off and come right back. I'm going to find out who's on this case," he said quietly.

"Right."

Gerald left the office and offered his arm to the waiting Emily. He modulated his steps, walking slowly enough for her to feel she was keeping pace, and they made their way out of the office building. The moment they were out of his office, Ransom was on the phone.

"Yes? Detective White is on his way out of the building right now with a little old lady. The name is Emily Charters...yes...he's taking her home. Follow them. I want her kept under surveillance. I don't *care* how short-handed we are, get on it!"

He hung up the phone and slid back into his chair, extracting one of his plastic-tipped cigars from his coat pocket. He lit the cigar, leaned back in his chair, and threw the match into the filthy ashtray on his desk. His mind raced.

SEVEN

Sara Collins had been very careful in choosing an apartment. It wasn't that she was antisocial, it was just that when it came to her home, she did not want to see or hear any of her neighbors at any time. She had come back to see the same apartment at different times of the day and night to make sure beforehand she would not be subjected to any extraneous noise in the building. The landlord, who in the end had become rather annoyed at having to show the same apartment to the same person so many times, assured her over and over again that the building, the other tenants, and the entire neighborhood were very quiet, and that she could be certain of safety and quiet in her own home. He was amazed that anyone as young as Sara, who on her application had stated her age as twenty-four, could be so concerned about peace.

As Gerald was walking Emily down to his car, Sara was combing out her long, frizzy blond hair, finally tying it back in a ponytail so that it wouldn't get in her eyes on her afternoon bike ride. She was all decked out in her riding apparel—pink high-tops, black tights, and pink leotard—and as she looked at herself in the mirror to apply her sunscreen, she was quite pleased with her overall appearance.

When she had finished, she retrieved the ten-speed racer she kept wedged under the counter that bordered her kitchen and living room and hoisted it onto her shoulder to carry it through the hall. Many of the other tenants, although she didn't see them, rolled their bicycles down the hallway, something that she would never have thought of doing. She knew the other tenants perpetrated this atrocity because she would sometimes spot wheel tracks on the carpeting between the apartments and the elevators. On such occasions, she clucked her tongue and reminded herself that most people were pigs.

She passed out of the doorway and closed the door behind her, quickly checking as it clicked shut to make sure she had remembered her keys, and turned down the hall with an only slightly irritated glance at the cheap metal 12 the building owners had tacked on the door to mark her apartment. Why are owners always so cheap? she thought as she often did when she cared to think about the building at all. She adjusted the bike on her shoulder and started down the hallway. As she passed number 11 she stopped and sniffed. The smell, she thought, was getting stronger. It was an affront. With all the care she had given to keeping herself free from the sights and sounds of other tenants, nothing could free her from their smell. The acrid odor emanating from number 11 had been growing day by day. They must be East Indians, she thought. Although she would swear that there wasn't a prejudiced bone in her body, she firmly believed that East Indians weren't the most sanitary people in the world and that they were always cooking things that smelled nasty. If she had known East Indians were living on that floor—if indeed, they *were* East Indians, since she had never seen her neighbors—she never would have moved in. "If they don't clean up whatever the hell is causing that stink," she said loudly, "I'm going to call the landlord!"

She paused by the door for a moment to see if she could hear any movement that might have been caused by her statement. Hearing nothing, she heaved a heavy sigh, continued down the hallway, and rang for the elevator.

Nobody had heard her.

The first official function of the Pennington Players, now "civilians," was held that Friday night, barely a week after their postmortem exercise at the Ridge Bar. This was a much happier event, held at Lorrie's apartment. This party was a celebration of one of their ranks finally making good: making good in this case translating to making money, and the rank in question being the soon-to-be-Hollywood-bound Damien Liddle. Damien had given in to the call for a party somewhat reluctantly, knowing he'd be leaving himself open to all sorts of snide remarks and barbs about selling out and the relative unrespectability of appearing on television. But Damien loved parties, especially when he was the guest of honor (although, had he been asked he would have been hard-pressed to name another occasion on which he had been the guest of honor, thus making the origins of his love for the position somewhat murky), no matter how dubious the honor might be or how insincere the other guests certainly were.

The party was in full swing when he arrived, having timed his entrance with his usual theatrical flair. He was greeted by what seemed to be the entire Chicago theater community, all plastic smiles and pats on the back and newly acquired friendliness. Damien, as usual, made sure he spent a decent amount of time talking to the important people at the party, although at the moment he was certain that he was the only really important person there.

"Damien!" said Lorrie, taking him by the arm. "It's so exciting! I can't believe it!"

"Yeah," he said, curling up the corner of his mouth, "it is."

"When do you leave? Do you know yet?"

"I have to go out to the coast right away. We go into

production in two weeks." Damien's internal smile grew even wider than the one on his face. He liked hearing the words coming out of his mouth and sounding so, well, real and professional. That was it, he thought, after all this farting around with the Players and the Chicago scene, he was at last a professional.

"You'll remember me when you get out there, won't you?" asked Lorrie. Although she tried to make the question sound like a joke, her eagerness was so thinly disguised it was almost painful to hear. "I mean, if a role comes up out there that I can do, you'll tell them about me, won't you?"

"Sure I will.'

"Have you seen Gail?" she asked coyly.

"No, why?"

"She's been moping around the corners of the room ever since she got here. She's just devastated that you're leaving her." She smiled at him, making a pretence of having accidentally used "her" instead of "here." "I mean, that you're leaving town."

"Really," he said flatly.

"Yes. If you work your way around the walls, you're bound to run into her."

He almost laughed. He didn't like Gail, but he liked Lorrie even less, especially now that she was using this conspiratorial tone of voice. "Thanks for the warning," he said. He glanced over her shoulder and saw Danny approaching with two drinks in his hands. He was once again reminded of one of Lorrie's reasons for liking the hulkish actor. Although Danny had one of those faces that betrayed a lack of intelligence, he was certainly able to keep himself looking good. This evening, Damien noted, he was wearing jeans so tight they appeared to be painted on and a cream-colored gauze shirt, equally tight, that showed his well-exercised pectorals, with a good amount of chest hair visible through the unbuttoned front.

"Here's the man of the hour!" said Danny congenially. Lorrie shot an annoyed glance at him over her shoulder, as if he were interrupting an important meeting and hadn't the sense to realize his mistake. Which, in fact, he didn't.

"Congratulations! Wow, a series! I mean, that's great!"

Lorrie took one of the drinks from his hand, spilling a drop or two on his right shoe, which also went unnoticed. He reached over and took Damien's hand roughly.

"When Lorrie told me, I said, 'Nobody deserves it more than he does!'"

"Thanks."

"I think it's vulgar," said Alice, who seemed to loom up out of nowhere to offer this pronouncement. Damien steadied himself against the sudden, brief dizziness he felt at her arrival, the manner of which accentuated the kaleidoscopic quality of theater parties, where Damien often had the feeling that he alone was standing still at a central, fixed point while the room revolved, so that he ended up talking with whoever swirled into his vicinity.

"Vulgar?" he asked with feigned incredulity, knowing full well what she meant.

"Vulgar," she continued, "that someone with an interest in classical theater should stoop to degrading himself in a medium like television."

It was odd that it had never struck him before, as it did now, how like a member of the Russian working class Alice seemed. Like a character out of *Ninotchka*. He half expected her to accuse him of being a member of the bourgeoisie.

"Oh, Alice, for God's sake, this is a party," said Lorrie in the voice of a petulant teenager.

"It'll free me up," said Damien, trying to control his temper, "it'll free me up to *do* Shakespeare."

"Without starving," she replied with a sneer.

"It will be nice to have money for once."

Alice's face was marred by a knowing smile that Damien found both disconcerting and infuriating. He reminded himself that Alice's views were more likely prompted by the theater's most injurious aspect: jealousy.

"I have nothing against you," she said finally. "Actually, I just fault myself for not having seen through you. You're not interested in the classics at all, you're only interested in money. You don't want to be an actor, you want to be a star."

With this pronouncement, the room shifted, revolving Alice away from them.

"Bitch!" said Lorrie loudly. "Don't let her bother you. She would do television in a minute if anyone *wanted* her to."

There was an embarrassed silence as the three of them searched for words to lift the pall that Alice had cast on the assembly.

"When you thinking of going out there?" said Danny, breaking the silence.

"Very soon," said Damien in a tone one uses when answering a child who asks the same question over and over. "I have to leave almost immediately."

"Wow, that's great! When is this series gonna be on? I'll have to look in the *TV Guide* for it."

Damien smiled. "You don't have to start looking yet. It probably won't be on till late fall—replacing something else—or midwinter. I don't have the date yet. I'm sure you'll hear about it."

"Lorrie will let me know, won't you?"

"Yes," she sighed.

"You'll call and tell her when it's going to be on, won't you?"

Lorrie perked up at this inadvertent mention of having Damien keep in touch with her, all the more important because Danny made it sound perfectly natural. For once, she wasn't sorry that Danny had opened his mouth.

"Yeah, I'll call her."

"That's really great. It couldn't happen to a nicer guy, Dame."

Damien winced. With all the care he'd given to choosing his vaguely British name, he had neglected to take into account the American penchant for abbreviation. It fortunately didn't happen very often to him, but it bothered him when it did. He started to ease away from them. "Thanks...uh, there's some people I have to talk to. Excuse me."

Lorrie turned a petulant glance toward Danny. "Idiot!" she said, giving him a sharp slap on the shoulder.

"What did I do?"

She sighed heavily, realizing that it was no use trying to explain subtleties. "I have to keep in good with the jerk now that he's going somewhere. I have to keep on his good side."

"Oh, come on," he said reproachfully.

"I mean it! You never know where these things can lead. And you're no help, you big idiot!"

"What did I *do*?"

"Well," she said, smiling unpleasantly at Damien, who was now halfway across the room talking to a small group of people who had attended acting class with him, "I'm sure he doesn't like being called Dame! He's really touchy about that."

"It's just short for Damien."

"You really *are* an idiot!"

Danny thought for a moment, and then, as if clouds were parting in his mind and a ray of sunshine had just broken through, he said, "Oh...you mean..."

"Yes!" she said, shushing him.

"I didn't know."

Lorrie laughed, as if enjoying a rather nasty private joke. "You're not the only one! Gail doesn't know, and she moons over him like a big wet puppy!"

Danny glanced over to the north wall of the apartment and there, slumped in an uncomfortable-looking easy chair, was Gail. She appeared very sad, but it was clear that her gaze was unswervingly fixed on Damien.

Lorrie reached up and nibbled on Danny's right ear, laughing lightly. "I wonder what she'll do when she finds out?"

"So what do we have?"

"Nothing that amounts to a hill of shit. A very frustrating hill of shit, if you ask me."

"I take it she had no enemies?"

"The Landis girl was twenty-five years old...."

"Hardly a girl."

Detective Robinson flushed slightly. He disliked being interrupted, but he wasn't about to argue with Ransom, whose reputation as an irreproachable expert was intimidating to the young detective. "She was only twenty-five, hardly old enough to have made the type of enemies that would have killed her. We would have thought it was some sort of sex thing, except that she wasn't raped."

Ransom smiled rather condescendingly at Robinson. The phrase "sex thing" reminded him of one of his pet gripes with the city, namely, that the public school system had deteriorated noticeably since he was young enough to be a student. Surely, he thought, even a novice detective could come up with a better euphemism for rape, if he felt he needed a euphemism at all. And, of course, given the opportunity, many twenty-five-year-olds had made deadly enemies.

"So," he said, "she wasn't raped and she wasn't robbed."

"That's right. There doesn't seem to be any particular reason she should have been killed."

"You've talked to her friends, family, coworkers?"

Robinson checked his anger at being asked such a basic question, which to him implied that he wasn't smart enough to carry on even the most rudimentary of investigations.

"Of course we did. It was the first thing we did."

"Sorry. I wasn't questioning your abilities. It was a rhetorical question."

"It's all right," said Robinson, somewhat mollified. He was in his late twenties and had been a detective for less than a year. It was particularly difficult for him because he was going through what could best be termed a "phase," during which he felt one thing but tried to do another. Robinson was still affected by the sight of death, yet felt that he needed to act as if any crime, no matter how heinous, had no effect on him at all. He also felt inferior to those older than himself, yet he was in a position where it was important to act as if he were on their level. Unfortunately, on his job he was dealing with life and death, which meant he had to control himself more thoroughly than someone who worked in a store or a bank.

Ransom, on the other hand, was only slightly more than a decade older than Robinson, and was painfully aware of the young detective's situation.

"What did the people you questioned have to say?"

"The usual," said Robinson, trying to adopt a more casual air. "That they couldn't imagine anyone having any reason to kill the girl. That it must have been a maniac. That she was a good girl, and nobody could have hated her or wanted to see her dead. The family was pretty broken up by it."

"As well they might be. What exactly happened?"

"Near as we can figure, he jimmied the lock—it had been worked over—whoever it was wasn't a pro—and waited for her to get home from work, and when she got there, he killed her."

"He?"

Robinson flushed again. "He or she, we don't know yet."

"I see."

"It's just natural to think that it was a guy that did this sort of thing."

"And this happened on Tuesday?"

Robinson nodded.

"How was she killed?"

"Her throat was slit."

Ransom shifted in his chair, clearly disappointed. "Really?"

"Yeah. The coroner said it was one clean cut—the area around the mouth and chin were slightly bruised, as well as her left shoulder."

"What did the neighbors have to say?"

"They didn't hear or see anything."

"There seems to be a lot of that going around these days." Ransom was disgusted at how inattentive or reluctant people seemed to be about helping with an investigation. And yet at the same time they always demanded that the police solve crimes immediately, presumably using a crystal ball and magic. The most ironic part of it was that they were always very insistent on the need to get involved when it was their own loved ones who were killed.

"So," said Ransom, staring off into space, picturing the scene, "whoever it was grabbed her from behind and presumably held her while slitting her throat. That would mean the killer was right-handed...." his voice trailed off.

"Well, yes..." said Robinson, a bit confused that Ransom seemed to be talking to himself, "that's what the coroner said. How did you know?"

"It just stands to reason. If the neighbors really didn't hear anything, then he obviously covered her mouth to keep her from screaming. The bruising around her mouth and chin would be from covering her mouth so tightly. He would also be trying to hold her still, so his left arm probably caused the bruising on her left shoulder. He reached around her from behind, holding her mouth and body with his left arm, and then used his right hand to slit her throat." There was a short silence as Ransom continued his reverie. He suddenly broke from it, remembering that he was not alone; "It *was* the left side of her throat that was cut?"

"Uh, yes."

"God, that must've been awfully messy," said Ransom, slipping back into his reverie.

"It was!" said Robinson, his earnestness betraying that he had been affected by the sight. But he couldn't help himself. Ransom's words had brought back the vision of Barbara Landis's body, lying in the center of her kitchen floor in what appeared to be a sea of blood, the refrigerator door hanging open and the groceries still sitting in the bags on the table, serenely blind to the hideous sight on the floor.

Ransom glanced at him knowingly. "It bothers you."

"No," said Robinson, a little too loudly and now turning a deep crimson in embarrassment.

"It's all right. You *should* be bothered by it."

Robinson looked up, not knowing whether to be embarrassed or angry. In the end he felt relief.

"I hope you stay affected by it. It's the only sign that you're still a human being."

Over Robinson's shoulder Ransom could see that Gerald had appeared in the doorway. He signaled for him to wait.

"Now," he said quietly, "have you discovered anything else about the Landis death?"

"Nothing. We've questioned everybody we can think of, and came up empty." He stopped, then added quickly, "We're still working on it."

"Good. If you come up with anything, let me know, will you?"

"Yes, yes of course," said Robinson rising, sensing that their meeting was over. "Tell me, why did you want to know about this? You're working on another case, right? Does this have anything to do with it?"

"Probably not."

"Then why…"

"I was just curious. I…saw her picture in the paper, wondered how she died."

Robinson looked at him curiously, and not very happily, then thought it was probably better to leave than to try to get anything further out of Ransom. He said, "I'll let you know if we come up with anything," and then bumped into Gerald on his way out the door.

"What's with the up-and-coming Sherlock?" said Gerald, as he seated himself in the chair that Robinson had just vacated.

"He's on the Landis case."

"That should keep it successfully unsolved."

"Be kind, Gerald."

"I noticed you didn't tell *him* anything."

Ransom sighed, knowing he had been caught. "Yes, I really don't want him looking around the same field we're in. He's a bit clumsy—I'm sure it's just because he's young."

"Uh-huh," said Gerald, smiling knowingly.

"Did you get Miss Charters home all right?"

"Yes. I noticed you had us followed. Sanders is settled in outside her house."

"Good. Sanders is a good woman."

"I take it that you give some credence to the old girl's story."

"Not particularly. It seems too farfetched. But it's better to be safe than sorry. I wouldn't like to see her killed while looking into it." He had tried to say this lightly, but was unconvincing.

Gerald laughed. "You really think there's a chance of that?"

"Well, look at the evidence, such as it is. Three people that were in the audience of a play on last Saturday night—a play attended by a handful of people—are dead. Now, if there'd been a thousand people there, I wouldn't think that much of it, but a handful? We've got to look at it logically. Watson, *our* dead man, doesn't have an enemy in the world, if the people we've talked to are to be believed, nor is there any reason we've been able to find that he should have been killed—and yet he's dead. The only thing we've come up with so far is delivered to us by this little old lady—and that's that he attended a play, and two other audience members are dead."

"Coincidence."

"Really? Look at the timing of it. Watson was killed

Monday night on his way home from work. Landis was killed Tuesday, ditto. Ferguson was found dead Wednesday morning. It very clearly appears that someone is killing off the audience members one by one."

"You sound as if you don't believe it even as you say it."

"Well," said Ransom, heaving a heavy sigh, "there's one thing I really don't like about it. The Landis killing isn't a bit like the Watson killing. Watson was shot in the street in what amounts to a hit. The only thing lacking was a black car speeding away from the scene of the crime. The Landis killing was quite different. Someone broke into her apartment and slit her throat. That sounds a lot more personal than our man Watson."

"I suppose so."

"Personal," Ransom continued, almost to himself, "and yet she wasn't raped. So it was a personal grudge, not personal passion."

"Once again, passion ruled out."

"Yes. It doesn't look like either Watson or Landis evoked much in the way of passion. So, it would look as if the Landis killing was personal grudge."

"Or a maniac."

"Oh, yes, the catch-all for unsolved murders."

"What about the old lady's friend...Meg Ferguson?"

Ransom shook his head, dismissing her. "I'm sure that was natural causes. In all likelihood, her heart just stopped beating. Now of course, there are ways to make the heart stop beating, but even if that's so, what are we left with? Three completely different murders."

"Then why have the old lady watched?"

A black look came over Ransom's face, and he rose from his chair, as if the faintly uneasy feeling he had about the old woman and her story could be handled better on his feet than sitting down. He propped himself up against the wall with one hand and looked absently at the map of Chicago that adorned it.

"Because, Gerald, if there *is* something to what she says, then for God-knows-what reason somebody is bumping off everyone who was in that audience last Saturday night. At the moment, we only know four of the audience members: Watson, Landis, Ferguson, and Charters, the latter being the only one still alive. I'd appreciate it if she'd stay that way until we can find out what's going on."

"You didn't tell her you're having her watched."

"No, of course not! I didn't want to *give* the poor old thing a heart attack! And at the moment, she doesn't seem to see the implication in what she herself suspects. She seems to only be interested in finding out who, if anyone, killed her friend. Now, it may be that she'll realize that if she's right she might be in danger—she seems a pretty sharp old bird, so I shouldn't think it would take long—and then I'll talk to her about protecting her. But I'm going to go on and have her watched for the time being without her knowledge, just in case."

There was another silence, during which Ransom appeared to be engrossed in studying the map, although if the truth be known he wasn't cognizant of the map at all. Gerald broke the silence.

"You know, there's one thing you haven't mentioned."

Ransom turned to him with a slightly quizzical look.

"Well," he continued, "there was a murder on Monday, Tuesday, and Wednesday. Today is Friday. You think somebody was killed last night?"

Ransom brightened as if this new idea had let a little sunlight into his brain, which had become darker and darker as they had pursued their discussion. Ruminating on the information they *did* have had made him completely forget the information they didn't have.

"Gerald, check around and see what came in in the way of murders yesterday. And—I think we'd better find out just as soon as we can who's in charge of the Pennington Players, and have a talk with him or her."

"Right," said Gerald, who was now on his feet. "We're going to have to see if we can track down the rest of the audience." He said this rhetorically, but Ransom wouldn't have answered even if the question had actually been directed to him. He had gone back to gazing at the map, lost in thought. Gerald left him to his reverie and went to see what he could find out about murders that had been committed on Thursday. Ransom didn't notice him leave.

"*Love's Labor's Lost*," he said quietly.

RANSOM FUMBLED with the keys to his apartment, even more exhausted than usual. He hated working late on Friday night, even after all this time, knowing that he almost always ended up doing it. He was sure this resentment about it stemmed from being brought up by parents who had a good old-fashioned work ethic: Do a good job forty hours a week, do your best, and the rest of the week is yours. What could he make of himself? he thought as he opened the door and switched on the lights. He found himself working sixty, seventy, eighty hours a week. What did that mean? Was it that he didn't do a good enough job in the allotted forty hours? Was it like school, being kept after for not having done your homework?

He shook his head, trying to dismiss these thoughts, knowing that they were counterproductive and just the outgrowth of exhaustion. He knew that he was no different from any other detective when it came to extra hours.

Even if they didn't stay at the station, how could you turn off your mind once you went home? It didn't matter if you'd turned over a case to the night shift, leaving it for them to dig up whatever they could. Your mind—at least, his mind—would continue working on it after hours whether he liked it or not, no matter what the union might say about it. So what was he to do rather than keep working? Unions! What a great job the unions have done for us poor little flatfeet, he thought sardonically. Ordinarily he would never have thought of using a term like that, but he was painfully aware of his feet at the moment, which felt as if they were burning their way through his shoes. He kicked off his shoes and sat on the ages-old couch in his living room and rubbed his aching feet through his socks. God, the others must think I'm some sort of obsessed workaholic. He shook his head again, and said aloud, "Jeez, it's not like you to even *think* about what other people might think of you! You *must* be tired!"

His exhaustion was not only physical, it was mental as well. It was early evening when they had started to look for information on the Pennington Players. At first he had tried the weekend section from the current paper but didn't find them in the theater listings. A quick rummage through the newspapers they had lying around the station turned up a weekend section from the previous week's *Tribune*. Unfortunately, only one name was listed, the director of the production, Damien Liddle. Ransom winced at the name. Through a phone call to the editor he turned up a few other names connected with the company, as well as the names of four of the leading actors in their last production. That was all right for a start, but calls to their homes had turned up nothing. None of the company members seemed to be at home, and he had listened to an endless number of sophomoric answering machine messages while trying to find someone in. Of course, he didn't want to leave anyone a message, first, because he thought a call from the police would unnecessarily alarm the innocent and warn the guilty, if there were a guilty party amid the company. Second, he was aware that even if he was getting their machines, there was a good chance that they were in and just screening their calls. That is, after all, what he did himself. After a long day of running down leads and calling all over the place, the last thing he wanted to do was return calls. It had come to the point that when he arrived home, if the light was flashing on his machine, he just reset it and erased the calls without listening to them. It was unfair, he knew, but it had been a gradual process of going from listening to the calls and not returning them, to playing the calls but not really listening to them, to not even listening to them at all.

Okay, it was Friday night, and these were, after all, theater people—although he didn't know what that had to do with it—and they could be expected to be out. Ransom couldn't remember the last time he had "gone out" on a Friday night, or any other night for that matter. Why did it seem that all he ever did was work?

While he made his calls, Gerald found that there had been two murders in their precinct on Thursday: In one a husband had killed his wife—he readily admitted to it, saying that he just couldn't take it anymore, although the detectives on the case hadn't been able to ascertain just exactly what "it" was. The other was an eighteen-year-old African-American man who had been shot in one of the housing projects. They were sure that this murder was either drug or gang related, or both. Ransom shook his head when he learned about it, sure that his killer wouldn't be caught dead, so to speak, in the projects. His own response surprised him, since he had no idea for whom he was looking, and therefore couldn't know what the killer would do or where he would go. Nonetheless, he was sure these killings were not related to the others. Why, then, had the killer presumably taken the night off? They were going to have to spread their search to murders outside their precinct.

Sitting there on his couch, rubbing his feet, he suddenly caught himself running through all this again in his mind. As if action was the only thing that could stop his mind from going off in these unwanted directions, he jumped up and headed for the refrigerator. Inside was a pitcher of instant tea he had made the night before, a few ounces of cheddar cheese, hardened to a dull, uninviting orange, a couple of sticks of margarine, and a few jars of assorted condiments. He sighed heavily and closed the door, remembering that he had meant to stop for some groceries—at least enough for the night—on the way home. And now he felt too tired to put his shoes back on and take what would seem an endless elevator ride back to the ground floor to get groceries, even though the nearest convenience store was just around the corner. With a momentary pang of desperation, he looked through the kitchen cabinets to see if he had any dried or canned food, anything that might be edible that he had forgotten, knowing all the while it was a fruitless search. The only thing he found was a box of cornflakes, and no matter how hungry he was, he just couldn't fathom eating a breakfast cereal at night.

In the last cabinet he found what he knew on sight would be his evening meal, a half-empty bottle of brandy. At first he stopped himself, realizing that since he hadn't eaten the drink would take effect more quickly than he wanted it to. But in the end, he went ahead, withdrawing a wineglass from another cabinet and heading into the bathroom with it. He ran a bath, letting the water run extra hot, as if he literally wanted to let the troubles melt away from him. While it was running he undressed, retrieved his book, and sat on the edge of the tub waiting for it to fill. The steam from the tub fogged up the bathroom mirror and the side of his glass.

In the short time he waited, he had emptied his glass of brandy. Warm inside and warm outside, he thought as he gingerly climbed into the steaming tub. His skin reddened slightly, but he didn't seem to notice. He slid back into the water and poured himself another drink. He took a couple of careful sips, set the glass down on the side of the tub, and picked up *Bleak House*. He was three-fourths of the way through the book and anxious to finish it, although he had read it before. But even as he opened it to the bookmark, he knew it was hopeless. The brandy and the bathwater were already well on their way to taking effect, and even though it wasn't all *that* late, he could feel his eyes go dry and his head start to fog. He closed the book, laying it on the bathmat where he hoped it would stay dry, and lowered himself further into the water, closing his eyes and feeling the steam flow up into his face. Sweat poured from his brow and underneath his hair, but it was a good feeling, a purging. He let his mind go wandering, and soon found fact and fiction melding, so that a strange, sweet little old lady seemed to be entering into Bleak House, telling him a story of people who looked familiar, but weren't familiar. Poor Esther, he thought, still seeing the little old lady, and what was the name of the other woman? Dedlock...Lady Dedlock. Esther saw someone who looked familiar, and yet wasn't familiar...the old lady seemed to be telling her the story of Esther...or maybe the old lady *was* Esther...or Lady

Dedlock. She looked familiar, and then something happened to her, he couldn't remember what, and she didn't look familiar anymore. Not totally familiar. The old lady and Esther and Lady Dedlock...the three women swirled through his mind as he drifted off to sleep.

EIGHT

IT WAS NOT a good idea to doze off in the bathtub. When he woke, he had been asleep for almost two hours, and his body ached from having been confined in such odd positions. To add to his discomfort, the water had long since gone from hot to tepid and was now becoming quite cold. He climbed out of the tub, pulled the stopper out of the drain, and toweled himself off. He then climbed into bed without bothering to don the shorts in which he usually slept, only to find that all this activity had robbed him of the ability to fall quickly back to sleep. He changed positions several times after laying in each position for what seemed hours. He tossed and turned for almost two and a half hours before sleep claimed him again.

The net result of all this nocturnal activity was that he awoke in the morning with a solidly aching neck and back and a fierce headache of the type that immediately drove him to overmedicate. He felt foggy and stuffy. He stumbled into the bathroom and retrieved the bottle of Excedrin that he kept open on the top shelf of the medicine cabinet—open because when he had one of his frequent headaches, he couldn't deal with childproof caps. It was a relief to find the tea waiting for him in the refrigerator, but he kicked himself again for not having gone to the store when he realized he had no milk for the cornflakes, and he didn't even have bread to make toast. He knew he'd have to stop on the way to the station for a doughnut, something—anything—that might help settle the faint nausea he felt, primarily as a result of the headache. He poured himself a large glass of tea and washed down three of the tablets with it. He really would have to eat something soon, he thought, or the pills themselves would make him sick. And this was not a day to be sick, since he had so many things to attend to. He intended to have a talk with Emily Charters in her home. Perhaps in her own surroundings she would feel safe and would be able to remember more about that night at the theater. But first he and Gerald would have to seek out the head of the Pennington Players. If they couldn't get any of these theater people to answer their machines, perhaps he'd have more luck by putting in a personal appearance.

He dressed quickly, deciding against wearing a tie, which he was sure would simply aggravate his headache, and slipped three more Excedrin in his shirt pocket, knowing he would probably need to take them later—and not much later, at that. He smiled to himself as he replaced the bottle in the medicine cabinet. For someone who had seen all manner of death and human suffering, he told himself, he certainly had a low threshold for pain.

Gerald had arrived at the station first, and after a quick check-in, they hopped into his car and were off to look up Damien Liddle.

"I got his address this morning," said Gerald.

"Good," said Ransom flatly. He could never understand how Gerald always managed to look healthy and happy. Gerald didn't seem to have a problem in the world, although Ransom was certain that he must have. Gerald was married, and as happy a marriage as it seemed to be, he was sure that they must at some time encounter problems. From Ransom's own experience, he knew that any long-standing relationship between a man and a woman was bound to see problems of one kind or another—probably big ones—but in all the times they had discussed his wife and the things the two of them did together, Gerald had never mentioned a problem, nor did he seem to show any of the little signs—sleepless nights, shortness of temper—that might indicate trouble at home. Ransom had met his wife, Sherry, on several occasions. They had even had him over for dinner, and their relationship had never appeared to be anything less than extraordinarily symbiotic. Ransom actually thought Sherry, with her long sandy hair, trim figure, and pleasing smile, to be a rather rare sort of woman: the kind that would get close, but not too close. The kind that would care deeply for her husband and still maintain a life of her own. The kind of woman, in fact, that he wished he could find for himself.

But the success of their marriage was not hers alone. Gerald White enjoyed an equanimity of temperament that was almost inhuman. In fact, Ransom found it quite irritating at times. He could never remember seeing Gerald angry, upset, or even short-tempered, although he did occasionally show a mild irritation at Ransom's unorthodox behavior. Gerald was the perfect...what was the word he was looking for? *Sidekick!* That was it. Ransom couldn't help smiling at the thought, despite his throbbing head, but the term wasn't far from the truth, and it was the first time he had really thought of it. He had always thought himself very lucky to have finally gotten a partner like Gerald White, but for the first time he realized that their success together might be because that was all Gerald was meant to be, at work as at home—a partner. Perhaps he was never meant to go on to other things: to climb the corporate ladder (so to speak) of the police department. Maybe he was meant to remain Ransom's helper and foil. But even Ransom couldn't bring himself to believe it, not really. Ransom felt sure that he was the only one who could ever "settle," he couldn't bring himself to believe that most people—himself notwithstanding—were not always hoping for something better for themselves, or trying to move up. He could remember a time when he himself would have held suspect anyone who didn't have a driving ambition. But if it were true...if Gerald really was content to be no more than a partner...they could end up together for quite some time, which certainly beat the hell out of trying to get used to a new partner once a year.

Ransom was beginning to feel the faint elation that comes from the mixture of caffeine and the aspirin in his tablets, along with a slight ebbing of the pounding that had been going on in his head since he woke.

"You're awfully quiet this morning."

"I was just thinking," said Ransom, rolling down the window a bit more to let in the cool morning air.

"You sure you're all right? You don't look too good."

"Yeah," he answered slowly, "I just didn't sleep very much. I woke up with a headache."

"Staying up late again with Mr. Dickens, I take it?"

Ransom smiled. "One of the things a single man still gets to do."

"I suppose if you're looking for an advantage that could be one."

"I'm not looking for reasons not to get married, Gerald. I have the best reason I can think of—I don't have anyone *to* marry."

"You could find someone if you wanted to."

"Spoken like a true housewife."

"Touché," said Gerald, with a smile that showed he wasn't taking his partner too seriously. He thought for a moment, then glanced at Ransom again before continuing. "You must not like the way the case is going."

"What makes you say that?"

"Because you're the only truly confirmed bachelor I

know. One of the Baker Street Irregulars following the Holmesian tradition of women being too hard on the brain for the thinking man. They get in the way, I can remember you saying on any number of occasions."

Ransom laughed at himself. "And yet I keep trying. You know the only time I've ever said anything like that is when my latest has given me the old heave-ho."

"Yes, but you still only ponder marriage when you don't like the way a case is going."

Ransom shot him a glance, a little annoyed that his partner would presume to know him so well. "I wasn't pondering marriage. You were the one who brought it up."

"It's true. *Are* you happy with the way this is going?"

Ransom sighed heavily and pulled out a cigar. It *was* annoying for Gerald to think he knew him so well, but it was even more annoying for him to be right. He tried to temper his response so that his partner wouldn't get to pat himself on the back. "Well, I wouldn't say I'm unhappy with it, exactly. It's more like unsure."

"What do you mean?"

"I mean, I feel like we're on the threshold of something. When we were looking at Watson's family and co-workers, I didn't have a sense right off the bat that any one of them had done it, although I suppose almost any of them could have. It was just a matter of finding a really good motive—not just adultery, but something substantial. With only that set of people to work with, I originally thought it would merely be a matter of time before we discovered *why* Watson had been murdered. But now, to be pulled in an entirely different direction, I feel like we're on the brink."

"Of what?"

"Of having something proven. I don't know exactly

what. But look at it this way, if the old lady's suspicions are true, and these deaths are somehow connected with this theater business, then we'll finally be on the right track. If there's no connection, then it'll prove that we've *been* on the right track, even though we don't have anything firm to go on."

"I'm not sure I follow you."

"If Watson was killed because he was in this theater last Saturday night, if there really is a connection, then I'm sure we'll be able to find it. If there really *is* a connection. If there isn't one, then we'll have to dig deeper into his private life, get tougher with the unpleasant Mrs. Watson, and the mistress...."

"And the corpulent Mr. Danners," said Gerald, enjoying the opportunity to remind Ransom of him.

"Exactly. We're on a threshold, Gerald. I think after today, we'll really know which direction to go. Either way, we'll know we're on the right track."

They fell silent for a time as Gerald maneuvered the car onto Western Avenue, which served as the main street for Damien Liddle's neighborhood.

"So I was right," said Gerald, breaking the silence.

"What?" Ransom had forgotten what they were talking about to begin with.

"You're dissatisfied with the case, so you start thinking about marriage. You're funny that way, you know. Case doesn't look right and you think your whole life's not right, and start thinking about uprooting it."

Ransom exhaled sharply in reply, and they fell silent again as Gerald looked for Damien's apartment building.

Ransom brooded to himself at the thought of being known. He was a loner, and as such had a distinct dislike for having anyone know, or presume to know, his inner thinking or motivations. In a marriage, he reminded himself, that was one of the things that happened. Your partner ended up thinking she knew you better than you knew yourself. Then she started finishing your sentences for you, then....

Gerald broke in on his thoughts. "There it is."

The building was one of the huge, U-shaped courtyards that are so common to the outer neighborhoods of Chicago. The brick of this building was a sort of sickly yellow, and the courtyard itself, which could have been beautiful and probably had been under earlier ownership, was unkempt and weed-ridden. No plants grew there that needed tending. The one concession that had been made to gardening was that the lawn in the court had been recently mown—but even that was done in the most slipshod fashion. Dead grass had been left to dry up on the walks and in the doorways of the building after being cut and blown about by a power mower.

The building itself seemed to be asleep, its windows dark, brooding, pupilless eyes that appeared to droop out of the face of the walls. It was clear that at nine o'clock on a Saturday morning, the inhabitants of the thirty or so apartments were not accustomed to being disturbed. But that was one of the reasons Ransom had chosen to come without calling ahead. He was a firm believer in the element of surprise, and the more the better. He was also sure that any actor worth his salt—and he had discovered that Damien Liddle acted as well as directed—could think fast enough on his feet without being given additional time to prepare for this interview.

There were four doors in the court, leading into the different sets of apartments, each door bearing the next higher number for an address. The second door bore the address of Damien's apartment. Inside the vestibule they found a row of mailboxes mounted on the wall. The floor was made up of small octagonal tiles, black and white, that hadn't been washed in years from the look of them, and the remnants of junk mail were scattered everywhere. Gerald checked the mailboxes and found the name Liddle taped across the one marked 1B. The doorbell was located just beneath the box, but he didn't push it. Ransom had tried the inner door and found it unlocked, so instead of giving Damien even this small warning, they proceeded through the door and up the short, dirty, carpeted staircase to the first-floor landing. Music was playing from somewhere further up the stairs, and given the somberness of the building's exterior and the deadly lack of movement around them, the music took on a strange, ethereal, disembodied quality, as if it came from nowhere and was heard by no one. Ransom knocked on the door of 1B, and in the following silence pulled his badge out of his breast pocket. There was no sound of movement from inside the apartment.

"Maybe he's not home," said Gerald quietly. He felt as if it would be unnatural to speak too loudly in this atmosphere. Ransom glanced at him over his shoulder and almost laughed. It was an obvious statement, and he had caught himself just short of saying it. He knocked again. At last they heard the soft sticking sound of bare feet on a wood floor, coming toward the door, though not in much of a hurry.

Both detectives were startled when the door opened not a crack, but wide enough for Damien to just fit between it and the jamb. Ransom sized him up immediately, trying not to rebuke himself for forming too quick a first impression. The man before him was about thirty years old and had light brown hair that was wavy and unkempt, which could be attributed to the fact that he had obviously just climbed out of bed. He was clad only in a pair of boxer shorts that were worn so thin they were almost transparent. Ransom supposed that Damien was considered handsome, though he was too thin by half, which was especially apparent in this uncovered state, where his rib cage was quite evident. Damien's legs and torso were lean and muscular, and his skin was nicely tanned in a way that Ransom felt always looked out of place in Chicago. Damien raised his arm up dreamily and leaned it against the doorjamb, cradling his head as if he were too tired to hold it up. Oh yes, thought Ransom, he's handsome and he knows it. Perhaps it was knowing that he was an actor that made the move look theatrical to Ransom, who was beginning to feel the all-too-familiar nudge of conscience at judging too quickly.

"Yes?" Damien asked drowsily.

"Mr. Liddle?" said Ransom. Damien grunted in assent. "I'm Detective Ransom, this is Detective White." Ransom showed him his badge.

"Detectives? Police?" Damien's green eyes opened a bit wider, pulling the badge toward him with one hand to get a closer look at it. His mind automatically raced through all the possible reasons he could think of for being visited by the police.

"We'd like to talk to you."

"About what?"

"Um, not something that has directly to do with you," Ransom answered cautiously. "We're looking into the murder of a man who attended a performance of your play *Love's Labor's Lost*, last Saturday night."

Damien stared at him blankly as if he were speaking in a heretofore unheard-of language.

After allowing the pause to go on as long as he thought considerate, Ransom spoke again. "Do you think we could step inside?"

Damien was startled by the question, as if he were a child again and an authority figure was taking him aside to scold him out of the earshot of others. He had the queasiness of one who had done something wrong and didn't know what it was. But he realized at once that this was just foolishness and that everyone must feel a vague sense of guilt when the police talked to them. He also realized that it would be idiotic—not to mention potentially suspicious—to keep them in the hallway, so he stepped aside, pushing the door open all the way for them.

As Ransom stepped into the one-room apartment, closely followed by Gerald, he was overcome by a sense of oppression. The apartment was small even for a studio and had obviously once been part of a larger apartment that had been cut down to two or more, the idea being that two rents were better than one. It had been years since the apartment had seen a coat of paint, and the rug was a study in filth. It had been virtually flattened by years of wear and had apparently never seen a wash. Ransom imagined that if he had woken in this apartment with the headache that was now making itself noticeable again, he would have had the impression of sinking further down into sickness. Some apartments are like that, so that they make the bad seem worse and even the good seem tainted. He blinked for a moment, picturing his own apartment and thanking God that he had woken up there. His, at least, was airy and sunny, so that waking as he had this morning he had the feeling of being helped on to health instead of being dragged further down.

The impression of Damien's apartment was not helped by the fact that the bed, prominent against the wall, was unmade and the torn coverlet exposed threadbare sheets; also, Damien's clothes were scattered everywhere across the floor. It was curious, thought Ransom, that actors—

well, not just actors, others as well—could live like this, and yet put themselves together with such dexterity and cleanliness that away from home they gave no indication that they lived in squalor. He could already believe that Damien was just such a person.

"Excuse the mess," said Damien. He threw the clothes onto the floor from two uncomfortable-looking wooden chairs placed on either side of the bed, and motioned for them to be seated. He quickly pulled on a pair of jeans and then sat on the bed.

"So somebody that was at the show last week was killed?" said Damien, with a bewilderment that was mixed with a rather disarming amount of interest.

"Yes. He was at last Saturday's performance."

"Our last performance."

"Really," said Ransom flatly.

"Yes. We had to close early due to a lack of interest by the theater-going public. Shakespeare, you know. Chicago doesn't exactly seem to be the place for fine arts."

"I don't know," said Ransom conversationally, "I would think this city had a lot to offer in the way of fine arts."

"Ha," said Damien, who continued in the tone of cynic who has the inside story on everything. "They have no sense at all here. They don't know anything of the arts. Even when you try to get some Shakespeare up here, you can't do the dramas, you have to do the comedies. If they're going to come out at all for Shakespeare, it has to be for the comedies—these idiots don't want to be 'depressed' by the dramas. We tried doing one once—I can't remember if it was *Hamlet* or *Macbeth*, and interest was so low we never got it off the ground at all. It's disgusting. I mean, of course, Shakespeare's comedies are better than anything else we could be doing."

Ransom saw instantly that this was a subject on which Mr. Liddle was prepared to jump up and stay up on his soapbox, so he carefully steered the discussion in the direction he intended. He pulled out the clipping on Lawrence Watson and showed it to him.

"Do you recognize this man?"

Damien took the picture in hand and squinted at it, looking as if he was trying very hard to place the face.

"Yes, he does look familiar. Yes, he was at the show."

"Good," said Ransom, taking the clipping back and slipping it into his pocket. "Was there anything unusual about last Saturday evening?"

"Other than it being the last performance, no. Of course, we didn't know at the time it would be the last."

"No?"

"I'm sure we all suspected. I mean, hell, we only sold six tickets to that performance, and had no reservations for any in the future. We met after the Saturday night show and decided to call it a day."

"Hmmm. You don't seem too broken up about it."

Damien sighed. "It's all that can be expected in this town, I guess. Our theater has never been exactly the most popular thing since Broadway. We weren't making it—and it had been more or less my idea to begin with, so it was kind of a relief to see it go, if you know what I mean."

"What about the others?"

"The others?"

"The other people in your company. How did they feel about it breaking up?"

"What on earth could that have to do with your investigation?" asked Damien, immediately realizing it was a mistake: He was sure as soon as he said it that it never paid to call the methods of the police into question.

"Nothing, really," said Ransom with a smile. "I'm just always curious about the way people react to change."

Looking somewhat confused, Damien explained the plans of his partners in the Pennington Players, at least those that he knew. He found it disconcerting that Ransom's expression didn't change as he spoke, making it impossible to tell if he was impressed, bored, or indifferent.

"Yes," said Ransom when Damien had finished, "and what will *you* do now?"

Damien perked up, thinking perhaps this ordinary detective might find his prospects exciting. "Well, I'm heading out to the coast—L.A.—to do a television kind of thing."

"Television," said Ransom in a tone that Damien found even more disconcerting, as it showed no interest and even less excitement.

"I'm going to be in a series. In the pilot of a series, at least. The prospects look good for it getting picked up."

"Congratulations. Now, getting back to last Saturday night, aside from it being the last performance, did you notice anything out of the ordinary?"

"Such as?"

"Oh, any unpleasantness between any of the audience members?"

"No, I didn't notice anything like that."

"Did you happen to notice whether or not Mr. Watson knew anyone in the audience? Did he speak to anyone, or sit with anyone?"

"No, I don't think so—at least I didn't notice it. Of course, we're all awfully busy during the show."

"Any...oh, unusual recognition between, say, a member of the cast and a member of the audience?"

Damien laughed. "You mean that you think maybe one

of our company murdered this man? I don't think so! We weren't exactly killing anyone in the audience, one way or the other."

"And yet, one of your audience is dead."

Damien immediately sobered up. "Sorry. I guess the idea having been near someone that's been killed is sort of unnerving."

"I understand. So, you didn't notice anything unusual with any of the audience?"

"No, and I would think I would have. I mean, like I said, we only sold six tickets—it's not like there was a whole lot of them to keep track of."

"Did *you* know any of these people?"

"Any of the audience? No."

"They were all people who just decided on Shakespeare that evening."

"Gluttons for punishment, I should say," said Damien, recovering his smile.

There was a brief silence. Gerald sat taking his obligatory notes, and Ransom paused for the moment as if digesting this information. Damien shifted a bit uneasily.

"Mr. Liddle," said Ransom finally, "do you have any way of knowing the names of the people who were in the audience last Saturday?"

"No, I don't know…" said Damien slowly. "Gail might. Gail Shelly—she's the one that takes the ticket orders, but I—" He stopped suddenly, his face going white. "Oh God!"

"What is it Mr. Liddle?"

"The break-in!"

"Break-in?"

"I got a call last Tuesday from Gail. We closed Saturday night, and Gail was the first one to go back to the theater on Tuesday. She found the theater had been broken into!"

"And?"

"Well, at the time, I—we—thought it was crazy—God knows we didn't really have anything valuable at the theater—but our answering machine was stolen."

"So?" asked Gerald.

Damien continued to address Ransom. "Well, it was the only thing that was stolen. At the time, I thought it was because it was the only thing we had there that was of any value."

"But what does that have to do with anything?"

"Detective Ransom, we're a very small company—like a lot of them here. All of our people have to work during the day, so like all of the other little theaters, we have an answering machine for a box-office staff. You see, people call into the theater and get the machine, and then they leave their names and telephone numbers, how many tickets they want, and for what night."

"Why do you ask for their phone numbers?"

Damien looked rather embarrassed at having to go into their past failures, but he sighed and went on. "Because, sir, a lot of times the cast outnumbers the audience. When ticket orders are really low, we cancel the performance. All the small theaters around here do that. But, you know, people get irritated if they travel all the way to a theater and find it closed. We take their numbers so that if we decide to cancel a performance, we can call the few people—if any—that ordered tickets and tell them."

Ransom's face hardened as he assimilated this new information. He spoke to nobody in particular. "So, the idea is that the names of the people who were in the audience last Saturday were on this tape."

"Yes," said Damien, not knowing whether or not he

was supposed to answer, or what he was supposed to make of the way the statement had been phrased, "and somebody stole it. Anybody could have stolen it. The theater is on Clark Street, in not what you'd exactly call a high-security building."

Ransom looked at Damien intently, then continued. "Would you happen to remember the names of any of the people who ordered tickets?"

"No, no..." said Damien after a contemplative pause, "I don't think I ever knew them. Gail listened to the messages just to count the number of tickets we'd have sold, and she told me how many. I *did* work the box office, and I suppose they probably each said who they were when they picked up the tickets...but no, no...." He shook his head and pursed his lips, as if trying to remember even as he dismissed the idea. "I'm afraid I wiped everything concerning that theater out of my mind the minute we decided to close it."

"Hmmm."

"Gail might be able to remember some of them," Damien added in a tone betraying the hopelessness of the suggestion. "She's the one who took care of ticket orders. She *might* be able to remember some of the names."

"ALL RIGHT, out with it. What did you think of our Mr. Liddle?"

"I think he's a liar," said Ransom flatly.

"Really?" said Gerald. He was genuinely surprised at the sharpness of the reply. "After that short interview?"

"I don't know," said Ransom with a sigh, "it could just be because he's an actor—acting is lying, isn't that what they say? Does that make actors liars?"

Gerald didn't respond, thinking it was best to let Ransom go on thinking out loud without interruption.

"It may be," he continued, "that actors have a harder time figuring out how to respond in real life than they do on the stage. Maybe that's why everything about that Liddle character seemed so damned insincere. Didn't you think so?"

"Oh, I don't know," said Gerald carefully, "I thought he was a bit on the theatrical side. I suspect they're all like that, don't you think?"

"I hope not. I pride myself on being able to see through lies. If everybody we talk to acts like Mr. Liddle, it's going to make life very difficult."

"You told him we were looking into one death."

"We are—officially."

"Yes, but..."

"And I want to stick to the idea that we're only looking into the Watson death—at least for the time being. I don't want to put the murderer—whoever it is—on his guard until we get some more information. I've a feeling if the murderer thought we were on to the other two deaths, he or she might bolt before we could get any evidence. And at the moment, I'm not sure we have enough to even tell people not to leave town, if you know what I mean."

"I'm not sure I do."

"Well, the performance of this play was on Saturday night. Watson was killed Monday night. There's no indication at all that there's any connection."

"But the other two..."

"I don't know how firm I am about believing the other two are connected. We have no evidence that they are, other than the wanderings of a little old lady—and that wouldn't stand up in court."

Gerald smiled, remembering Emily. "I should think any jury would believe her."

"Believe that she believes, yes—but there's still no evidence. Except..."

"The answering machine?" said Gerald helpfully.

"Yes," said Ransom slowly, gazing out the car window. "The answering machine adds a new wrinkle that I really don't like. It at least points to the idea that someone wanted to know who was in the audience last Saturday."

"Unless it really was just a burglary, and the machine was all they got."

"Yeah..." said Ransom doubtfully. "Just too damned coincidental. I think whoever broke in got just what they were looking for."

"But with the theater broken into like that, the murderer could be anybody."

"That's right," said Ransom, pushing the cigarette lighter into the dashboard, "it could be anybody."

"THAT'S HORRIBLE!" said Gail Shelly, ushering the two detectives into her apartment. "You mean he was killed right after seeing our show?"

"Umm, not *right* after—but not long after," said Ransom, examining the apartment as he entered. Gail's apartment was the antithesis of Damien's. It was in a much nicer building, although it wasn't far from Damien's, and she had a one-bedroom instead of a studio. But the biggest difference was that it was clean. Gail seemed to live by the credo "A place for everything and everything in its place." He could see through the open partition that separated the living room from the kitchen that all her coffee mugs hung neatly on a rack beneath the kitchen cabinets. The kitchen, like the living room, was spotless. Also unlike Damien's, Gail's apartment was not a hodgepodge of castaway furniture. Her sofa matched her two chairs, and it was fronted by a low, beautifully polished maple coffee table. In a rack underneath the coffee table several theater magazines were neatly displayed. As Ransom glanced at the titles, he was surprised that each was devoted to a different aspect of the theater: design, costuming, acting, even directing. There appeared to be more to write about the theater than he was aware of. The room was comfortable, despite the rather prominent desk in one corner on which sat a personal computer. However, even desk and computer were in perfect order. There were no loose papers or stray pens. All of those things, thought Ransom, were probably kept in very neat order in the desk drawers. It was no wonder she was useful to the theater, where there were so many details to keep track of.

The apartment was a direct contrast to Gail herself, whose mousiness did not go unnoticed by Ransom. He sized her up immediately as being clean and efficient but without any of the quirks or vitality that would make her a noticeable personality. She was the type of girl who would work hard in the background most likely without anyone being able to remember her name.

Gail motioned for the two men to sit on the couch, which Ransom did readily. Gerald, however, took a seat off to the side in his usual nondescript manner. He firmly believed that it was important for him to be off to the side during interviews his partner conducted, so that he could take his notes as unobtrusively as possible, and the people being questioned had a sense of intimacy with Ransom. It was surprising how effective he had found this method. On several occasions, as Ransom had been ending an interview, the suspect would turn and notice Gerald almost with a start, as if they had no idea there was someone else in the room. Handy talent, Ransom had often told him.

"Tell me, Miss Shelly..." Ransom began.

"You can call me Gail."

He pulled the clipping from his pocket and showed it to her. "Do you recognize this man?"

Gail looked at the picture for a moment, her face betraying no recognition at all. "No, I'm afraid I don't."

"He was at your play last Saturday night. I understand it was the last performance."

A cloud passed over her face. "Yes, it was." She handed the clipping back to Ransom, who replaced it in his pocket.

"But you didn't see him."

"Actually, I worked props for the show. I was responsible for seeing that everybody had everything they were supposed to go onstage with."

Probably very good at it, he thought. She'd be crushed if she missed a cue.

"You didn't see any of the audience."

"Not really. I usually arrived before everybody else got there. We didn't open the house—I mean, we didn't let people into the actual theater, until about twenty minutes before we were about to start, and by that time I was stuck backstage. The only time I ever went anywhere near the audience was during the play—during blackouts, to do any setting up of the next scene. And during blackout the house is...black. You can't see a thing."

"What about during intermission?"

"Oh," she said, in a tone that indicated she had forgotten something. "During intermission I set up the stage for the second act. And...sometimes when the audience was large I helped serve coffee in the lobby."

Ransom's expression remained unchanged, but he found it odd that she would be assigned such a duty in a theater that admittedly never had a large audience. He wondered what was considered large for them.

"And was last Saturday night one of those times?"

She looked away from him, doing her best to look confused, and finally said, "You know, I really don't remember."

Ransom thought this unlikely, but decided not to pursue it at the moment.

"Hmmm. So you don't know if anything unusual happened Saturday night?"

"What do you mean?"

"Like, a disturbance in the audience. Any unpleasantness between any of the audience members?"

"No," she said slowly, shaking her mousy head, her eyes narrowing behind her brown-rimmed glasses. "I'm sure there wasn't a disturbance of any kind. The theater is—was—so small, I don't think there's any way anything like that could have happened without everyone knowing about it. Damien—Damien Liddle our company manager, might be a better person to ask about that. He was working the box office, so he would have come into contact with the audience."

"How about the cast of the play?"

"What do you mean?"

"You were backstage with them. Did any of them mention knowing anyone in the audience, or seeing someone in the audience that they recognized?"

"No, I didn't hear anything like that. And I would have. We had an almost nonexistent backstage area. It was all we could do to keep from tripping over each other, let alone say anything without everyone hearing it."

"Did any of them come in contact with the audience? Maybe, go out to the lobby during the performance...or after?"

"Oh no!" said Gail, aghast at the suggestion. "Damien

never would have allowed that! That would be totally unprofessional! Nobody in our company would do that!"

Ransom could sense from the strength of her reply, and the fact that she flushed slightly when she made it, that Gail was hopelessly devoted to this theater company. He wondered whether or not the company was worthy of that devotion. He doubted it.

"I'm sorry," he said kindly, "it was just a thought. I have to explore all the possibilities."

"We may have been a small company, but we really were a good theater!"

"I'm sure you were." He paused for a second, then added gently, "It's a shame it had to break up."

"It's a shame for me," she said, her voice coming irritatingly close to a whine. "I don't think anybody else cared that much that it was over."

If Damien Liddle were representative, you're right, thought Ransom.

"Lorrie's already rehearsing with another company, and her boyfriend Danny doesn't care one way or the other. And Damien..." She fought back tears, and cleared her throat so that she could go on. "Damien is going to leave."

He considered Gail as she dabbed her eyes with the cuff of her sleeve, the only messy gesture he'd seen her make. She reminded him at this moment of someone else, and he couldn't quite place it. After a moment, it hit him: Gloria Forsyth, Lawrence Watson's secretary. It wasn't that the two women looked anything alike; certainly Gloria was much lovelier than Gail. It was this expression of honest emotion in the midst of so many who didn't care. It was obvious that Gloria Forsyth was fond of her boss. It was equally obvious that Gail Shelly felt the same about hers. The only difference was that Damien was still alive.

"I'm sorry to be such a baby," said Gail, blushing at having cried in front of strangers. "I like Damien. We've worked together at the theater for a couple of years now. He's really a wonderful actor. I guess I should have known he'd go sometime. He was far too good for our little theater, even though he did start it himself. Nobody was as dedicated to it as he was. I'll be sorry to see him go."

"It was Mr. Liddle who thought you might be able to help us."

"Really? How?" There was a definite easing of her tension at the idea of being thought useful, especially by Damien.

"We need to know who was in the audience last Saturday night. Mr. Liddle thought you might be able to remember some of their names."

"Oh, I can do better than that," she said, getting up and crossing the room to her desk. "I have them written down."

Ransom rose and followed her over to the desk.

"Really? Was there some special reason for doing that?"

She opened the top left-hand drawer of the desk and extracted a small pad of paper on which were written four names. "Yes, I've been preparing a mailing list. That's the way you build up an audience, you know. You keep the names of the people who have been to your theater before, and then when your next show comes up, you send them all flyers telling them about it. Damien's been talking about doing this sort of thing for a long time, but he's kind of...disorganized. He doesn't have a head for business, and I do, which is why we worked so well together. Anyway, I took it upon myself to start one up, sort of to surprise him with for our next show, especially since it's easy for me to keep on the computer." Her face clouded over. "It looks like we won't be using it, though. Anyway, I like to take care of things right away or I'm afraid I'll forget to do them. So every time I listened to our answering machine for ticket orders, I copied down the names on a second sheet and brought it home. It's a good thing I did it right away, too. I suppose Damien told you about the break-in."

"Yes. He said you were the one that discovered it."

"It gave me chills—I mean, just to be in a place that was burglarized."

"Nothing else was taken, just the answering machine?"

"We didn't have anything else, except the sets—and they were all that cheap board, I can't remember what it's called."

"Pressboard."

"Yes. They weren't worth anything."

"Did you report the theft to the police?"

"No," she said, another cloud passing over her features. "I guess Damien thought there wasn't much point with the theater closing and everything. We really didn't need it anymore—the answering machine, I mean—and it didn't belong to anyone in the company. It was a gift, and it was old."

"Hmmm."

Ransom scanned the paper, reading it aloud. "Lawrence Watson, Mark Benson, Barbara Landis, Meg Ferguson." He looked up from the paper to Gail. "There's only four names on this list. I thought you sold six tickets to that performance."

"Yes," she answered, going over the orders in her head, "two of them were for two tickets each. Um, these two." She pointed to the names of Mark Benson and Meg Ferguson.

"Hmmm. You didn't get their addresses?"

"No. You see, their phone numbers are there, and I call that number—it's in my address book. You know, the number that you call and give them a phone number and they give you the address that goes with it. That way we didn't have to bother the audiences for their addresses. The oddest things can make people feel put out."

"You haven't called for their addresses yet."

"No. I guess there just didn't seem much point. I would've gotten around to it, though. You never know when you might need a mailing list."

Ransom smiled to himself. He now realized that Gail was the type of person who couldn't keep herself from being efficient even if it weren't necessary.

"Would you by any chance have the names and addresses of the cast of *Love's Labor's Lost?*"

"Sure I do," she said, opening the middle desk drawer. Ransom glanced over her shoulder and saw it was organized much in the same way the rest of her apartment was. Her neatness extended into her drawers, he thought to himself with a smile. There was a small stack of papers on the left side of the drawer, and a holder on the right that was full of pens and newly sharpened pencils.

She pulled out a sheet and handed it to him. "Here's a list of the names of the cast with their addresses and phone numbers. I made up a cast list for all our shows."

"Thank you, you've been most helpful." He and Gerald started for the door. Ransom stopped for a moment and looked back at Gail. "Tell me, Miss Shelly, what do you do for a living?"

"Me?" said Gail, lighting up at the idea of interest being directed to her. "I'm an administrative assistant at Walden and Baker. They're an advertising firm on Sheridan."

"Do you like it?"

Gail flushed, betraying the fact that she did like it but felt embarrassed to admit to it. "Well, it's a job, I guess."

Ransom smiled at her kindly. "I'll bet you're very good at it."

"VERY EFFICIENT GIRL, don't you think?"

"Uh-huh," said Gerald, turning the key in the ignition. The car jumped to a rather noisy start. Gerald put it in gear and pulled away from the curb.

"A bit too efficient," said Gerald with a smile, delighting at rubbing it in. "She seems possessed of that presence of mind you're so famous for."

"Yes," Ransom said slowly, "but I got the impression she wasn't exactly telling the truth."

"About what?"

"About being in the lobby during intermission. Did you notice what she did? She couldn't even look me in the eye and say she couldn't remember."

Gerald shook his head. "I was busy being your secretary. But you're right. It's hard to believe that one couldn't remember everything in great detail. Much, much too efficient."

Ransom smiled back at him. "If the world were run by more of her sort, it'd be going around better, eh?"

"And be a damn sight more boring."

"It's a good thing for us she *is* so efficient. Now we know who was in the audience last Saturday night."

"Three of whom are dead," added Gerald.

"Yes. We have a lot to do, and some of it we have to do quickly. I want you to get back to the station and call this Mark Benson. I don't want to alarm him, but it would be nice to know whether or not he's still with us. And then I want you to call all of the cast members—there are only ten."

"The cast? What for?"

Ransom sighed in exasperation. "To see if *they're* still alive, Gerald. So far we don't know if it's only the audience at risk, or if the actors are being knocked off, too. I don't want you to set up appointments for them yet, just find out if they're still alive. I want to think about it a bit first before we tackle the actors."

"A lot of people to go over, and the murderer has a head start."

"We have one thing that he doesn't."

"What's that?"

Ransom smiled. "We have Emily Charters. Her name wasn't on the list because Meg Ferguson ordered the two tickets in her name. If we're lucky, the murderer doesn't know who she is."

"You like the old bird, don't you?"

"She reminds me of my late grandmother," said Ransom wryly.

"I thought maybe you were developing an interest in history."

"You're a heartless clod, you know that?" said Ransom genially.

There was an amused silence, and Ransom's hand absently traveled up to the window control. He spun the wheel on the handle and gazed out the window, speaking softly in a confessional manner that Gerald had seldom heard him use.

"I have a thing about age, you know. I realize that as you get older you change. You get little aches and pains and things, but I've never quite understood why some people seem to disintegrate, while others keep going. You know what I mean? Some old people get *old,* and bit by bit they stop functioning: They stop going out, or doing things for themselves, or even trying. All they seem to do is complain. Others keep going. Others keep living into their eighties and nineties, and they remain vital, doing everything. I admire that. I really do. And I'm just certain it has to be in the mind. It has to be that they choose to keep going. Look at Miss Charters: Eighty if she's a day and she's still sharp enough to put this case together before we did. She still goes everywhere and does everything. Yes, I like her."

"I suppose there's something to be said for her." Though a kind man, Gerald White was a bit younger than Ransom and not quite as understanding of the perils of the aging process, while Ransom, in his late thirties and able to look back to the perils of youth and forward to the perils of age with equal clarity, was naturally more understanding. This was something Ransom recognized in his partner, knowing also that time would be the determining factor in Gerald's view of the aged.

"There's one thing you didn't mention," said Gerald.

"What's that?"

"Neither of us knows the name of the sixth person. The one that came with Mark Benson."

"Maybe if he's still alive he can tell us."

"And what are you going to be doing while I'm making all these phone calls?"

"I have a date."

NINE

Ransom stood for a moment on the sidewalk looking at Emily's house. It was different from so many other houses he had seen in the years that he had been old enough or aware enough to give the meaning of an individual's dwelling place any consideration. Indeed, since becoming a detective he had grown morbidly aware of the environments of the people with whom he came in contact. He had been instantly aware, for example, of the coldness and austerity of the interior of Marian Watson's home, which he knew was a reflection of the lady of the house. And Virgil Danners's office, with its opulent furnishings that gave the impression of an oversized world, mirrored the corpulent lawyer himself. The office, in fact, had been especially interesting to Ransom in that it was opulent, yet contained nothing in the way of personal items that would distinguish it from any other office, almost as if it were a display of an office rather than an inhabited room. That lack of individuality matched Danners himself, whose size obliterated the distinction of his features. An amorphous office for an amorphous man.

It was different from the outside of a home. In driving around the city, Ransom had found that with most homes, the outside revealed very little. You couldn't tell by looking at the frame or the porch or the yard anything about the people who lived inside. It was as if the outside of the houses jealously guarded the personalities of their owners.

But he thought it probably wasn't as deep as all that.

With mobility what it is today, and families failing to dig their roots in as deeply as earlier generations, the personalities of the inhabitants don't have time to seep through from the inside to the outside. The houses stand tired and confused, determined to exist on their own as facades of family dwellings rather than family homes. Houses of today reflect the architect, not the owner.

Emily's house was different. It had what was now sneeringly referred to as "old-world charm." Ransom was sure that if he hadn't known the address, he could have walked down the street and automatically picked out this house as hers. Partly this was fancy, he thought with a smile. The wood-frame house was painted a pale gray, with white trim around the windows. There were three steps up to the screened porch, and the steps were bordered with wrought-iron railings, which were painted with a similar shade of gray, but with heavier paint. The short bushes on either side of the steps and running along the house were kept trim, but probably not quite as trim as they had been in the distant past. A stray branch grew here and there, longer than the rest, and seemed to demonstrate not a lack of care but a care that was growing tired and weak. Unlike other houses, this was a house that had finally succumbed totally to the personality of the dweller within. This was Emily's house.

Ransom approached the house quietly and once again laughed inwardly when he realized that the idea of noise or hurry in the presence of Emily (and by extension, her house) seemed an affront. He paused for a moment on the steps and glanced down the street. Three doors down was an unmarked police car. Sanders, who had spent the night there watching the house, had been replaced by Henderson. Ransom reminded himself that Henderson was a good man. He proceeded up the steps and pressed the doorbell, which rang out with two muted tones. As he waited, he looked through the screen door at the porch. It was painted an off-white and was kept very clean. Although the porch was small, along the right wall stood a wicker love seat where he imagined Emily passed her quiet summer evenings. Directly above the love seat, screwed into the ceiling, were two large hooks set approximately three feet apart, which indicated that there had once been a porch swing. The hooks had been painted over the last time the porch had been done.

The lace curtains on the front door quivered, and then were pulled to one side by Emily's frail hand. She smiled sweetly when she saw Ransom and opened the door for him as he let himself in through the screen door on the porch.

"Detective Ransom, how nice to see you," she said with a tone of surprise that almost made him forget that he had told her he would be coming.

"Ma'am," he said, smiling broadly.

"I was just making some tea," she continued, shutting the door behind him. "Would you like some?"

"Sure."

Emily had continued down the hallway into the kitchen as she spoke, leaving him with the impression that it would be natural to follow her. This is what he sensed from the outside of the house, he thought as he passed into the kitchen: the air of hospitality and familiarity Emily exuded that made one feel not only like a welcome guest but like a very old acquaintance. He felt almost as if he had been here hundreds of times before. He took a seat at the kitchen table without being asked, and Emily retrieved the teakettle from the stove and poured the steaming water into a china teapot from which three strings with Lipton tags dangled. While letting it steep, she put her favorite blue china cup and saucer in her usual place, and its sister in front of Ransom.

"So," she said with an air of finally getting down to business, "how are you coming with our case?"

He stifled a laugh at her choice of words, her prim schoolteacherish manner making him feel something like a young boy who'd forgotten his homework. It didn't even cross his mind that if someone else had asked him this question—Sergeant Newman, for example—he would have been, if not offended, at least put off.

"Well, Miss Charters..." he said, clearing his throat, "we haven't—"

"You can call me Emily."

"Emily," he said, smiling partly because she had asked him to call her by her first name, and partly because it sounded so natural coming out of his mouth. So often, he thought, elderly people seem like they should be addressed formally. He was glad to have his impression of Emily thus reinforced. "I'm afraid we haven't—"

"What shall I call you?"

He stopped, confused. No one had ever asked him this question before, the other detectives just naturally called him by his last name, and now that he was being given a choice of what to be called, he wasn't quite sure of what he liked.

"Well, most people just call me Ransom."

"Is that your Christian name?" she asked, with a noticeably raised eyebrow.

"Jeremy."

"Jeremy," she repeated, savoring the sound and looking quite pleased with him. "I think that's what I'll call you, then.

"So, Jeremy," she said, pulling the tea bags out of the pot, "how is our case going?"

"Well, as I was saying, we really haven't had much time to make any headway since I last saw you—that was just yesterday, you remember." As soon as he had added these last two words, he winced, and hoped she would let it pass.

"I remember quite well," she said and smiled.

"I've been able to talk to a couple of people from the theater company, and they were both very helpful. I was able to get a list of the people who were at the theater last Saturday, the last performance of their play. As it happens, the last performance of their company. They've disbanded."

"Since last Saturday?"

"Yes. Apparently, it had been expected."

"Oh dear, this is distressing. It seems so hard for theaters to make a go of it nowadays. Heaven knows, they weren't the best of the lot, but one hates to see any venture of that sort fail. It just seems like a sign of the times."

"The company members I talked to today—at least one of them—don't seem too broken up about it."

"They're very young, and I imagine quite resilient. They can do other things, find other groups to join." She lifted the teapot, her hand trembling just slightly under the weight, and filled his cup, then hers. After declining milk and sugar, he carefully lifted up the china cup, which was ridiculously delicate for him, and took a sip.

"You're probably right, there seems to be enough little theaters around Chicago for them to get into. Except for the theater manager. He's going to California to be in a television show."

"Oh!" she said, impressed. "It's just like I was telling you yesterday about my programs. I'll have seen him here, and I can look his name up in the program. I got it out for you this morning."

"That's all right, I don't really need it. I was given a cast list, with all their names and addresses. I'm afraid you're out of luck with this particular actor, though. He was working the box office; he wasn't in the show."

"Oh yes, well, I suppose I can say he sold me my ticket once."

He laughed. "Yes, you can."

"Of course, television is an awfully low step down from Shakespeare. Do you like Shakespeare, Jeremy?"

"I'm afraid I'm a Dickens man, myself," he said, taking another sip of tea and marveling at the fact that it didn't seem peculiar to be called by his first name, even though she was the first person in his adult life to use it.

"Ah yes, Dickens. He's good too," she said in an offhand manner that made Dickens seem acceptable but minor.

"I've read Shakespeare, though—at least all the plays, and I've seen several of them. I really do like the language of them. It's beautiful."

"I love Shakespeare. The words are pure poetry. It is especially so now, when we live in an age where our language has for the most part lost its meaning. I really think that that's a major part of what's wrong with our society—when language loses its meaning, everything starts to crumble."

"I'm sure you're right," he said, and with that they fell into a brief contemplative silence, during which they both sipped their tea and reflected on the state of the English language.

"Getting back to this case," he said, more than a little embarrassed at sounding as if he were trying to direct the conversation of someone who was his elder, "there doesn't *appear* to be any connection between the three dead people."

"You mean murder victims."

"For the moment, I'll say dead people," he said firmly, still unwilling to believe, or at least admit to believing, that Meg Ferguson's death had been the result of anything other than natural causes.

"I see."

"The company members—at least, the two I've spoken to so far—didn't know anyone in the audience. And it seems to me that the only thing the audience members had in common is the Pennington Players themselves. Do you see what I mean?"

"I think I do. You mean that if someone is actually killing the audience members, it must be someone from the acting company that's doing it, because it's the only thing the victims have in common."

"Yes," he said, thinking it better not to mention the stolen answering machine and the possibility of someone else being involved in the killings.

"You *are* going to talk to the rest of the company?"

"Of course. My partner is looking them all up now."

"And the rest of the audience?"

What's left of them, he thought. "Yes."

"You sound like you're being very thorough," she said, with a hint of approval in her voice.

"Well," he said, trying to put her mind at ease, just in case she was inclined to worry about her own safety, "it's not that I'm convinced that there's a connection between these deaths, but I always think it's best to be thorough and follow up any possible leads."

"So you don't think *I'm* in any danger?" she said with a coyness that Ransom missed.

"Oh no. Even if there is something to the idea that the deaths are connected, we have no way of knowing if they need to continue. Perhaps the people that *had* to be killed for whatever reason are already dead. And as I told you, we have a copy of the list of audience members, presumably the only list available, and your name isn't on it."

"It isn't?" she said, sounding almost disappointed.

"No. They are only able to list the people who actually order the tickets, because those people left their names on an answering machine. Since your friend made the reservations, her name was on the list, but yours wasn't. So even if someone *is* killing off the audience, they'd have no way of knowing who you are."

"Hmmm." Emily was lost in thought for a moment. Ransom drank some more of his tea and looked at her with an innocence that was supposed to convey his assurance that she was safe.

"I'm not in any danger at all," she said rather suddenly.

"No." He smiled at her.

She replaced her cup firmly in the saucer and looked at him sternly.

"Then why are you having me watched?"

Ransom felt his jaw drop and stared at her in wonder. Once again he felt like a schoolboy who had been caught doing something he shouldn't. And like that student, he thought it best to feign innocence.

"Having you watched? What makes you think I'm having you watched?"

"Jeremy..." she said in a tone of mild rebuke. Ransom was immediately contrite.

"I was just being cautious. I can't say I'm fully convinced of your theory, but I don't believe in taking any chances, and we didn't know about the list yesterday. And I wouldn't want to think of anything bad happening...." His voice trailed off as he realized that what he was about to say was bound to sound ridiculous to one he had known for just a day.

"Oh," she said, her cheeks turning pink with embarrassment.

"You noticed you were being watched?" he said, clearing his throat.

"Oh, yes. I don't know that many people on the block personally, just to say hello to and that, but you get a certain sense for the people around you and their comings and goings, who belongs and who doesn't, and many times you hear about whether or not people are having visitors before they actually arrive, so when you see a strange car, you know it belongs to the people who are visiting the Smiths or the Joneses."

"So how did you know it wasn't just someone visiting one of your neighbors?"

She straightened herself in her chair and cocked her head in his direction with a look that was highly incredulous. "Why Jeremy, when someone comes to call they generally go into the house. There's been someone sitting in that car since last night."

This time he laughed and blushed simultaneously, no longer able to contain his amusement at her frank logic. "Very sound thinking. You seem to be very astute."

"Well," she said, slightly embarrassed, and Ransom realized that this one word had been meant as a sort of rebuke, letting him know that it wouldn't have taken a genius to figure out that she was being watched.

"You seem to notice quite a bit."

"I try to stay aware of what's going on around me."

"Emily," he said, taking another sip of his tea, which was now becoming cool enough to drink without trouble, "have you given any thought to what we talked about yesterday? I mean the play last Saturday night. Was there anything unusual about it?"

"Well, you know, that's the interesting thing about it."

"What?"

"I was up half the night thinking about that, and I can't remember there being anything unusual about it, except for the fact that the performance was not very good, there wasn't anything to set it apart from any other."

"Nothing unusual happened in the audience, or between any of the audience members?"

"Nothing."

"What about during intermission? Where did you go?"

"Meg and I went out into what they call the lobby—it's actually the very front of this store. They'd built this thin wall to separate the small area up front to act as a lobby, and Meg and I went out there because they were serving coffee, and to stretch our legs—I'm afraid that aside from everything else, they were doing the play quite slowly, and I was a bit uncomfortable on the hard chairs they provided. We wanted to stand up for a while."

"I see."

"And it's a good thing, too, because there wasn't anywhere to sit down in the lobby. We each had a cup of coffee—I didn't drink very much of it—it wasn't very good—and then we went back into the theater."

"And the rest of the audience?"

"Oh, all of them went out into the lobby."

"You saw all of them during the intermission?"

"Yes."

"None of them stayed in the theater."

"No. And just when they were ready to begin the second act, we went back in." She added confidentially, "There were a few muttered remarks about being gluttons for punishment, but we went."

"There was *nothing* unusual. You're sure."

"Quite sure."

"Hmmm." Ransom tried not to let his disappointment show, but he did not have such complete control over his emotions that he could control his body, which now slumped visibly. The picture of the night in question he held in his mind was not of the normal evening out that Emily had described. Of course, he knew absolutely nothing of the local theater scene. His forays into the theater had been limited to the Shubert and the Blackstone, seeing only the odd touring company of large shows, specifically musicals. All he knew of the local theater was from the large spread of titles offered in the Friday and Sunday entertainment sections in the papers: a seeming sea of plays, each indistinguishable from the other. However, his idea of the theater in which Emily and Meg had spent their last night together was of something dark and sinister, where there had hopefully been something quite noticeable (upon reflection) that had tied all the audience members together in a secret for which they were now being killed. It was now apparent that if Emily was at all representative, these unsuspecting people were being killed for something, presumably something they had seen, but they had no idea what it was they had seen, or that they had seen anything at all.

He felt something that he rarely if ever felt before: a warm, sick feeling in the pit of his stomach that he was facing a much more difficult, inscrutable problem than he had ever faced. What could these people have seen that would have been so innocent that they wouldn't even remember it and so important that it would cost them their lives? And if those who were still alive didn't know they had seen anything, how would he proceed? He sighed very heavily, the energy seeming to drain from his body.

It was not like him to give way to these irrational feelings of inadequacy. And he was conscious of the need to fight an even more irrational fear: that failing to solve this case would be failing Emily. What's worse, failing to solve it in time might cost her her life.

While Ransom was engaged in contemplation, Emily watched him with the loving concern that so many of the elderly seem to be able to spare for mere acquaintances. Like others of her age, she found it easy to give away that which she didn't have much time left to give. She didn't interrupt his thinking and quietly poured him another cup of tea. He stirred, as if the action of the pouring water had brought him back to the present.

"Thank you," he said quietly.

"So," she said, replacing the teapot on a small, quilted potholder she kept at tableside for this purpose, "what will you do next?"

He did not want to alarm her with his growing anxiety concerning the case and thought it best to continue with her as if he were following up her story as a matter of course. "Well, I think I'll talk to the members of the theater company, just to be sure, and of course we'll talk to the remaining audience members."

"There aren't many of *them*," she said with a gleam in her eye.

"No, I suppose not," he said, smiling ruefully. He continued to find her directness rather disarming. Surely the other elderly people he had met in his adult life were not as direct or clear as Emily. They had always struck him as vague and wandering, or worse, endlessly reminiscing as if forever lost in the past. But Emily was alert and certainly aware, and he was beginning to realize that whatever caused his growing desire to protect her, she was not a woman to be shielded or protected.

"I'm sure we'll have this whole thing cleared up in no time," he added casually. "But in the meantime, I want you to keep trying to remember anything—*anything* that might have happened last Saturday. Even the smallest detail, even if it doesn't seem important, might be."

"I'll try," she said, smiling warmly.

"And if you don't mind, I'll keep having someone watch you. That will make you feel safe, won't it?"

Emily heaved a rather tired sigh, her gaze traveling back to the lightning-marred oak tree and off-center bird feeder. "I haven't really felt safe, I don't think, since my husband died. It's not that I feel frightened, oh no. But...it's funny. Even though I've always been a fairly self-reliant person, there's always a great feeling of safety in having a husband, even if you don't feel the need for his protection. You believe that if ever anything does need to be handled, you will have help doing it. It's not quite feeling afraid, to be left on your own, as it is an unpleasant sense that you will *have* to handle anything that comes along by yourself."

"We'll be looking after you now," said Ransom, knowing as he said it that the phrase would sound empty but needing at the same time to find some way to let her know that she was being taken care of. He knew that nothing could replace her long dead husband, or her recently lost friend, but he also sensed that this would be yet another one of the transitions that faced all humanity throughout their lives. For Emily, the time of being cared for by her husband had long passed, and the time of being cared for and surrounded by many of her friends was fading quickly away. It was, he felt, a delicate time in her life. She could decide to continue moving out among people, making new friends and finding new people to care for and to have care for her, or she could simply decide that she was too old for another of life's changes, slowly cutting herself off from the world and fading away into nothingness. He could see Emily, as strong a woman as she might be, going either way. Even a strong flower must eventually wither. At the same time, he wondered what more would happen during this transitional period, and if whatever happened would decide the matter for her.

TEN

RANSOM HAD SPENT much more time at Emily's house than he had originally intended, so it was late Saturday afternoon before he got back to the station. He thought it was the approaching Saturday night with its usual festivities that filled him with expectation. One thing he had always loved about Chicago was that Saturday night was never dead. There is always this feeling that no matter what the weather—and the weather could be pretty risky—there was a party going on all over town. It was not a party that one necessarily needed to attend, but it was there for you when you needed or wanted it. But as it grew later he realized that his expectation stemmed from the fact that this particular Saturday night marked the one-week anniversary of the curtain going up on that fated Shakespearean performance that had presumably cost three people their lives, and might cost more. This sense of the curtain going up, the play about to begin (as of course many curtains must be going up on plays all over the city on this very night, if indeed the theaters still had curtains) was inescapable, almost palpable. He could picture the lights dimming in the audience, much as the light of day was now waning around him, and the curtain rising in the darkness, almost imperceptible to the naked eye, and the lights quickly rising on the stage, the story about to unfold in front of you. He stopped himself in amusement when he realized that his heart had begun beating faster in anticipation.

Upstairs and back in his office, he found Gerald waiting

for him, weary and trying to hide his uncharacteristic irritation with his partner for having been gone for so long, leaving him to do the part of their job that he considered the work. Of course, it was only through weariness that he would dare to think of such a thing, since even he had a great deal of admiration for the way his partner seemed to be able to solve murders. But Gerald would not discount his own contribution to their partnership. He knew that he was methodical and thorough, and there was something to be said for legwork, even that done by phone.

"What did you find out?" said Ransom without preamble.

"Over the course of the day," he replied, which would be the only concession to his irritation, "I've been able to contact all the members of the cast. All ten are in town, and alive, and I told all of them to stay in town. Whether they'll stay alive is the part I can't vouch for."

"You've left your preposition dangling, Gerald—go on."

"Anyway," he continued with a sigh, "I told all of them we would need to question them."

"I bet that set the theater world to buzzing."

"Two of the actors—these two—" he checked off two names on the cast list "—were pretty miffed about being kept in town. They said they'd been planning to go camping, and as they were both men, I can only guess what that may mean."

Ransom raised a curious eyebrow at the tone of his partner's voice. It was unlike him to demonstrate anything in the way of prejudice, and Ransom wasn't quite sure if it was actual prejudice, or if Gerald was directing his irritation at strangers instead of at Ransom himself. He tried not to smile, although he was quite pleased to see this tiny crack in his partner's equanimity.

"I didn't press them for their destination. I told them they may have to put it off, but we'd try to finish with them as soon as possible."

"What about the crew?"

"Their crew appears to have been Gail Shelly. The lighting man was Damien Liddle."

"The Shakespearean cum television star?"

"The same. It doesn't exactly call for a lot of lighting expertise, from the little I've been told about their theater so far. All they had was a dimmer they used for lights full up or full down. They'd never made enough money to rent proper lighting."

"And now for the sixty-four-thousand-dollar question. What about Mark Benson and friend?"

"The proverbial good news and bad news. The bad news is that there's no sign of them...and that's the good news, too. I tried to get him by phone all morning and he didn't answer, which under the circumstances worried me, so I went over there, got hold of the landlord, and had him open the apartment. Nobody was there. So, he wasn't there and we don't know whether or not he's dead or alive. But at least we didn't find a body."

"Any leads on the lady he was with?"

"His wife. There were pictures in the apartment, and the landlord identified her for me. Here, I took the liberty of taking this from the apartment."

"Gerald, I'm shocked," Ransom said wryly as he took the snapshot from his partner and looked it over. They were a very handsome couple, he thought, telling himself at the same time that the expression was hopelessly outmoded. The couple in the picture were both very tan and wearing broad smiles. They both had dark hair, though hers was darker and straighter than his. It was apparent from their dress, their manner, and the fact that they were on a beach that this had been taken during some sort of vacation or holiday. Ransom couldn't help thinking that they, like most other people, were probably pictured on their vacation in the Bahamas, but he knew this island idea of his was becoming an obsession because of his inability to get away on a trip. For all he knew, the beach in the picture could be the Indiana Dunes. There was certainly nothing in the picture to serve as a landmark.

"So these are the Bensons."

"Yes," said Gerald, "Mark and Stephanie. The landlord told me her name. He didn't know where they had gone, but he couldn't remember seeing them for a while."

"Did he define 'a while'?" Ransom asked, tossing the picture back to his partner.

"No. He said he couldn't remember the last time he'd seen them—I mean, he literally couldn't remember. I pressed him a little but he got pretty mad—he said it wasn't his job to keep track of his tenants' comings and goings."

"Well, I suppose he's right."

"It seems to me things would be better all the way around if someone *was* watching our comings and goings."

"Perhaps for us, but I have no desire to live in an Orwellian society."

They fell into a silence that for once was neither contemplative nor reflective. Gerald gazed at the picture of the Bensons, feeling neither one way nor the other about their choice of vacation spots, and Ransom smoked quietly. It was Gerald who finally spoke.

"How did your date with your little old lady friend go?"

"She couldn't remember anything more than she told us yesterday."

"Figures."

Ransom shot him an amused glance. "The little old lady was sharp enough to notice that she was being watched by the police."

"You're kidding!"

"No, I'm not. She keeps her eyes open. She noticed him right away. I didn't have the heart to tell her that sometimes it's safer to keep surveillance rather obvious."

"How did she know it wasn't the murderer?"

Ransom blushed, answering his partner more sharply than he ordinarily would, purely out of embarrassment over having asked Emily virtually the same thing. "Honestly, Gerald, I really wonder sometimes how you ever got on the force in the first place. She probably figured that the murderer would come in and kill her instead of sitting in a car on the street all night."

Even Gerald couldn't help laughing at this. There were times, and this was one of them, when Ransom was transparent to him.

"You keep on like this and I'm going to end up with Emily as a partner."

"Emily?"

"Miss Charters. The old lady."

"If she's so sharp, didn't she see anything out of the ordinary at the performance?"

"No," said Ransom, growing more serious, "and that's what bothers me. I would think that if there *had* been something odd there, she would have seen it. But the only thing that seems to have been memorable about the performance is that it was what she calls an 'unfortunate version' of the play. I assume she meant by that that it was a bad production."

"Hardly a thing worth killing for," said Gerald, beating his partner to the punch.

"I UNDERSTAND that we're now running a nursing home," said Sergeant Newman, his voice rising louder than was normal for him. It was a clear indication to Ransom that he really was angry, since Newman preferred being quietly effective to histrionics. Raising his voice was something Newman believed to be a sign of weakness rather than an indication of anger. And it made him all the more angry when he felt he had been pushed to the point of doing it.

"You know how shorthanded we are?" he continued.

"What are you talking about?" said Ransom, knowing full well in advance what the sergeant had in mind, but thinking it might calm him down to say it openly.

"I understand that you're using up our resources by having a little old lady under surveillance twenty-four hours a day!"

"If by 'resources' you mean people, I don't think they'll be 'used up' by watching the old woman."

"Don't be a smartass! You know what I'm talking about! We can't spare the manpower for something so damn stupid!"

Despite himself, Ransom grew angry. Newman always knew how to press the right buttons when he wanted to. Ransom couldn't abide having his decisions, nor preserving Emily's safety, be referred to as stupid. "I have evidence that Miss Charters's life is in danger."

"What evidence?" Newman snapped.

Ransom, as calmly as he could, related the story that Emily had told him, and what their subsequent investigation had turned up: the murders, the stolen answering machine, and the missing married couple. Newman remained unimpressed.

"So you really don't have any evidence to support twenty-four-hour surveillance of one person."

"I have three dead bodies! Possibly five, since we can't find the other audience members. What the hell more do you need?"

"I need my men here, working!"

"Doing what? Protecting the people? Isn't that what we're paid to do? That's what we're doing by watching Emily—Miss Charters."

"Emily, is it?" said Newman, finally sitting in his chair and calming himself. "So now we come to it. She's a friend of yours."

"I want her watched because she's in danger. Look, if it were up to me, we wouldn't just be watching *her*, we'd be watching the Bensons' apartment, too. We need to get to them before..."

"Before what?" said Newman, raising his voice again and sitting up in his chair. "We don't know that they're in any danger at all. All we have are the wanderings of some old bag that you're fond of."

"The *lady*," said Ransom, emphasizing the word warningly, "has been right about everything so far. If the audience that was at that play last Saturday night is not being systematically killed off one by one, they're sure as hell giving a good impression of it!" If Ransom was surprised to find his voice now raised to the same level as Newman's, he could not waste energy thinking about it. He knew it was important now, maybe even a matter of life and death, to not give in or let his intensity drop.

"We need to keep Emily Charters under surveillance, and we need to have the Bensons' apartment watched. *We* have to be the first to see them when they get back, assuming they're not dead already!"

Newman took a couple of deep breaths to calm himself down, but it was too late to even attempt quiet effectiveness now that he had let his anger get the best of him. He seldom had run-ins with Ransom, and he always disliked it when he did, feeling that somehow or other he always ended up on the wrong end of the fight.

"We do not have the manpower to spare watching an empty apartment, and we don't have it to spare to watch some little old lady with an overactive imagination. I'm calling off the surveillance. I *need* our men here. Our case load is too heavy for this sort of thing. And you know, the public doesn't think we're doing our job as it is— every time some idiot gets himself killed, they act like we're to blame."

Ransom leapt out of his chair, slamming both fists down on Newman's desk with so much force that it actually gave the sergeant a start. Ransom leaned so far over the desk that his face was less than a foot away from Newman's.

"You think we have a heavy case load? People don't think we're doing our jobs? Well let me tell you something," he shouted. It was all he could do to keep from grabbing Newman by the lapels, but even in anger he knew his limits. He could get away with yelling at the sergeant; he would not get away with manhandling him. "If you take surveillance off of Emily Charters, she's going to die! And what the hell do you think the papers and the public are going to think of you then, huh? They're going to think we're as big a slime as the bastard that kills her. Take them off, get her killed, and the newspapers are going to have a field day with you! You'll never live it down! That'll be it!"

"And how do you think they would find out about such a thing if it happened?" said Newman warily, pushing his straggly gray hair out of his eyes.

"I'll tell them!" Ransom spat back as he stormed out of the office.

THE DAY HAD BEEN very long, and although the pounding in Ransom's head had long since subsided to a dull ache, he was still aware of it, and he had taken the last of his Excedrin long ago. He was keenly aware of the need for a good night's sleep. It didn't help to know that tomorrow he was going to have to start the long and arduous task of questioning all the actors who had appeared in *Love's Labor's Lost*. He felt even more weary at the thought, made worse by the nagging suspicion that it would all be in vain.

Despite the lateness of the hour and the fact that he didn't intend to make the same mistake as yesterday—he would have to stop at the grocery store—he took the time to swing by Emily's house before heading home. As he turned his car down the block, he was greatly relieved to see Sanders back at her post. He was afraid that despite the histrionics, Newman would go ahead and take surveillance off the old woman. Fortunately, the bluff had worked, or so it seemed.

He drove past Sanders's car, acknowledging her with the barest nod of the head, and started for the store. Tonight, he knew, he was simply too tired. There would be no bath and no Dickens. He thought ruefully that his job was encroaching further and further into his time, so that he not only had no personal life, he was in danger of ending up with no off-duty life at all. But as he had realized long before, as long as he was on a case, especially a challenging one, it didn't matter whether or not he stayed at the station, his mind went on working. As he drove, he mentally constructed the theater and the performance. Fortunately the play was one he could remember fairly clearly. He knew that he and Gerald would have to go and look at the theater to get some idea of whether or not the cast could actually see the audience and how exactly the audience was set up. Perhaps Emily could help him recreate the seating arrangement, since she seemed to notice a great deal. And with careful questioning, he might be able to get some of the cast members to tell him just how visible the audience was. He simply couldn't discount the idea that one of the cast members was involved. But why? The only thing...the only thing he had to go on was the performance: The only thing Emily had noticed about it was that it wasn't good. Damn, what could it have been?

He glanced suddenly to the right, through the passenger window, and realized that he was turning the car into the parking lot of his apartment building. He had driven himself home without thinking, without stopping at the grocery. He pressed the brake quickly, cursing himself as he did, and rested his head briefly on the steering wheel. Finally, he sat up, taking himself in hand. There was nothing for it but to drive back. He sighed and wearily pressed the gas pedal.

ELEVEN

SARA COLLINS COULD stand it no longer. It had been bad enough when the odor from the suspected Indian apartment was seeping into the hallway, but it was insufferable to have it permeating her own apartment. That was something she wouldn't stand for. Mr. Luddin, her landlord, wasn't at all amused about being rousted out of his home the first thing on a Sunday morning by a tenant complaint, especially one about a smell, but Sara was most firm about it, and of course she knew that threatening to withhold the rent until the problem was taken care of would get prompt action.

After assuring Sara that the tenant of number 11 wasn't East Indian, and that he couldn't imagine what the young man in the apartment was doing but he'd come up and look into it, Mr. Luddin hung up the phone and swore to his wife that he was going to have to go into some other kind of work. He just couldn't tolerate anymore the constant interruptions of his leisure time by the idiotic tenants who thought he should be at their beck and call twenty-four hours a day. His wife, as usual, reminded him very unsympathetically that it was his *job* to be at their beck and call twenty-four hours a day, more or less.

After having to go back down to his apartment because he had forgotten his passkey, Luddin traveled up to number 11 on the elevator, muttering oaths under his breath and trying once or twice to pull the front of his solid khaki T-shirt down over his protruding spare tire.

When the elevator doors opened on the third floor, the

odor was immediately apparent. Luddin got off the elevator, reluctantly admitting to himself that the smell *was* pretty bad and that this was probably going to lead to a rather unpleasant confrontation between him and the inhabitant of the apartment. The smell grew stronger as he approached the door. He stopped and rapped solidly on it with his knuckles, directly under the metal numbers. To his surprise, the door to number 12 opened to his knock, and Sara poked her head out into the hallway.

"You *can* smell it, can't you, Mr. Luddin?"

"Yeah, miss, I can smell it," he said, glaring at her. It didn't matter to him whether or not she was correct about the smell; he still didn't appreciate being called out of his quiet apartment on a Sunday morning. It was obvious from the strength of the odor that it hadn't developed overnight. It was always this way with these tenants, he thought, waiting until it was a crisis to report any problem. He was sure this could have been taken care of during normal working hours.

"It's been getting worse all week!" she said.

Then for God's sake, why didn't you call me earlier, he thought, why wait until Sunday morning?

A minute or two had gone by, and there had been no answer to his knock. He rapped on the door a second time, this time calling out "Mr. Sands?" as he knocked. There was no answer, and not even the sound of movement within the apartment. He pressed his ear closer to the door to see if he could detect any sound, but there was nothing. Sara watched silently as Luddin sighed and pulled out his passkey, which he fitted into the doorknob. He unlocked the door, swung it open, and as he stepped inside was immediately slapped in the face by the strength of the odor pouring out of the apartment. As large and strong as he was, he couldn't help recoiling. Sara covered her mouth and nose with her hand.

He took another step into the apartment, which slightly obscured him from Sara's view, and then with a sudden slam, he flung himself back against the doorjamb. Sara's eyes opened wider at the sight of him. His fleshy cheeks had been drained of all their color, and his eyes looked as if they would dart out of his head. Sara started to speak, to ask him what was wrong, but he stopped her without moving.

"Call the police!"

"What..." she said, hesitating in her own doorway.

"Call the police!" he yelled again.

Sara, terrified by the expression on his face and the tone of his voice, turned immediately into her apartment to make the call. Luddin, all his composure and all trace of his irritation now destroyed, turned out into the hallway, unable to let go of the wall for fear his legs would give way. He leaned against the wall just past number 11, still holding fast to the doorknob, and vomited.

THE FIRST ORDER of the day for Ransom was a much more leisurely breakfast than he normally allowed himself. He usually restricted himself to a bowl of cold cereal and a glass of iced tea, but this morning he was experiencing a weird mixture of elation and serenity, coming with the absence of his headache from the day before and the good night's sleep from which he had just awakened. He feasted on soft-boiled eggs, warm toast with butter and blackberry jam, and the obligatory tea. When he had finished, he sat back in his chair, sated and happy, and pulled out one of his plastic-tipped cigars. He rarely indulged in a smoke this early in the morning, but he felt that this would be the only thing that could improve his enjoyment.

He did, in fact, enjoy it so much that the tip was beginning to melt before he stubbed it out in the ashtray on the small all-purpose table wedged in the corner by the windows. On mornings like these he was struck by the beauty of the city. Seeing it spread out before him now from the window of his high-rise apartment, with the sun glowing and the early-morning haze long since burned off, it was hard to believe that the inhabitants of this city had a tendency to kill each other.

Of course, the moment this thought entered his mind, he was reminded that it was time to go to work. As he left his building, his hair was immediately blown out of place, which normally irritated him, but on this morning he felt so good that he literally brushed it aside with his hand and continued on to work.

Gerald was waiting for him at the station, and they immediately started out together on what would be a long day of asking questions of some overtly nervous young actors, beginning with the lesser actors and working their way up to the leads. Of the eight that took up all the smaller roles, none were able to help the two detectives. It seemed that none of them had known anyone who had been in the audience on that fateful night, and all as one disavowed even paying any attention to the audience on that or any other night. It seemed, Ransom learned from one rather short actor who had appeared in no less than three roles in this production, that good actors were supposed to act as if they really existed in the world of the play, and that the audience wasn't really there. Ransom found this disconcerting, since he felt that for the price of a ticket your presence should not go unnoticed.

Gerald studiously took notes as Ransom asked each actor in turn about what had gone on backstage during the performance and the intermission, hoping that one of them might have heard another mention knowing someone in the audience, thereby exposing a lie, but in this, too, he was stymied. It seemed that the lesser actors had been forced to double in so many roles that they barely had time to breathe backstage, let alone talk, since they constantly had to change costumes and makeup during their time offstage. The leads spent most of their time onstage, and even when off there was certainly no one with whom to carry on a conversation.

Two of the actresses were particularly incredulous over the suggestion that they could talk backstage, explaining to the detectives that *backstage* was a very loose term to use for the area in which the actors had been "trapped" (their word). It was an area of approximately eight feet square, separated from the right side of the audience by a black scrim. They assured Ransom that if they so much as whispered backstage, their voices were heard quite as audibly as if they'd been sitting in the audience's collective laps. It was, after all, a *store* they were performing in, not the Shubert!

Ransom was careful during these interviews not to let his facial expression or the timbre of his voice betray his anxiety at the lack of progress he seemed to be making. Inwardly he grew wary of hearing the same answers from these young and energetic yet ultimately self-possessed people. He could feel his mind growing cloudier and cloudier as the earnest answers droned on, all the while his heart sinking further at the disconnectedness of the whole situation. He was beginning to find the whole theater experience, at least that which he was hearing of today, to be oddly comparable to Emily's grappling with the familiar but unfamiliar, knowing and yet not knowing. The picture of the relationship that these young actors drew between themselves, the stage, and the audience, was similar in his mind to Emily's plight: the audience being there, but not there, the actors huddled together backstage, unable to communicate with one another. All these ideas whirled around in his mind.

But at the same time, he couldn't dismiss the idea of art reflecting life, if the Pennington Players could be considered art. As the actors talked of noncommunication, Ransom's conscience continued to nag him about his reluctance to even listen to the messages on his answering machine, especially since the importance of messages seemed to be primary in the case at hand. He tried to ease his conscience by reminding himself that his decision concerning phone messages or communication of any sort was purely a matter of choice, unlike these people, who seemed to have drifted into a land of noncommunication. This was very little consolation, though, since while one rather plain actress explained the rigors of changing from one wig to another in the dark, he tried unsuccessfully to remember exactly when it was he had started to ignore his calls.

Gerald coughed suddenly, and Ransom started and glanced over at him. Gerald flashed a smile at him, and he realized that the cough had been designed to bring him back to the present. As his mind had wandered, the plain actress, whose name he couldn't recall at the moment, had stopped talking and was looking at him expectantly. It had taken Gerald more than a moment to realize that his partner wasn't pausing for effect, he simply wasn't paying attention. Ransom thanked her for her help and the detectives took their leave, going on to the next on the list.

Ransom asked each actor in turn what had transpired during the intermission, and this, too, met with uniform responses. The actors, though they were allowed to talk during intermission, were still required to keep their voices hushed in deference to the audience. They were also required to *remain* backstage during the intermission (in deference to professionalism), so none of them had had an opportunity to mingle with the audience. None could remember any of the audience members coming backstage to use the bathroom.

The only exception to this sequestration was Gail, who set up props both backstage and onstage during the intermission and helped with refreshments for the audience on particularly heavy nights, which they never had. However, it seemed to be understood that she would help Damien whether he needed it or not. Gail alone of the people backstage during the performance would have possibly been able to see the audience. However, most of the actors and actresses doubted if she had, since she was universally thought to be a colorless, officious doormouse who was laughably dedicated to their theater. She was so single-minded she wouldn't have noticed someone from the audience unless they came up on stage and got in her way. Gail, it seemed, was a joke.

None of the actors could remember anything in particular that had been talked about during the intermission, but they all assured the detectives that it certainly hadn't been the audience. Their conversation was usually restricted to what they had each auditioned for, what they would be auditioning for, and why they hadn't gotten what they had auditioned for. In fact, by the time they were through questioning the minor players, Ransom had a fairly comprehensive list of the coming attractions for the Chicago theater scene.

The only exception to the virtually endless stream of banality was Alice Hardwick, a young woman who took herself and her acting very seriously. Alice told them of the high expectations she had originally entertained for the company and her growing discontent with her fellow members, none of whom were as serious about it as she was. She had originally been fired up to be a charter member of the company by Damien's apparent dedication to classical theater. It had been a crushing blow to her to find that Damien, to put it in the vernacular of the sixties, was a sellout. "He would drop his dreams to become a wealthy television star," Alice had proclaimed with venom.

Because of these feelings about her compatriots and her seriousness about the theater, she was singularly unhelpful to Ransom. Being a method actress, she concentrated on her character backstage as well as on, and given her feelings about the rest of the company, she was even less inclined to pay any attention to what they said or did.

The only person that Alice could spare any sympathy for was Gail. Gail, Alice told them, was a nice but foolish girl, and it was particularly sad that she was so infatuated with Damien (so, thought Ransom, not everything escaped Alice's notice). Alice felt that Gail was simply fooling herself, but she had said this in a way that made Ransom believe she was sympathetic to the girl: an emotion that made him like Alice despite her seriousness.

When they finally stopped for lunch, it was almost two, which was late for Ransom, who liked to eat punctually at noon. Both he and Gerald were tired and hungry, having spent the morning driving from apartment complex to apartment complex, all alarmingly alike, to question the actors, stopping between each interview to call Mark and Stephanie Benson's apartment to see if they'd returned home. Though Ransom's threat of media interference had coerced Newman into continuing the surveillance of Emily, it had not succeeded in getting surveillance for the Bensons, and Ransom feared that the safety of these last two audience members depended on his getting to them first, assuming they were still alive.

They stopped for lunch at a restaurant that had been one of Ransom's favorites before it had become yuppified, its name being as simple as the food they served: Eat Inn. As they waited for their burgers and chips, he remembered wistfully the days when you could always walk into this restaurant and find a seat, the service was always good, and the food plain but appetizing. Then one day the restaurant had inexplicably become "the" place to eat. There never *did* seem to be an explanation for why a place that has stood quietly and discreetly for forty years will suddenly become a hot spot, but like so many places before it, Eat Inn was now enjoying its turn. Ransom begrudged the crowds, but as a longtime patron he was still always treated well, and he knew that in time the crowds would fade as another restaurant was "discovered" and took its turn, and he felt he could suffer in relative silence until the wave had passed.

As they ate their hamburgers (which Ransom always ordered burnt), their chips, and small slaw cups, they discussed the morning's work.

"None of them know a damn thing!" exclaimed Gerald, sucking into his mouth a bit of coleslaw that was left dangling on his lip from the last forkful.

"So it would seem," said Ransom. The music playing in the background, always classical, had switched from Bach to Mozart, and he had become aware that the music seemed to be causing him to eat faster.

"You think we learned anything this morning?" asked Gerald.

"Well," he answered with a sigh, putting his sandwich down until the music changed again, "I do, as a matter of fact."

He pulled a cigar out of his pocket and tapped it on the table, but Gerald caught his eye and an understanding glance passed between them. Gerald didn't mind Ransom's smoking. In fact, he found the aroma of Ransom's brand of cigars faintly pleasant. But he couldn't stand the smell of smoke while he was eating, so it was understood between them that Ransom could smoke any time except meals.

"I think we know at least a little *because* the cast doesn't seem to know anything. First, it doesn't appear that any of them knew any of the audience. I can't imagine that in the time they spent together backstage, no one would have noticed it if one of the actors had recognized someone in the audience, especially in such close quarters. In that sense, they all seem to corroborate each other in one way or another."

"Hmm," said Gerald, taking a large bite of hamburger.

"It's like that one said…"

"Which one?"

"I can't remember!" said Ransom, only mildly exasperated. "It's no wonder so few actors are truly memorable—all these people seem alike. I can't separate them in my mind."

Gerald laughed. The music switched from Mozart to Bach's "Air on a G String," so Ransom felt safe to resume eating at a more peaceful pace. He continued with his thoughts between bites.

"And then there's the fact that these actors are all still alive. Unless one of the actors is the murderer, it doesn't seem like whatever happened has anything to do with the actors at all."

"Unless our murderer is very methodical," said Gerald, taking a sip of the Bud Light he had ordered with his meal.

Ransom paused in his chewing just long enough to give his partner a quizzical glance.

"Perhaps," explained Gerald, "he simply wants to finish off the audience before he starts with the actors."

"Sort of like finishing off one course before you start on the next," said Ransom, laughing.

RANSOM STOPPED briefly at a pay phone on the way out of the restaurant to call the Bensons, but the phone was answered once again by an answering machine. He slammed down the receiver angrily, wondering if they realized that their insufferably cute message became very annoying if you had to listen to it repeatedly.

Back in the car, he continued his dissertation on the matter at hand.

"No, if we're to believe what we're hearing from these people, then the cast is not involved in what is happening. They had no knowledge of or contact with the audience."

"Except," Gerald reminded him, "for the Liddle fellow, and probably Gail Shelly."

"Gail Shelly and the Liddle Fellow," said Ransom, correcting him with a laugh. "Sounds like the title of a Disney movie." The faint irritation he had felt at going so long without lunch had now faded, and he sat contentedly smoking his cigar on the passenger seat. Gerald steered them to their next interview. "But you're right, we need to remember they came in contact with the audience."

"Right," said Gerald, pleased to have added something to Ransom's ruminations.

"I'm still annoyed with our mousy little Gail that she 'can't remember' whether or not she helped in the lobby during the intermission. I really don't know what to make of it."

"She doesn't seem like the mass-murderer type."

"None of them do," said Ransom, tapping his ashes out the window instead of using the ashtray on the armrest. "So, assuming that we're getting the correct impression from the actors—"

"Do you think we are?"

Ransom stopped and looked out the window, thinking for a moment and releasing a stream of smoke. "Yes, I do," he said finally.

"I mean, after all, they *are* actors. Wasn't it you who said that all actors are liars?"

"I said I had heard that," Ransom said with a smile. "But liars or not, I do believe we're getting the correct impression. If they were lying, it seems at least one of them would have to trip up sometime. But they all agree. I can't believe they've all gotten together to match their stories and are able to stick to them so religiously while looking so innocent. It's impossible for them to be that well rehearsed."

"So where does that leave us?"

"Well, if the cast was, indeed, unaware of the audience's identities—if they were completely separate from the audience—what does that suggest?"

"Oh jeez," said Gerald testily. As much as he liked his partner, he hated these pop quizzes Ransom was wont to give when he was onto something. "You tell *me!* What does it suggest?"

"The audience and the actors were together, so to speak, when the play was going. If the audience saw something that the actors didn't, it would indicate that whatever happened, happened during the intermission, when the audience was completely separated from the actors."

"Almost completely."

"Almost completely," repeated Ransom. "We've just two actors left—the two that were onstage the longest, Rosaline and Berowne."

"Who?" said Gerald, taking his eyes off the road long enough to look at his partner.

"Lorrie Reed and Danny Leming, Rosaline and Berowne."

Gerald still looked perplexed, and Ransom sighed, fearing that Damien Liddle's assessment of Chicagoans' lack of knowledge of the fine arts might be painfully true.

"Rosaline and Berowne. You really should brush up on your Shakespeare, Gerald!"

As the two detectives pulled up in front of Lorrie Reed's building, Ransom marveled again at how alike the actors and actresses seemed. This was sparked by the fact that Lorrie lived in a courtyard building much like Damien's, albeit cleaner. In this court there were flowerbeds along the walls of the building, planted mostly with marigolds and petunias, and in the center of the lawn stood a huge fountain, the top of which was mounted with a cherub that ostensibly poured water from an urn into the pool of the fountain below. In this case the urn had long since run dry, as no water was in the pool and apparently hadn't been for some time. The pool had at one time been painted blue, but lack of use and exposure to the sun had caused the paint to dry and chip away.

The first door in the court bore Lorrie's address, and Gerald found the mailbox with her name and pressed the doorbell below. They were almost immediately buzzed in and passed through the wooden lobby door with its heavy lead-glass inset. The two men hesitated just inside the door, since the mailbox had not been marked with an apartment number, and Lorrie hadn't given them the number when they'd called. After a brief moment, they heard a door open above, and a young female voice called out to them. "Who is it?"

"Detectives Ransom and White," Gerald called into the air.

After a split-second pause, the voice called down to them, "Come on up, we're on the top floor."

Ransom speculated on who "we" were as they trudged up three flights of stairs. At the top landing, Lorrie Reed stood leaning over the railing, watching them climb. Her long blond hair hung down from both sides, enveloping her face. The moment she came into view, Ransom began to register his impression of her. She was wearing a light pink, sleeveless T-shirt and a very tight pair of jeans that showed off to full effect her beautifully curved hips and slender legs. Around her waist was a thick leather belt clasped with a ludicrously large silver buckle in the shape of an eagle.

Ransom, having a fair knowledge of the classics himself and having both seen and read *Love's Labor's Lost,* was at first taken aback by her appearance, and assumed that this was not Lorrie but her daughter, since the girl on the landing was far too young to have played the aging Rosaline. But his doubts were dispelled when they reached the second-to-last landing and she announced rather proudly that she was, indeed, Lorrie Reed. She said her name, thought Ransom, almost as if she expected them to have heard of her before, not from the case they were investigating, but from the many plays in which she'd appeared.

As they climbed the steps to the last landing, Ransom was relieved to find at last that *this* actress was somehow different from the others. She was different in a way that he could not quite put his finger on, though several words ran through his mind. It could be what they call "star quality," but somehow to his mind that didn't fit any actress, no matter how talented, who was still in her early twenties. "Presence" was another word that he'd often heard in reference to actors who in some way had a bit more to them than others, but it was a term that was foreign to him in this context and so he dismissed it. As he stepped onto the landing, a phrase came to mind that he was sure was more appropriate to Lorrie and would set her apart from the other actors he had questioned: the killer instinct. That is the quality the others lacked, and the thing that would aid her in rising above the others no matter how much or little talent she might possess.

Oh God, he thought to himself, the girl had so far uttered two short sentences and her own name, and from that you've decided she would walk over people to get what she wants. But he couldn't seem to help himself, especially in this case, and he tried to quell his conscience by attempting to analyze his speculation about her character. Part of his impression was based on the fact that of all the actors and actresses he had questioned so far, Lorrie was the only one who displayed no nervousness. It was as if she were queen and the rest of the world her court and not anything she needed to be bothered with. No, he told himself, that's not quite it. She was not aloof to her audience (remembering, of course, that the more "serious" actors had felt they weren't ever supposed to be aware of the audience), she was in charge. Here on this landing, and everywhere else, she was giving a performance. "All the world's a stage and all the men and women merely bit players," he paraphrased to himself.

He smiled without thinking and then took himself in hand, reminding himself of his resolution to stop judging suspects so thoroughly at first glance. But try as he might, he couldn't shake this impression of her. It seemed, in fact, obvious, even in the smile she flashed at them as she waved them into the apartment, that his impression was correct.

Inside, the apartment was completely different from Damien Liddle's. Not being a slave to the profession as Damien felt himself to be, Lorrie held down a full-time job during the day, and that job had paid for furnishings that gave her apartment a sense of order lacking from the director's. The furnishings were cheap but functional. The shelves and stereo rack were pressboard that had been coated with a mahogany stain and varnished in a misguided effort to disguise their cheapness, and the rest of the chairs and the couch, though they matched, were old and obviously inexpensive. The walls were decorated exclusively with pictures of Lorrie and other actors from plays in which she'd appeared, each enclosed in the type of frame used to display diplomas or degrees.

Also in the apartment was another of Lorrie's possessions, Danny Leming, standing rather nervously by the windows looking as if he didn't know whether he should stay or go, or whether he should be standing or sitting. During Lorrie's hasty introductions he shook hands with the detectives with the air of a man who thinks he's not dressed properly for an engagement.

Ransom's assessment of him required much less mental activity than was necessary for Lorrie. He summed him up in one word: dolt. Danny, he thought, was an oversized Ken doll, genitalia notwithstanding. The problem for this empty-headed doll was that his mate was obviously not a fresh-faced California Barbie doll. No, Ransom thought gleefully as he took the offered seat, the situation here was "Ken meets Lolita."

"Now," he said as much to stop his mind from racing

as to begin the interview, "I believe Detective White told you on the phone that we wanted to ask you a few questions in regard to a murder investigation. We're interested in the last performance of your play, *Love's Labor's Lost*."

"Oh yes," answered Lorrie as she sat down on the left side of the couch, folding her legs up under her. She pulled Danny down next to her and cuddled up next to him kittenishly, as if this were the way they received all visitors. Danny appeared dazed and perplexed. He sat stiffly, taking no notice of the arm slipped through his. Gerald had quietly taken a seat by the windows where he was slightly obscured from view by a very large anonymous plant. He took out his notebook and began scribbling notes.

"We're anxious to help you in any way we can," she continued.

"Good." Ransom leaned back in his chair and crossed his legs casually. "I was wondering what you could tell me about that night."

"Huh?" said Danny, looking even more perplexed.

"The night of the last performance."

"Oh, yeah," said Danny. "Well—"

"What do you want to know?" said Lorrie, cutting him off.

"Was there anything unusual about the evening?"

"In what way?"

Oh, she's shrewd, thought Ransom. Not likely to give anything away. But he also thought that perhaps, if he tread carefully around her, he might be able to get her to say more than she intended.

"Well," he said, "did you notice anything unusual in the audience?"

"Aside from the fact that there *was* an audience?" she

said with an artificial little laugh. "We so seldom had one."

"Did you happen to notice if there was any unpleasantness between any of the people in the audience?"

"Unpleasantness?" she said, still smiling, as if she thought his choice of words was very quaint.

"Did you notice anything?" he said flatly, hoping that the seriousness of his demeanor would transmit to her the seriousness of the situation.

"I didn't notice anything about them," she said, oblivious to his tone. "I never do. I mean, I would have noticed if somebody had been talking or something."

He was certain that she was telling the truth. If the audience had been performing its primary function (watching her every move), this young lady would have paid them no mind. She would have noticed them only if they had not been paying attention to her. Like a cat.

"You didn't recognize anyone in the audience?"

"Well, you can't really see them from the stage, and I don't really like to look at them, because if you do look out in the audience it breaks your concentration."

No doubt, thought Ransom. He turned his gaze to Danny and raised a questioning eyebrow.

"Oh," he said when he realized that he, too, was expected to answer, "no, I didn't notice anything. I'm kinda nervous when I'm onstage, and so I can't think of anything else but what I'm doing...at the time. God, if I looked out at the audience, I think I'd shit!"

He laughed nervously, and Lorrie shot him an annoyed glance. It was obvious to Ransom that Danny was not kept around for his brains.

"Tell me about what went on backstage."

"You mean during the show? Not a whole lot. I mean, we were on and off quickly all the way through the show.

It was one of those stupid plays where the minute you go off you're waiting for your next cue to come back on. And then everybody else in the cast was back changing makeup and costumes and stuff. They had a lot of quick changes."

"Yeah," Danny added, as though he felt he should say something. "I didn't go offstage very much during the show."

"Did you know if anyone you *knew* was in the audience? Any of your friends or family there that night?"

"No one I knew. And nobody stayed around after the show. I'm sure if any of my friends had come that night, they would have told me ahead of time. And if not, they always wait around after the show to tell you how good you were. But most of my friends came during the first week, anyway." She leaned into him secretively with a sharp, wicked little smile. "They had to with the Pennington Players—there might not be a second week."

"I didn't know anybody there," added Danny dully.

"Do you know if anyone else in the cast knew any of the audience?"

"Nobody said anything about it, if they did," said Lorrie.

"Didn't anybody say *anything* backstage?" Ransom's tone reflected his disbelief that they could have spent so much time together without talking about something.

"Oh sure," laughed Lorrie, "they said things like 'get the hell out of my way' and stuff like that. Nobody had a chance to chat."

"What about during intermission?"

Lorrie sighed heavily to demonstrate that she was quickly becoming bored, as she would with any conversation of which she was not the subject. "Nobody talked about the audience, if that's what you mean. A couple of the girls said they'd auditioned for *Grease* and they were waiting to hear whether or not they were cast, but I didn't say anything because I knew they hadn't been. I mean, I'd already been cast in the lead—Sandy—we're in rehearsals now—a couple of days before, and the director told me who else was in the cast. They didn't get anything." A little smile darted across her pale pink lips, signifying a certain delight in the misfortune of her fellow actresses, and she sat back in her chair as if she'd finished all she had to say.

Ransom fought the urge to applaud.

"And?" said Ransom, in a tone that Lorrie found very disconcerting. For the first time she seemed unsure of herself.

"And...well, nothing, really," she said slowly. "The usual stuff. We couldn't talk a lot—I mean, we had to keep it down because that idiot Damien thought it was unprofessional for the audience to hear us backstage, even during the intermission."

Ah, here it is, thought Ransom. I've kept her talking long enough to get something.

"And you didn't agree?" he said, coaxing her along.

"At *that* theater?" she said with a sharp laugh. "For Christ's sake, we were separated from the audience by a sheet! The whole thing was a joke, and everybody seemed to know it except Damien!"

"You thought it was a joke?"

"Uh-huh."

"Then why did you work with the Pennington Players?"

She looked at him as if he was alarmingly dense and clucked her tongue. "For the credit, of course!"

"The credit?"

"Yeah, so I could put it on my résumé that I did Shakespeare."

"Did Shakespeare," thought Ransom, was probably an apt description. But what exactly she had done to him was questionable.

"I mean, it really doesn't matter to anybody *where* you did him. As long as you've done him people think you can act. You don't even have to have been *good*," she said with a glance at Danny.

"You were great as Rosaline," said Danny defensively, missing her point.

"So the Pennington Players was a joke...to everyone?"

"Everyone except Damien. He's such an—" She checked herself, thinking it might be out of character for her to swear in front of the detective, especially to use the word she'd intended. "He was so serious about the whole thing! Like Shakespeare is the end-all and the be-all of everything, and he was born to present him to the adoring public."

"Come on, Lorrie," said Danny reproachfully, and then continued nervously to Ransom: "Damien's a great actor. He's going to be on TV, you know."

"Yes, he mentioned that to us."

"He *would*," said Lorrie petulantly. "Probably within the first five minutes of the conversation."

"The *questioning*." She took the reproof icily, snuggling more closely to Danny in a feigned attempt at vulnerability.

Ransom gave her an appraising glance and unfolded his legs. "Was there anything else discussed backstage that night during the intermission?"

Lorrie sighed more deeply than ever before. It was quite clear that she was tired of the whole thing and wanted to get on to something else. "The usual stuff," she said, sounding more and more like a petulant little girl. "Who's sleeping with whom, who's planning to sleep with whom. Janet—that's Janet Kinney—she played Jaquenetta, the country wench—and she was just *made* for the part, if you know what I mean—all she talked about was the guy she's been going with for a few weeks. It was really a bore. The other girls talked about pretty much the same thing. The guys mostly talked about going out and drinking after the show, which I'm pretty sure they did."

"What about Gail?"

"Gail?" She spat out the name with an uncanny degree of contempt, as if she resented having to say it.

"What did Gail talk about?" he said, unperturbed.

"I'm sure I wouldn't know," she said with an air of superiority. "Damien, I suppose. He's all she usually talked about: 'Where's Damien? What's he doing? Does he need any help? Isn't he wonderful?' She's absolutely gaga over him. It's disgusting!"

"Why?"

"*Why?*" she repeated, then continued in a tone that Ransom would later describe as sniggering confidentiality. "Because *he's* not interested in *her*."

She smiled at Ransom in a way that he thought was meant to imply that she had been very subtle and clever. He decided he would enjoy making her spell it out for him.

"Was he interested in another woman?"

Lorrie clucked her tongue again, annoyed with him for being so thick. "Honestly! He's not interested in *any* woman. He's a faggot!"

"Lorrie!" said Danny, finally losing some of his nervousness. "You don't know that!"

"Get off it!" she said, pushing him away. She turned back to Ransom rather intently, making it clear that she relished smearing Damien's character at every opportunity. "Everybody knows it! I understand from some of the other company members that Damien was quite a little tramp before the AIDS crisis. These days, he's trying to act the respectable, monogamous little homebody!"

"For crying out loud, Lor, what'd he ever do to you?" Danny, in his dull way, was proving to have a strong moral sense, which precluded speaking ill of anyone, especially anyone not present to defend himself. This was one of the few aspects of Lorrie's personality that he really found disturbing, and Lorrie was not blind to the effect her cattiness had on him. When she had tried his patience about as far as it would go with her rude and insinuating remarks about people, she would turn from cat to kitten, calling all her coquettishness into play until she had him back in hand. But for all her work and as thick as Danny might be, he harbored a sneaking suspicion that Lorrie was simply not a nice person.

"He bitched at me all the way through the last show!" she spat back at him. "He was always picking at me during rehearsals, telling me I wasn't doing my part right!"

"Well, you know how he is," said Danny, trying to placate her. "He's crazy about Shakespeare and wants everything to be perfect!"

"He just picked at me because he doesn't like women."

None of the gentlemen present knew what to say to this outburst, but they didn't have to think for long. Lorrie, presumably fearing that she had protested too much, relented. Of course, her relenting was imbued with the air of one who is being "big about it" by making allowances for a lesser creature.

"Of course, he *did* want the show to be good. Honestly, I don't understand a word he says!"

"Mr. Liddle?" asked Ransom.

"No, *Shakespeare!*" she said, rolling her eyes. "I was in *Love's Labor's Lost,* and I still don't understand it. Do you like Shakespeare?" She directed the question at Ransom, who had been resting his right elbow on the arm of his chair and propping up his chin with his hand. It was a position that made him look decidedly bored, which Lorrie would not stand for. She hoped to remedy his intimidating attitude by asking him a question and making him talk, thus requiring him to shift position.

"Yes, I do."

To Lorrie's surprise and consternation, instead of simply shifting, he stood up entirely, motioning for Gerald to do likewise, obviously calling an end to the interview. Lorrie hopped up, confused and annoyed that control of the situation was not in her hands. Danny remained sitting, too confused to do anything.

"Tell me, Mr. Ransom, did you see *Love's Labor's Lost?*"

"I didn't see your production, but I've seen it and read it."

"Well, then, maybe *you* can tell me what it's about!" she said, thus hoping to put him on the spot. But her effort immediately backfired. She was totally unprepared for his response.

"Yes, I think I can. It's about a group of people who are playacting and playing games until someone comes to them and tells them of a death...and then the playacting has to end and they have to face reality."

Lorrie's mouth grew so tightly closed that her pink lips disappeared into one thin slit. She glared at him, and her face turned bright red, but by the time she had thought of a rejoinder, the detectives had taken their leave.

"Did he mean something by that?" asked Danny.

"I TRULY LOVE stumbling across hatred!" said Ransom as he lit his cigar.

Gerald climbed behind the steering wheel without acknowledging his partner's statement. He knew all too well Ransom's tendency to make the occasional odd comment, which Gerald firmly believed was simply designed to get a rise out of him. For his part, Gerald enjoyed his own capacity for frustrating Ransom by not giving him the desired reaction.

"Hatred is, at least, an honest emotion; there's something almost clean about it," continued Ransom, slightly perturbed at his partner's lack of response. Gerald noted his barely altered tone and was suitably pleased with himself. "An honest emotion is one that I can deal with."

"You think she was honest, then?" Gerald asked.

"Oh yes, I think she was honest. She fancies herself an actress, but she's got a long way to go before she's any good at it. She couldn't be convincing if her life depended on it. She's one of that rare group of people whose face and manner will expose their thoughts every time."

"But she didn't tell us anything," said Gerald, giving in to playing the prompting partner despite his resolve of only seconds earlier.

"She told us lots of things. She told us the subject matter of the backstage talk, which I think we have every reason to believe. As stuck as she is on herself, I think it's safe to assume that she hangs on every word spoken anywhere near her in hopes that she'll be the subject or at least hear something to her advantage. She corroborated everything we heard from the other actors about their proximity to the audience, the lack of recognition between anyone in the cast and anyone in the audience, and the generally innocuous, quiet talk that went on backstage during the intermission. I think we can definitely rule out the idea that anyone *said* anything backstage that was unusual, or that we can connect them to the murders, because I can hardly believe that our Lorrie Reed would suppress it. Much as she thinks herself a star, I imagine she would like to play the part of the star witness, giving us very dramatically the one piece of evidence that would fry the murderer.''

"Unless she's waiting for a more dramatic moment."

"Hmmm. There's a thought."

"Then, of course, it may just be she was intimidated. She did seem to find you intimidating, you know."

"Yes," he said with a gleeful smile that he simply couldn't repress. "Then there is the business about Gail. Gail, it appears, has quite a little thing for our Mr. Liddle, which we can assume will remain frustrated."

"Now that's exactly what I meant," said Gerald, stopping Ransom with a gesture of his right hand. "Are we supposed to take this girl's word for it that Liddle is gay?"

"Why not?"

"Well, for one thing, it's pretty damn clear that she hates him, and I'm sure she's vindictive enough to go around spreading rumors about him—that's common enough."

"I agree," said Ransom, which seemed to stop Gerald. Ransom took a sharp puff of his cigar and said, "And?"

"And what?"

"You said 'for one thing'—was there another thing?"

"Well...for another thing, he just didn't *seem* gay to me."

"That's why they call it acting, Gerald."

"Dammit," Gerald exclaimed, banging the steering wheel once with his fists, "you're insufferable when you're happy!"

"All right, all right," said Ransom, laughing. "I hate to admit it, but frankly, I agree with you. He didn't strike me as gay, either, but I'm inclined to believe that he is."

"The long-term relationship he supposedly had."

"Yes," said Ransom, his laughter having subsided. "Lorrie must have known that that would be an easy thing to check out."

Gerald brought the car to a halt just as Ransom finished his sentence, and they sat in silence for a moment as they waited for the traffic light to change. It was almost as if the red light had called a time-out in their conversation to let them assimilate the whirl of information they'd been discussing. Ransom puffed away thoughtfully, his teeth nibbling at the plastic tip of the cigar, and Gerald stared straight ahead, as if their spoken words were now replaying themselves in front of him. The light changed to green, and as Gerald smoothly pressed down on the gas pedal, Ransom began to speak once more.

"It seems to me there's something missing," said Ransom finally. "We have a lot of information, but nothing to tie it together. We have a prop girl—a gofer—who is infatuated with a homosexual. Suppose she found out about him..."

"And what?" said Gerald, happy to have the upper hand. "She kills the audience?"

The right side of Ransom's lip curled up, and he gave his partner a look that was supposed to be withering but could only be described as comical. Gerald saw this and despite himself burst out with a hearty laugh. Ransom, who was not entirely above enjoying a joke at his own expense, especially in his present state of exhilaration, merely smiled and said, "I was just thinking out loud."

"Go on," said Gerald.

"Then we have the leading lady, who obviously detests

Damien Liddle—and before you say it, you're right. Why would that make her kill the audience? And we have Liddle himself—the prospect of a new and lucrative move in his career..."

"...and absolutely nothing to hold him here," Gerald pointed out.

"That's true," said Ransom thoughtfully. "We have Damien Liddle, frustrated with the theater doing poorly and with the prospect of a rise in his career, Gail Shelly, frustrated in her love for him and with the prospect of losing him, and Lorrie Reed, who hates them both. All that anger and frustration. The answer must be in there somewhere."

"We're back to square one," said Gerald with a sigh.

"What do you mean?"

"It seems to me this is right where we were when we were just investigating Watson's murder—these people seem to have motives for killing each other, but not for killing the audience. The wrong people are dead."

"Which leads me to believe that my theory is right," said Ransom, stubbing out the remains of his cigar in the ashtray on his armrest.

"What's that?"

"If the audience was indeed that separate from the actors, and it's the audience that's being killed off, it must have something to do with the intermission. They must have seen something, however innocent at the time, that is costing these people their lives."

"Where does that leave us?"

"With Emily."

"And with the Bensons," added Gerald.

They fell into a contemplative silence as Gerald directed the car back to the station. Ransom, exhilarated as he was with the fact that he now had a wider body of information with which to work, was at the same time painfully aware that a week and a day had passed since the fateful performance, and he was no closer to a solution. Worse yet, tomorrow would be the one-week mark for the murder of Lawrence Watson, the one murder with which they were primarily supposed to be concerned. Even with his established reputation as a renegade and a loner, he was not totally insensitive to the pressure to get results, and he knew that the longer you took in tracing the killer, the colder the trial became. He was trying to decide whether or not to smoke away the mild anxiety he was beginning to feel because of these mixed feelings when they arrived at the station. He decided to wait until he was at his desk.

It was just after 5:00 p.m. when the two detectives finally walked into his office, and Ransom was tired. As he took his seat behind his desk and pulled out a cigar, he thought ruefully of how he had spent Sunday evenings in his younger days, before he had joined the force. Sunday evening was a time for rejuvenation—not a time to make plans and go out on dates or to parties, but to kick off his shoes and read or watch television, resting up for the beginning of the week ahead. He had done that all through school and all through his early days in the "work force" when he would take any job he could find, work at it until he got bored, and then find another job, repeating the pattern endlessly. He had worked everywhere and sold everything: in offices, department stores, factories. He couldn't even remember the names of all the employers for whom he had worked. There was a dull sameness in all the jobs he had taken that stupified the mind and the senses. But then there were the Sunday evenings. Looking back on his early employment now, he could see what many find attractive in the dullness he had found so stultifying: life continuing at a measured pace, without emotional upheaval but with plenty of happiness. A life that is lived for the pleasure of the individual. He could understand people being enamored of that kind of life, no matter how dull he himself had found it. But then there were the Sunday nights...

He was rescued from his life of sameness by his decision to join the police force. The mental alacrity he knew he possessed was given full sway once he became a detective. For him, detective work was not marred by an inherent distrust of his fellow man, or even by the cynicism of so many of his peers. For him it was invigorating: a chance to exercise his inherent ability to solve puzzles. He enjoyed solving crimes much in the way other people enjoy solving acrostics or crosswords.

What he hadn't anticipated in becoming a detective was that in escaping the mental torpor of other vocations, he was entering a world of mental exhaustion. His mind was always working out puzzles, and with the current rotation system, he didn't have the set night, those blessed Sunday nights of what he now called his youth, to relax and restore. Fortunately, he had with minor success been able to train himself to take what time he had to himself and use it to its best advantage; hence the nightly forays into the bathtub with Dickens and smoke had become almost spiritual release.

As he sat at his desk now, releasing another stream of smoke into the greasy air of his office, he anticipated the evening's respite in *Bleak House*, but he knew Esther and Lady Dedlock would have to wait. He felt sure that if Mark and Stephanie Benson had to return to work tomorrow morning, they would have to return home tonight, and he wanted to be the first to talk to them. He picked up the receiver of the old black phone on his desk and dialed the number, which he now knew by heart, dreading the idiotic answering machine. The phone rang twice as Ransom glanced at his partner, who sat quietly beside the desk looking over the notes he had taken that day.

On the third ring, instead of the click of the machine answering, the phone was picked up by a human hand.

"Hello?" said the voice, which did not match the man in the picture that Gerald had taken from the apartment.

"Hello!" said Ransom, sitting up in his chair. "Is this Mark Benson?"

"Who is this?" asked the voice, sternly.

"This is Detective Ransom, I—"

"Ransom!" said the voice loudly, cutting him off. "This is Robinson! Detective Robinson! There's been a double murder here!"

TWELVE

THEY HAD ARRIVED home at what Mark thought was about three-thirty, but he had promised Stephanie he wouldn't wear a watch during their camping trip, and the clock in the dashboard of their car didn't work properly. Stephanie had often called him an inveterate clock-watcher, which he knew was true. He had even proved it on the trip up to Wisconsin. Without anything to tell the time, he found himself disoriented rather than relaxed, a feeling that Stephanie could only relieve him of by engaging him in fishing, or canoeing, or sex. In this situation it was the sex in particular that had enthralled him. He found the timelessness of the sex both appealing and exciting, in a way that he hadn't experienced when they were at home, although they had been married for about two years. Somehow, sex back in their apartment was always performed in the constraints of time, whether real or imagined. He could never truly release himself within the act of love in their own bedroom, feeling all the time that once the act was complete there was something else to be taken care of or looked into or someplace else to be. In the timeless regions of the wilds, he was free—free of the clock that incessantly ticks away lives of most city dwellers—free to fondle and caress, to discover his wife's body in ways he never had before. When their bodies parted, he would feel drunk, and satisfied, and exhausted.

At the same time, Stephanie, once she had been able to stop him from trying to remember the workings of sundials from his Boy Scout days, was able to discover her husband, mind and body, in ways that were new and exciting. As they clung together on the last night of their camping trip, she congratulated herself on having achieved something she hadn't been sure would be possible: She had gotten her husband to take time for her.

It was with great irritation that they had arrived home to a ringing phone, signaling that though one may escape temporarily, the constraints of time are with us always. The phone rang angrily as Mark fumbled with his keys, yelling "Wait a minute" to the unknown caller, though he hadn't been able to open the door yet, let alone answer the phone.

The phone continued to ring as Mark swung open the door, dropping his backpack on the floor just inside. Stephanie followed and did the same.

"I'll get the phone," he said over his shoulder as he went into their bedroom.

"I'll get the sleeping bags," she said vacantly, the apartment seeming unfamiliar after the week in the relative wilderness. She left the apartment and walked back down the two flights to the front of the building where they'd left their car double-parked long enough to unload it. She pulled the two sleeping bags from the open trunk and thought for a moment about trying to take the cooler up by herself, then thought better of it, even though she knew she was going to have to make another trip up and down the stairs, the very thought of which exhausted her.

She hoisted one of their sleeping bags, the ones her parents had given to them on their first wedding anniversary by request, over her shoulder, letting the other dangle at her side. She slowly made her way up the stairs, and young as she was, she had to stop at the first landing and rest. The long ride in the car had taken more out of her than she thought.

When she reached their apartment, she dropped the sleeping bags and called out to her husband:

"Who was on the phone?"

She glanced over at the bedroom and saw that the door was closed, and realized he must not have heard her. She walked to the bedroom, trying to control her irritation with him for having returned to his old ways immediately upon returning home, but she realized her anger was irrational and only caused by her weariness. She pushed the door open quietly in case he was still on the phone.

"Mark, who..."

Her voice trailed off. The phone was sitting on their nightstand with its receiver in place, and Mark was lying on the bed, his arms outstretched and his legs dangling down to the floor as if he might have flung himself backwards on the bed, exhausted. But something was wrong. His eyes were open and staring with a deadly glaze at the ceiling, and a very thin red line, which she didn't recognize as blood, ran from the corner of his mouth down his right cheek.

"Mark?" she said as she stepped into the room, trying to make out the cause of the stain that was prominent in the center of his shirt. As she drew closer, she noticed that the stain was growing. She reached out to touch it when she realized to her horror that it was blood, and that it was flowing from a gash, dead center in her husband's chest.

It was at that moment that she became aware of another presence in the room.

Her husband's name was the last word she spoke.

The killer, though having admitted to a high degree of intelligence in the past, was frankly astonished at the untapped store of mental dexterity used in removing these potentially dangerous people. Murder was simply another skill that could be easily mastered, and the police, without a doubt, were no match. There was now only one person left who could be a potential problem, but the killer was confident of being able to track her down and eliminate her without the police posing any difficulty—if it were even necessary to find her at all.

IT MIGHT HAVE BEEN through a quirk of fate that Detective Robinson, who was still new to the job and still squeamish, had received the call to the scene of the crime almost as grisly as the one in Barbara Landis's apartment. If Ransom had been asked, he would have said that the gods were showing their worst to the novice detective at the outset to prepare him for the years ahead.

The momentary shock of hearing Robinson's voice on the phone passed quickly, and Ransom and Gerald raced from the station to the Bensons' apartment, Ransom all the while battling a raging sense of guilt and anger. Gerald remained silent in the passenger seat, his eyes glued to the road. One of the worst faults that Gerald would readily acknowledge in his partner was his insistence on driving when he was angry. Gerald had been told as a boy by his father that you should never get behind the wheel of a car when angry, and Ransom was proof positive that this was an axiom to be trusted. Ransom's driving was wild and erratic when he was in his present state, but he was immovable in his insistence on driving.

When they reached the crime scene, miraculously in one piece, it was almost six o'clock. The bodies had already been taken away, evidence bagged, but the apartment was still being dusted for fingerprints, an action that Ransom recognized at once would be futile.

"How long have they been dead?" he asked Robinson without preamble.

"A couple of hours, no more than three, according to the doc."

"A couple of hours..." His voice trailed off.

"In there," said Robinson, motioning to the bedroom. Ransom walked passed him without so much as a glance and glared at the room in which the bodies had been found. There was a moderate amount of blood on the bed, and another large, separate stain on the floor beside it.

"The husband was found on the bed," said Robinson, who had followed Ransom into the bedroom. "He was stabbed once through the heart...with this." He proffered a bag that contained a medium-sized butcher knife.

"The killer left it here?" Ransom said, staring intently at the knife.

"He left it embedded in the wife's chest."

"It wasn't his, then."

"No. I checked the kitchen drawers. It seems to be part of a set." Robinson looked a bit proud of himself at having thought to do this routine check. "We're dusting for prints, but we probably won't find anything."

"Tell me," said Ransom, shifting his intense stare to Robinson, which went a long way in making him even more uncomfortable, "how did you hear about this so quickly?"

"From the young lady downstairs. It looks as if the two of them were in the process of unloading their car when this happened, and they had double-parked right outside. The lady in the first floor apartment went to leave at about four-thirty and found her car hemmed in. She knew it was theirs, so she came up to ask them to move it. She didn't get an answer when she knocked, the door was ajar, and the rest, as the saying goes, is history."

"Where is this..."

"Susan Bart."

"Where is she now?"

"She's been taken to the hospital. She's in a really bad state of shock." The young detective's eyes grew wider, once again losing his own perspective at the thought of what he'd witnessed when he arrived at the scene. "You would be, too, if you'd seen this place when I got here."

"Yeah, yeah," said Ransom, waving him off. As momentous as the case was becoming, and as much as needed to be done and sorted out as soon as possible, Ransom felt he could no longer spare the time to placate feelings. "I want to know the minute you discover anything."

"Hey look, Ransom," said Robinson, the memory of the scene being overshadowed by the offense he took at being treated so offhandedly by someone who was supposed to be his peer, "just what's your interest in this case, and in the Landis case? Are they connected to something you're working on?"

"Apparently," he said, his expression not changing.

"Then *you* let me know if you turn up anything pertinent to my investigation." With this he adopted an expression that was meant to be stern but was so unnatural to his countenance that he only succeeded in looking ridiculous. For the first time since the news of these latest murders, Ransom smiled.

"Yes, I'll do that," he said, without a hint of contrition in his voice.

The soberness of the situation returned to him at once when he glanced down and saw the large bloodstain on the floor by the bed where the body of Stephanie Benson had been found. He silently berated himself for not having prevented the scene that was now before him, but his guilt was partly quelled by reminding himself that he couldn't watch everyone, and the extra manpower he had requested was denied. There was nothing to do for his anger, though, knowing that Sergeant Newman would not feel any sense of guilt or remorse over the death of this young couple. Newman had his own method of dismissing any negative feelings that might erupt. Although Newman might admit to a bad call in this matter, he would chalk up their deaths to the luck of the draw and shrug the whole thing off, saying that life would go on for those of us left alive.

Ransom signaled to Gerald that it was time for them to leave, and on their way out the door, Gerald glanced back at the scene and sighed.

"And then there was one," he said under his breath.

THE MOOD IN the car was decidedly sober as the two detectives drove back to the station. Failure was not part of Ransom's repertoire, and to him the death of the Bensons was a failure, something that could have been avoided. Gerald, having been with his partner for some time now, had a good idea that the silence was a sign that Ransom was trying to find something in his handling of the case that could have prevented these most recent murders, but he knew better than to offer his partner hollow words of comfort. He was sure that Ransom would work out for himself that there was no way he could have prevented the Bensons' murders before they'd even clearly grasped the situation they were facing. Of course, surveillance might have prevented it, but Ransom was not responsible for the lack of surveillance, nor was Gerald really willing to blame Newman on that point. He wasn't sure he himself would have granted it on the evidence they'd had at the time.

But now it was different. If there had been any doubt before about the first three deaths being connected, the additional two had dispelled them. When Ransom finally spoke, it was to review the case.

"So, we have five murders," he said, breaking the silence suddenly as if they were in mid-conversation. "One shot, one throat slit, one...well, we don't know what happened to Meg Ferguson...and these two, stabbed through the heart."

"All by the same person?"

"Yes," said Ransom emphatically. "Yes, definitely. I assume our murderer has chosen to use different means for each murder to try to keep the murders from being connected, so that even if someone *suspected* they were connected, it would muddy the waters."

"Which worked. Sound thinking."

Ransom looked at him. "That's an interesting description to use for someone who's murdered five people."

Gerald blushed. "I meant sound thinking for someone who's killed five people."

"I hate to admit it but you're right," said Ransom with a weary sigh. "Obviously the killer believed the same thing we did: that if the Bensons were unreachable this week, they must be away, and if that were the case, it was likely they would return today, assuming they had to work tomorrow."

He pulled out a cigar but didn't bother with the dashboard lighter, using instead a book of matches he had picked up free in a convenience store. He took a couple of puffs.

"Of course," he added, "the *killer* was able to keep their apartment under surveillance—at least for today." This would be the only verbal concession he would make to his inner thoughts.

"And of course, he didn't count on Emily Charters," said Gerald.

"Ah, I see you're ready now to admit the worth of my little old lady." Ransom couldn't help saying this with a smile, pleased to hear his belief in Emily affirmed by his skeptical partner.

"Well," said Gerald, blushing once again, "I have to admit that if it wasn't for Miss Charters, the killer would have been right. The murders probably wouldn't have been connected."

"Yes," said Ransom thoughtfully. "I wonder..." His voice trailed off like the wisps of smoke from the cigar as he paused between puffs.

"What?"

"I wonder where our little theater friends were late this afternoon. Up till now we haven't really gone into who was doing what when, but I think it's time we did—with a vengeance."

"*All* of them?" said Gerald, the thought of requestioning these vacuous actors making him feel wearier than he had before.

"Not all of them," said Ransom, a smile growing on his face that Gerald knew signified the dawning of an idea. "I think we can safely narrow it down to the two who presumably came in contact with the audience."

"Assuming it's not someone entirely outside the whole thing."

Ransom glanced at his partner and took a puff of his cigar, slowly shaking his head. "The answering machine. No, the murders were committed in four different ways to throw us off the track, and I'm sure the machine was 'stolen' for the same reason. So that if we ever connected anything with the theater, there would be the possibility of an outsider."

"Thereby throwing the whole thing open."

"Exactly. First thing in the morning we should question

the staff of the Pennington Players. But before we do that, after I drop you off, I'm going to have another talk with Emily."

"Don't you want me to go with you?"

Ransom was startled by the question, almost as if his partner were asking him if he should accompany him to a family gathering. He recovered himself quickly, though, and answered with a tinge of embarrassment. "No, no—I think she'll be more comfortable talking just to me."

"Right," said Gerald, who then feigned coughing into his hand to cover the smile he felt spreading across his face.

"We're going to have to act very quickly now," said Ransom, choosing to ignore his partner's gesture. "Emily's the last of the audience, and I don't want anything to happen to her."

"But how could the murderer know who she is? He couldn't have her name."

"That's our only hope—that he still *doesn't* know who she is. But we can't discount how the killer has proceeded so far—he's been using his head."

He fell silent for a moment and gazed out the passenger window, inhaling the cigar and releasing the stream of smoke into the open air.

"I want to catch this bastard," said Ransom finally. "He thinks he's too clever."

"I'M SORRY to stop by so late, but it's very important that I talk to you right away."

Emily, who had been mildly surprised to see the detective through the lace curtain on her front door at the unusually late hour of eight-thirty on a Sunday evening, was perfectly startled by his statement. Her eyes were wide open and quizzical, and the wisps of hair that had come unfastened from the bun at the back of her head frizzed around the top of her head, making her look even more startled. Still, she was able to remain gracious and genteel.

"Come right in," she said, ushering him through the hallway and into the living room, which was through the first doorway on the right, halfway between the front door and the kitchen.

As they entered the room, she switched on a tall floor lamp that stood between an easy chair and a sofa. The fringes of the lamp were decorated with small prisms that jangled and clanked together even from the gentle touch of the old woman's delicate hand. In light of the murders he had been investigating, Ransom found the tinkling sound positively eerie. It vaguely reminded him of the wind chimes that forever heralded impending doom in the horror movies of his youth.

Shaking off the feeling, he surveyed the room as he took his seat on the brocaded sofa—the same sofa in deference to which Cyril had sacrificed his claws—Emily having explained with her usual candor that she reserved the easy chair for herself since it sat higher off the floor and was therefore easier for her to get in and out of. His attention was immediately drawn to the dark tan carpet, over which rainbows danced from the jangling prisms. The easy chair and the sofa, as well as the other pieces of furniture, were of the overstuffed variety that seem to be very comfortable to the aged and very uncomfortable to the young, and all were patterned in various shades of rusts and tans. It was a comfortable room, one that Ransom imagined had been decorated to suit the taste of Emily's late husband. If he had any quarrel with the room, it was that the antique floor lamp was equipped with a light bulb that was too weak to adequately light the space. Apparently this was because Emily used her easy chair for reading, and the weaker bulb shielded her eyes from the glare. Ransom was sure that if he tried to read in this room he would fall asleep. He drummed the fingers of his right hand absently on his knee.

"You needed to speak with me?" said Emily, breaking the silence into which they had fallen.

He looked at her thoughtfully, appraisingly, wondering how the news would affect her.

"Emily, I don't want to alarm you—"

She smiled as she interrupted him. "You've already done that. It would probably be best if you'd simply say what it is."

He smiled back at her, continuing to find her directness both disarming and refreshing.

"It seems that you were right. These murders we're investigating are connected. Lawrence Watson, Barbara Landis, and Meg Ferguson. I'm not sure how Meg's death was accomplished, since no violence was apparent on her body. Even if she'd been strangled, it would have been noticeable. But I don't think it would have been difficult to kill her."

"Oh yes," said Emily sadly, "she was the same age as me but she was much more frail. I'd imagine it wouldn't be hard, especially in her sleep."

"There was no autopsy done?"

"No...no. She was old...old and forgotten. I sometimes think the world looks on the death of the elderly as a relief more than anything else. It's like I told you before, had she been younger there probably would have been many more questions asked, but does it really matter whether a frail old woman died because her heart stopped beating or because she couldn't draw another breath? Nobody gives it a second thought."

He looked at her and thought of his grandmother, who

had spent the last decade of her life in a nursing home. Emily was probably right, he thought. People seemed to be continually dying in the home, but no explanation was ever given. He remembered once asking his grandmother what had become of the woman with whom she had shared a room, and she told him that she had woken one morning and the roommate was gone. The nursing staff told her that the woman died, but no further information was offered, and she was never mentioned again. This, he believed, was from whence the term "passed away" had come: It signified going from life into a dark void where you were neither explained nor remembered. An involuntary shudder passed through him.

"Jeremy," she said, once again interrupting his thoughts. "I had the impression before that you didn't quite believe my suspicions. Why do you believe me now?"

This, he thought, was the hard part. "Because two more people have been murdered. A young married couple."

"Oh dear," she said, deeply concerned, "that is terrible."

"It also means that you're the last audience member left alive."

"Oh," she said, her mouth retaining the roundness of the word after she'd said it. Her thin eyebrows raised just a little, and then her face relaxed into its normal expression from the slightly startled look it had worn since his arrival.

"Oh dear," she said finally, matter-of-factly. "That is most distressing."

"So you see, it's imperative that we do everything in our power to catch this murderer before he or she has a chance to...kill again."

"Oh yes, I quite agree. Anyone who murders must be brought to justice. But what do you want me to do?"

"I need for you to think—think very hard. I want you to think back to the night of the performance and tell me what happened."

"I have been thinking of little else since this whole business started," she said, looking down at the carpet and moving a piece of fluff with her toe. "It's just difficult. The whole event was so *ordinary*."

"I realize that, but it's not the whole evening that I'm interested in. It's the intermission."

She looked at him, her face a picture of puzzlement. The wisps of gray hair that framed her face shined in the faint light.

"You see," he explained, "none of the actors have been killed, only the people in the audience. Now, that leads me to believe that the people in the audience saw something, something significant—something that didn't mean anything at the time but might in the future, that the people onstage didn't see. And the only time that would have happened was during the intermission."

"I see," she said slowly, already picturing the scene in her mind.

"So," he said, sitting back on the sofa casually to try to get her at her ease, "tell me about the intermission."

"Well," she said hesitantly, "as I told you, Meg and I went into the lobby, or the little area that was used as a lobby. We wanted to stretch our legs and they were serving coffee—not very good coffee, as I said before. I didn't finish mine."

"And was any of the staff of the theater there?"

"Oh yes, the young man that sold us our tickets—he was there. He's a very handsome young man, but a trifle thin."

Ransom smiled at the fact that her assessment of Damien's physique coincided with his. "That would be Damien Liddle."

She shrugged, indicating that she didn't know his name but was sure Ransom must be correct.

"What about Gail Shelly?"

"Who?"

"The young woman who set up the stage and handled props for the show."

Emily thought for a moment. "Is she the rather plain young woman—she wore glasses and had sort of dull, brown hair?"

"That would be her."

"Oh yes, she came out into the lobby—at least, into the doorway. She was only there a moment."

Ransom checked her off his mental list. This proved that Gail was out there, whether or not she remembered it herself. Maybe she'd remember it now. "You said when we first talked, I believe, that the rest of the audience came out into the lobby also. Are you sure about that?"

"Quite sure."

"So all six of you came out of the theater?"

"Six?" she said, her forehead wrinkling deeply and her eyebrows almost meeting atop her tiny nose. It was clear she was quite confused.

"Yes," he said, not knowing what to make of her reaction. "There were six people in the audience."

"Six," she repeated faintly, her eyes gazing off into space. It appeared as if she were staring at the scene and trying to reconcile the picture to his words. Suddenly, she turned to Ransom, shaking her head. "I'm sorry, there were seven."

Now it was Ransom's turn to be confused.

"There couldn't have been. There were only six tickets sold to the performance."

"Nevertheless, there were seven," she answered with finality.

"Are you sure?" he said, leaning in closer to her and studying her face.

"Oh yes," she said, her features relaxing once again now that she had cleared up her confusion. "Quite sure."

"But how can you be?"

"Because I've gone over it in my head." As she continued, she counted out the people on her fingers. "Meg and I sat in the third row near the entrance to the theater—we sat there because it was level with the entrance—you had to go down steps to the first two rows and up steps to the rest of the rows. Meg and I are two. Now, the man I first saw in the paper, the first that was killed..."

"Lawrence Watson," said Ransom, his interest growing.

"He sat way over to the right in the second row. That's three. And the poor girl that was murdered..."

"Barbara Landis."

"Yes, she sat in the middle of the second row. That's four. And this couple you say was just murdered...well, there was only one couple there, and they sat in the row behind us."

"That's six," said Ransom, shrugging to indicate that his point had been proven.

"Then," she said tolerantly, "there was the young man who sat in the back. He arrived just before the play began."

"The young man? Are you sure it wasn't just Damien Liddle? He *did* have to come into the theater to run the lights when the show started."

"Oh no, this was quite another young man."

"How can you be so sure?"

Emily drew herself up as much as she could in her chair, amused by the detective's disbelieving gaze.

"Because, he left during the intermission."

Ransom sat bolt upright, his face draining of its color. He knew that this bit of information would prove to be the key to the whole thing. He fought the irritation toward her welling up inside him.

"But Emily, why didn't you tell me this sooner?"

"Do you think it's important?"

"Important! This could be exactly what we needed to know! I asked you if anything unusual happened! Why didn't you tell me this before?"

"I told you it was not a very good production," she said primly. "In my day, it was not unusual to leave a bad performance during the intermission. Back then we thought our time was more important than the money."

Ransom sat back sheepishly, once again shamed into contrition by her mild tone of rebuke.

"You're right, I'm sorry I raised my voice."

"I'm sure you're just anxious about your case," she said, patting his hand gently.

"Do you remember what he looked like?"

"He had very dark, long hair—the front of it came all the way down to his eyes—and he had very light, smooth skin—surprisingly light for having hair so dark. He wasn't very tall...he was fairly well built, but not exactly what you'd call muscular...and..." Her voice trailed off and she looked at Ransom as if she didn't think it would be polite to proceed.

"And?"

"Well," she said with a sigh, "he didn't seem at all pleasant, if you know what I mean. I don't know why.

He didn't say or do anything to *us*, but he just didn't seem pleasant."

"Did he say or do something to draw himself to your attention?"

"Oh yes—although the lobby was so small he wouldn't have had to do much to get our attention. He didn't...yell, or anything like that, but he seemed to be threatening to raise his voice—you know what I mean—as if it might be worth his while to make a scene."

"Who was he talking to?"

"The young man from the box office."

"Did you hear what they said?"

"Not really. The box office man was, I think, trying to make him keep his voice down—probably because he didn't want the rest of the audience upset."

"But you didn't hear anything they said?"

Her face clouded, as if she wished she could be more specific since she knew the importance of the question, but it was no use. "To be perfectly honest, I don't know what they were talking about—but I believed at the time the young man wanted his money back. I think I remember hearing him mention money, but I didn't think anything of it. As I said, in my day it wasn't unusual to leave a play that wasn't very good, and it certainly wasn't unusual to ask for your money back. But really, it was a silly request. Theaters never refund your money nowadays, no matter how bad the production. That's what makes going to a play so expensive and risky. You're really taking your chances when you go to the theater."

Yes, thought Ransom, sometimes more than others.

"I have one more thing to ask you, and this is very important. You said that Gail Shelly came out into the lobby. Can you remember—was it during this little scene between the two men?"

Emily thought for a moment. "I couldn't be sure...but I think so. I think she was there then."

Ransom sat back on the couch and smiled broadly at her. "That, my dear Emily, is very interesting."

HE LAY IN the bathtub as it filled, the swirling water easing the aching muscles in his legs and feet. He was tired, as usual, but not as tired as he'd been the night before, and his mind was quite alert, darting back and forth like a computer processing information in the background while its operator carried on with other functions. For Ransom, the other function this evening consisted of some well-deserved relaxation and the continuation of *Bleak House*. Unfortunately, when he turned off the water and tried to read, he found when he'd reached the bottom of a page that he had no idea what he'd just read, but rather had been listening to his mental computer trying to put together all the information on his case.

It had been like this since he'd spoken with Emily a little over an hour ago. His mind immediately went to work on the problems involved, assimilating the new information greedily as if somewhere within it, and all the other information he'd been given, was the answer. He had driven himself home only to find he'd arrived and had no recollection of having driven there. He had eaten, undressed, and climbed into the tub, all the while unaware of anything he was doing.

He groaned in exasperation and set the book beside the tub when he realized he'd just finished another page and didn't know what he'd read. He was relieved to find that though he'd been on automatic pilot when he came in for his bath, he'd remembered to bring his pack of cigars and matches along and had laid them on the bathmat within reach. He'd been afraid he was going to have to get out of the tub to retrieve them, and the thought of leaving the deliciously warm water for anything was very uninviting. He pulled one out of the pack, lit it, and slid further down into the water, his eyes closing out the tan-and-white tile of the walls and the rather harsh light over the sink. He allowed his thoughts to lead him, every now and then letting out a quiet "hmmm" as different ideas passed through his mind and taking an occasional drag on the cigar. The quiet murmuring of the water, which seemed to move a little even though he was keeping still, helped ease his mind and control his thoughts. He realized that the information he was trying to compute was slightly incomplete, and he felt that tomorrow, Monday, might just be the day when he'd have all the information he needed. There were still several questions to be answered before he would be able to put together any viable theory. For example, who was the seventh audience member? Did Damien Liddle know him or was he just a disgruntled theater patron? Was he still alive? Why wasn't his name on the tape? Ransom was certain that with these questions answered, and a few others, he'd know who the killer was. Proof was another story, one that he would not let his mind entertain at the moment.

Having finally quieted his thoughts, he felt confident he could read again. He picked up the book and turned back to the section he'd been trying to read. Poor Esther, the heroine of *Bleak House,* had just discovered that her natural mother was really none other than the upright Lady Dedlock, and the guilty secret of Lady Dedlock's infidelities was becoming a pressing problem. Ransom admired the character of Esther, finding her strength (mixed with naïveté) quite appealing. He quickly found his place and started at the beginning of the chapter.

Suddenly, he sat up as straight as he could in the tub,

drawing his knees up and resting the book on them. He peered at the page. In the middle of the first paragraph, Esther revealed her fear of coming near her mother and vowed to stay away, knowing that if their relationship became known, her mother would be ruined. The words burned into Ransom's mind, and he said aloud, slowly, pondering the phrase: "knowing that my mere existence as a living creature was an unforeseen danger in her way."

He laid the book down beside the tub and rested his back against the walls, squinting as if he was trying to see his own thoughts. He took another puff of his cigar and sighed.

"Hmmm...an unforeseen danger...in *her* way, or *his* way?"

THIRTEEN

"Mr. Liddle, we have a few more questions we'd like to ask you."

Damien stood in the doorway of his apartment eyeing the detectives, looking as if he were undecided on whether or not to be cooperative.

Damien Liddle fully awake was quite different from the man they had woken for their first interview, thought Ransom. In the few moments before Damien responded, Ransom gave him a second appraisal that was less flattering than the first. The young actor was still quite handsome, his curly brown hair now combed and in place, and he was dressed casually but well. However, fully awake there was a cunning in his expression and a sharpness in his deep green, penetrating eyes that was so apparent that Ransom was surprised it hadn't been noticeable the first time he questioned him. He realized much to his dismay that his plan to take the actor by surprise last Saturday morning had backfired: Catching Damien offguard had only succeeded in giving them the false impression that he was insincere if not a liar. In the cold light of Monday morning, with Damien awake and alert, the impression was quite different: that of a cool, calculating actor. Ransom was sure that if he saw this man onstage, he wouldn't believe a word that came out of his mouth.

"May we come in?" said Ransom, with a politeness that was perfectly ominous.

"Sure," said Damien curtly after a moment's pause. He pushed the door open and led the way into the dingy apartment, leaving the detectives to close the door behind them. "I'll have to work while we talk. I have to be out to the coast at the end of the week, and I've got a lot of packing to do, and a lot of stuff to get rid of."

"We'll try not to disturb you too much," said Ransom with an unmistakable gleam in his eye, making it clear from this statement alone that he would receive great enjoyment from disturbing the actor.

He and Gerald took the seats they had occupied only two days earlier and watched in silence for a couple of minutes while Damien took books from a makeshift bookshelf and placed them carelessly in a box sitting on a nearby chair. The silence had the desired effect on him; he seemed to be exerting a great deal of effort to maintain his composure under the scrutiny of the great detective.

Damien, for his part, thought it best to take the offensive. "You seem to like dropping in on people early in the morning," he said with a glance toward Ransom as he rearranged a couple of the books in the box. "If I didn't know better, I would think it was a tactic to catch people off guard."

"But you know better," said Ransom with a smile.

Damien was stopped short by this and broke into a wide, ingratiating smile. "Of course."

He took another handful of books from the shelves and began arranging them in the box.

"Would you mind if I smoked?" said Ransom suddenly.

For the first time since they had begun questioning the people connected with this case, Gerald's expression changed: He raised an eyebrow. It was extraordinary for his partner to smoke during an interview, and he wasn't sure what to make of it.

"Sure, go ahead," said Damien.

Ransom pulled a plastic-tipped cigar out of his shirt pocket and unwrapped it while Damien, almost without a pause in his packing, moved an ashtray from the table to the arm of the chair in which the detective was seated. Ransom tossed off a "thank you" and lit his cigar. He leaned back in his chair, took a long, leisurely drag, and exhaled slowly.

"So, you really are going to go ahead with this television series."

"It's a job," said Damien with a smile and a shrug.

"I'm surprised. I wouldn't have thought you were the type of actor to give in to such a...second-class medium."

"Well, even the best actors—not that I consider myself the best—but even the best have to make a living."

"Hmmm. Won't this damage your Shakespearean career?"

Damien stopped for a moment, his jaw tightly clenched. "Sometimes it takes a star to bring people in to see Shakespeare."

"Ahhh."

"But surely you didn't come here to discuss my career," said Damien curtly.

"Mr. Liddle," said Ransom after a calculated pause, "it appears you lied to us about the number of people that were in the audience the last night of your play?"

"What?" said Damien, standing bolt upright, books still in his hands. He looked as if he didn't know whether to be worried or outraged.

"There were more than six people in the audience."

"We only sold six tickets," said the actor emphatically. It was clear he didn't like being called a liar. "I mean, it's easy enough to prove, you only have to check with Gail. She should know how many tickets were sold." He shoved the books he was holding into the box roughly, without bothering to arrange them, then grabbed another handful. Ransom thought with a slight twinge of conscience that he could never trust a man who handled books so indelicately.

"Whether or not you sold six tickets doesn't matter now. The fact of the matter is there was a seventh person in the audience."

"A seventh?"

"A medium-built young man, very dark hair, very pale skin. He left during the intermission."

Damien stopped for a moment, looking as if he was searching his memory, then his face cleared. The act of remembering, thought Ransom.

"Oh, you mean Eric," said Damien, relieved to have remembered. He continued to put the books away.

"Eric?"

"Eric Sands—he was one of the company members. That's why it didn't hit me before what you were talking about. Company members who weren't in the show dropped in now and then. We never considered them audience. At least, I didn't. Hell, they were always in and out. And they never stayed for the whole show."

"Really," said Ransom, taking a puff of his cigar. "How impolite."

"Yeah," said Damien, hesitating a moment. He didn't know what to make of the detective. He went on packing.

"I should have thought that *Love's Labor's Lost* would require the use of your entire company."

"Not really. Aside from the people that worked with us all the time, we had a lot of hangers-on, like all the other theaters do."

"And that is what this Eric Sands was to the theater?"

"Not exactly," said Damien with the heavy sigh of one who knows a truth is about to come out that he would rather not reveal. "He was a member of the company—when the company was still together, that is—but he was more a friend of mine than anything else, I guess."

"Is it possible that by friend you mean lover?"

"No, Mr. Ransom," he said, bristling, "we were sex partners."

"Really," said Ransom, surprised at the candor.

"Yes. The term 'lovers' implies something that simply wasn't there. You know, hearth and home, long-term commitment, that sort of thing. That's not the way it was with Eric and me. The only commitment we had was sexual. It's too dangerous to sleep around these days, so we sort of stuck together." It was evident that the young actor resented having his dirty laundry aired, even if it was before only two members of the public. "I suppose you're shocked."

Ransom tapped his cigar ash into the ashtray. "I'm simply surprised that anyone would make so fine a distinction."

"It's an important distinction," said the actor, any sense of amusement now gone from his demeanor. "I assume that you have slept with more than one... woman."

Ransom inclined his head slightly.

"Then I would think that you know the difference between sleeping with someone—even on a long-term basis—and entering into something like a marriage."

Ransom didn't respond.

Damien continued, the growing defensiveness in his voice apparent. "That's the way it was with Eric and me. We had sex—no commitment."

"You keep using the past tense."

"Yes," he said, his eyes clouding, "I broke it off with him a while back."

"Why?"

Damien heaved another sigh, even heavier than before, realizing that he would have to go all the way in explaining his intimate life. "Because Eric was sleeping around, and like I said, in this day and age it's too dangerous to do that. It's also too dangerous to sleep with someone who's sleeping around. So I called it quits."

"*You* called it quits."

"Yes."

"I see."

Ransom released another stream of smoke into the oppressive air of the apartment, then added, as if in afterthought, "We will want to talk to him. You have his address, don't you?"

Damien stared at him blankly, then all the haughtiness that had been in his voice dropped away as he attempted to be more ingratiating.

"Of course I do."

He wrote the address on the bottom of a sheet from a spiral notebook.

"I really have to hand it to you," said Damien as he tore off the bottom of the page and handed it to the detective, "you must be awfully good at your job. I'd forgotten all about Eric being there. How on earth did you come by him?"

"We have a witness," said Ransom flatly, accepting the paper.

"A witness?" said Damien with feigned amusement. "A *witness!* A witness to what? A rotten production of one of Shakespeare's lesser plays? God, we've called our audiences a lot of things, but never witnesses! It makes our production sound like a crime!"

"Perhaps it was," said Ransom with a calmness that made him sound positively menacing. "Are you aware,

Mr. Liddle, that five of your audience members are now dead?"

Damien was halted in the midst of his joviality by this. His face went deathly pale and his legs looked like they were about to buckle. He grabbed the book box with one hand, using it for balance, and lowered himself onto a wooden chair. His face was a study of shock and dismay. A study, Ransom thought shrewdly, not necessarily being the real thing.

"My God," gasped the actor. "But why?"

"That's what we're endeavoring to find out," replied Ransom, unmoved by Damien's reaction. Gerald looked up from his note taking just long enough to smile to himself at his partner's brand of questioning. He was sure that Ransom was the only detective in the city who would use the word *endeavoring*.

"The last two victims were killed just yesterday afternoon."

Damien sat staring dumbly, his deeply furrowed brow indicating his inability to believe what he was hearing.

"By the way," continued Ransom after a calculated pause, "where were you yesterday afternoon between three and five p.m.?"

The directness and implications of this question startled Damien out of his daze.

"What?"

Ransom repeated the question.

"Why, I was here," said Damien falteringly. Then he added: "Packing."

"Nobody saw you? You didn't speak to anyone?"

"No," he answered vacantly.

"Nobody stopped by here?"

"No."

"So there is nobody that can verify your whereabouts?"

"No." Damien stared at him, his mouth hanging slightly open.

Ransom looked at him appraisingly, his face not revealing whether or not he believed the actor's answers. He was very glad to have reached this point. The vagaries of the case, the multiplicity of ideas, the dozens of possibilities—all were quickly fading away as the suspects were narrowed down to those directly connected with the victims on the night of the play. And now they had a victim who was involved with the theater itself. It was now a matter of identifying the killer from among them, Ransom thought, and then the burden of proof. He was vastly enjoying himself.

"Wait," said Damien, suddenly returning to himself as the full impact of the situation hit him, "you don't think *I* had something to do with all this?"

"I really have no idea," said Ransom with a casual wave of his cigar.

Damien struggled to control himself against what he felt was the infuriating behavior of the detective. He thought that Ransom didn't seem to understand the seriousness of his accusation and the ramifications it might have for an actor on the brink of possible stardom. Ransom certainly didn't take the actor seriously, which infuriated him even more.

"We'll need your help this afternoon," said Ransom, standing up as if to leave. Gerald immediately stood up as well, folding his small notebook and slipping it into his breast pocket.

"What? What can I do?" asked Damien, his composure slipping away.

"We'll need to see the theater. You can let us in, can't you?"

"Yes...yes, I still have the keys. I haven't turned them in yet."

"Then could you meet us over there at, say, one o'clock?"

"Uh, sure," said Damien, following them to the door.

"Is everything still there?" said Ransom, stopping suddenly.

"What?"

"At the theater? You haven't taken anything down yet, have you?"

"Oh...no. I think we were just going to leave that for the landlord to deal with." He managed a weak smile.

"Quite right," said Ransom, smiling broadly. He opened the door and started to leave, then paused in the doorway. "Oh, there's one thing I don't understand."

"What's that?" asked Damien, his apprehension evident in his stance. Acting and posturing had been forgotten.

"Your company members—when they came to the show, they didn't pay for tickets, did they?"

"No, of course not. They just went in."

"Funny. I understood he asked for his money back."

"His money?" Damien looked positively perplexed. Then his face cleared. "Oh—he was probably...he asked me for some money. He was always broke, and he borrowed money from everyone."

"Hmmm." Ransom considered this, then as he stepped out the door: "One o'clock, then. Please don't be late."

Gerald followed him out.

Damien closed the door softly after them and turned back to look at his apartment. For once, the oppressiveness of it was apparent to him.

"WHAT WAS ALL that about?" said Gerald with a smile as he steered the car out into the street.

"What do you mean?"

"I've never seen you smoke during an interview before."

"Ah!" said Ransom, a broad smile spreading across his face. "I was setting in for a performance, and a performance is what I got."

"You think he was lying?"

"I'm sure of it. I can never trust anyone with so convenient a memory."

"Meaning?"

"That he didn't remember his ex-lover was at the play that night."

"Well..." said Gerald, not believing what he was about to say himself, "you have to remember that when we first spoke with him we asked specifically about the audience. I suppose it's possible that what he said was true, that he just didn't connect Eric, a company member, with the audience."

Ransom's eyes narrowed as he appraised his partner. "We asked him if he *knew* anyone who'd been in the audience. I'm sure he knew what we were looking for."

"So you think he's the killer?"

Ransom sighed deeply and pulled another cigar from his pocket. "I think he's one of the possibilities." He pressed the lighter into the dashboard. "Two people have lied to us."

"The other is Gail Shelly."

"You've got it. She lied to us, too, when she said she couldn't remember whether or not she'd been in the lobby during intermission."

"So the two of them have lied to us—at least that's what you think," said Gerald, working it out aloud. "Of course, they don't necessarily have to be lying because of the murder.''

Ransom laughed despite himself at his partner's propensity for playing devil's advocate. The lighter popped out and he lit his cigar.

"No, but I'd say being a murderer is a strong motivation for lying." He took a couple of puffs on his cigar and grew more serious. "More to the point, being involved in a murder is rather big motivation for telling the truth—unless you were afraid you'd implicate yourself or someone else in it. I don't know why they would lie—by omission or otherwise—about something so significant. I'm sure one or the other did it, I just don't know which one—or why. They were the only two to have any contact with the audience. And we've, at least, discovered a connection between them and one of the people in the audience."

"A pretty strong connection," added Gerald in that same oddly prejudiced tone he had used before when speaking of another male couple.

"But I still don't see any motive for either one of them to kill the audience."

"With apologies to Agatha Christie," said Ransom wryly, "sometimes you find the motive *after* you find the killer."

Gerald rolled his eyes.

"What we have now are five people who are dead and two people who are lying."

"But how can you be so *sure* that Liddle was lying?"

"For one thing, he must have mentioned half a dozen times that there were only six tickets sold, even though there were seven people in the theater. Looking back on it, he seems to have made quite a point of it. It would almost seem that he was covering his tracks, so that if we discovered the presence of another audience member, we couldn't accuse him of lying."

"Yes, well..." said Gerald, not really believing it, "for another thing?"

"For another thing, just from the way he reacted when I told him about the five audience members being dead. It struck me as if he'd had his reaction ready for us—you know, in case he ever had to play a scene: 'young man given shocking news, take one.'"

"Really?" said Gerald. "I thought he really was shocked."

"Ah, but why?" said Ransom with a gleam in his eye. "Because they were murdered, or because we knew about it?"

THE ELEVATOR DOORS opened and the two detectives stepped out onto the fourth floor. After a false start to the wrong end of the hallway, they doubled back and found the door to number 11. Just as Gerald raised his hand to knock, the door to number 12 swung open and Sara Collins struggled out into the hallway with two very large suitcases. She set them outside the door and disappeared back into the apartment. Gerald rapped on the door just under the cheap metal 11. As they waited, Sara reappeared with a large handbag slung over her shoulder. She closed and locked her door, heaved the suitcases off the floor, and started down the hallway, noticing the detectives for the first time.

"You're wasting your time," she said.

Ransom and Gerald turned to her in unison and saw what they took to be a healthy, attractive young woman who hadn't slept the previous night. The rims of her eyes were blazing red from crying, and her hair, though clean, was completely disheveled, even though she had put clips in it in an attempt to pull herself together.

"I beg your pardon?" said Ransom politely.

"They took him away yesterday."

Ransom glanced at his partner and then back at Sara. "I'm afraid I don't know what you're talking about."

"The guy that lived there—his body—they took it away yesterday." Her eyes began to fill.

"Eric Sands—the man who lives here—he's dead!" said Ransom incredulously.

"I don't know what his name was, but he's dead."

"This happened yesterday?"

"He wasn't killed yesterday," said Sara, tears now running down her cheeks. It was evident that the thought of what had happened was overwhelming to the girl. "I heard...I heard one of the policemen say he must have been dead for a week."

"He was just found yesterday?" said Ransom excitedly, his mind already beginning to race.

"Yes. And I told Mr. Luddin—the landlord—lease or no lease, I'm not staying here! I'm not staying here!" Her voice became choked with sobs. "How can I? Right next door to where someone's been murdered!"

"HEAD BEATEN IN," said Ransom thoughtfully as Gerald drove them to the office of Walden and Baker, the advertising firm where Gail Shelly served as administrative assistant. He was repeating aloud the words that Mr. Luddin had used to describe the corpse of Eric Sands.

"I never seen anything like it," he had said, a look of bewilderment on his fleshy cheeks.

Luddin had struck Ransom as a rather stupid man of the beer-guzzling, television-watching sort that he held in contempt. He had been no further help to them except to confirm Sara's statement in that he, too, had heard the police say that Sands had been dead about a week.

"Head beaten in," Ransom repeated, mulling it over. Then he turned to his partner and added brightly, "Well, now we know the motive!"

Gerald White refused once again to be forced into the role of a bumbling Dr. Watson, forever asking, "But why?" or "But how?" of his genius partner. Gerald had taken, on occasion, to simply not responding, thereby robbing Ransom of the opportunity to play the enigmatic Holmes. Much as he liked his partner, he feared that Ransom enjoyed hearing his own voice a bit too much and was inclined to be a little too pleased with himself. This was one such occasion. Instead of asking him what motive he was referring to, he asked about the purpose of their visit to Gail's office.

"I should like to pin her down as to whether or not she was in the lobby on the night in question. At least, I'd like to get her to admit to it. Emily saw her there."

"Ah, yes."

"But most of all, I would very much like to know if she knew that our Mr. Liddle, with whom she is so obviously infatuated, is homosexual."

"You don't think she knows?"

"I think she knows now," said Ransom with a knowing smile that Gerald found insufferable.

Walden and Baker was located in an old four-story office building that was only a few blocks from the theater. The detectives walked up to the office, which was on the second floor, and found that despite the age of the building and the absence of what Ransom referred to as "modern conveniences" (by which he meant an elevator), the offices were quite clean and orderly.

The receptionist stationed in the outer office was a

young brunette who was quite lovely, despite not being nearly as expensively dressed, coiffed, or trained as the receptionist at the office of Virgil Danners, the corpulent attorney. This young woman, who did not have a nameplate on her desk, was much more genuine and accessible than the lawyer's receptionist. Ransom liked her.

"Can I help you?" she said with a wide, pleasant smile.

"We've just stopped in to see Gail Shelly. Is she in?"

"Sure," said the receptionist, pointing to an open door down the short hallway that ran back past her desk, "she's the very first door on the left. You can go right in."

Ransom thanked her, and he and Gerald went down the hallway. None of the secretive planning and phoning, none of the announcement of their arrival as there'd been at the lawyer's office, thought Ransom as they entered Gail's office.

She sat behind a medium-sized metal desk, busily working over some papers as seriously as if the fate of the world hung in the balance, which Ransom thought with some amusement was not possible, given that this was an advertising agency. The room was, as he suspected it would be, neat and clean, everything in its proper place.

Gail looked up at them through her brown frame glasses as they entered, startled and dismayed that they had intruded into her "working life," a life that she kept quite separate from her nonworking life. She looked almost as if she expected two violently opposed cosmic forces to come crashing together right at her feet.

"Please close the door," she said with a little gasp. Gerald obliged.

"Forgive us for disturbing you here," said Ransom.

"That's all right," she said, catching her breath. "What can I do for you?"

Ransom took a seat in front of her desk; Gerald remained standing by the door.

"Well, there've been some new developments, and I wanted to check in with you again to see if you remembered any more of the evening of the last performance."

"New developments?" she said, her eyes widening. Ransom stifled a laugh. Her widening eyes, her straight, drab hair, and her large glasses made her look almost like a caricature of a bookworm. He coughed lightly to cover his reaction and smiled at her in a friendly fashion in an effort to quell her fears.

"Yes. I was wondering if you'd perhaps remembered whether or not you'd been in the lobby during the intermission."

That same reserve that had crossed her face at their first interview when he asked this question appeared once again.

"I...I don't—"

"Okay, let me ask you this," he said, maintaining a conversational tone. "Did you know that there was someone else at the play that night?"

"Someone else?" said Gail, confused.

Ransom looked at her steadily, trying to decide if she didn't remember or hadn't known. Then he said the name.

"Eric Sands."

"Oh, Eric," Gail said, her face relaxing a little. "I didn't even think of him. Yes, he was there."

"You saw him?"

She nodded in response.

"When?"

"During..." she stopped as she realized what she was saying, dropping her head. She looked up at Ransom over the rims of her glasses. "During the intermission. That must mean I *was* in the lobby during intermission." She said this as if it was a revelation to her, but so unconvincingly that Ransom was embarrassed for her.

"I didn't remember Eric. Lots of the company members come in and out during the performance," she said, then added almost by rote, "I think it's rude, you know, to leave in the middle of a performance."

Apparently this had been another one of Damien's rules, which had gone ignored by everyone except Gail.

"You saw him leave, then?"

"Yes," she said, her eyes beginning to glaze. "Well, not actually leave. He didn't come back after the intermission."

"Would you have happened to have heard anything he said while in the lobby?"

"Said. No. Not really. I didn't really stay in the lobby, I just looked in to see if Damien needed any help."

"Help?"

"With the coffee," she added quickly.

"You didn't hear what he said to Mr. Liddle?"

"No."

"So you wouldn't know if he'd asked him for some money? A loan?"

"It's likely. He's always asking for money. Eric... doesn't usually have a job. He gets money from his friends."

"But you didn't actually hear what he said?"

"No," she answered more emphatically, "I only went out there to serve coffee during intermissions sometimes."

"Only when crowds were heavy," said Ransom, watching her face.

"Yes," she said weakly.

Ransom continued to gaze at Gail with a compassion that he felt would continue even if she were proven to be the murderer. He sensed a deep hurt within her, most likely a hurt that had come from years of being insignificant. She was the unfortunate type of person who was not attractive enough or distinctive enough in other ways to hold her own in any sort of relationship. She was doomed, he imagined, to either be browbeaten or ignored completely by those to whom she was attracted, and he didn't know which would be worse. But then he realized it would never come to that for Gail. Nobody would ever notice her at all. Keeping that in mind, it was with a pang of guilt that he asked his next questions.

"Miss Shelly?" He paused and waited for her to look up at him. "Did you know that Damien Liddle and Eric Sands were lovers?"

Tears immediately welled up in her eyes, and she looked away from him as they dropped onto her round, pale cheeks, splattering on her pink silk blouse.

"Yes...everybody knew."

"Bastard," Ransom said to himself, although he wasn't sure whether or not he was referring to Liddle or himself.

"So you know that Mr. Liddle is homosexual."

She nodded in assent.

He paused for a moment, his sense of compassion at war with his need to know the truth. But he knew the importance of remaining objective and continued, trying to keep a touch of formality in his voice.

"How long have you known about him?"

Gail's hands had fallen carelessly into her lap, and as she spoke she stared down at them, her tears falling on her entwined fingers.

"I guess I've known for a long time. I mean, he wasn't...interested in me, but...well, and I've heard people talking about him. People say things in front of me because...I think sometimes they forget I'm there. But I guess I knew about Damien all along."

"You did," said Ransom quietly, not quite sure, if this were true, how she had managed to stay so infatuated with him. As if in answer to his thoughts, she continued.

"I guess I was just fooling myself. It's just...Damien was so kind to me."

"Was he?" said Ransom pointedly, "was he really?"

Gail shot him a brief, angry glance that was so uncharacteristic it took him by surprise. Almost as quickly, she regained her composure.

"No. I guess he wasn't."

Ransom considered her silently for a moment. Gerald had stopped taking notes. It somehow seemed vile to him to be recording the emotions now being displayed before him, and he didn't think he'd be likely to forget the scene.

"So, you went out to help Damien with the coffee that night, and...?"

"And I saw him there with Eric...so I turned around and went back into the theater."

He waited a moment before continuing quietly. "Miss Shelly, I have to ask you where you were yesterday afternoon between three and five o'clock."

She turned her wide, tear-filled eyes to him. "I was at home. Alone." She lowered her head again, a fresh stream of tears running down her face.

The sight of this pathetic creature crying silently moved him, and he decided to end this interview. He had found out the most important piece of information he needed about Gail.

"Miss Shelly," he said, rising from his chair, "what time do you go to lunch?"

She looked up at him, dabbing her eyes with a tissue

she'd pulled from the box sitting on her desk. "Whenever I...it doesn't matter."

"Could you take it at one o'clock today? We're meeting Mr. Liddle at the theater at one. We need to see how it's laid out."

"Damien will be there?" she asked with a whisper. Ransom couldn't decide if the tone indicated she would be happy or unhappy to see him.

"Yes."

"What do you want me for?"

"It might be helpful to have both of you there," he said, not explaining any further.

"All right. I'll be there."

Gerald opened the door, and Ransom passed through without another word, his partner following and closing the door behind him.

As they walked down to the street, Ransom appeared to be lost in thought.

"You didn't confront her with Eric Sands's murder," said Gerald, interrupting Ransom's reverie.

"No. I didn't want her to know that we knew about it. And I don't want Liddle to know either. I think that their thinking we're in the dark about Sands will prove to be to our advantage."

"Why?"

"Because the murderer will think he or she is still safe—at least, partially safe."

He didn't elaborate any further, and Gerald realized that this was one of those occasions where he wouldn't. Gerald decided to change the subject slightly.

"Well, we now know she knew about Liddle and Sands."

"We know more than that. Even though she says she must have known all along, I think it's more likely that she discovered it recently. It may be that she finally admitted the truth to herself when she saw Liddle and Sands together at the theater. The wound hasn't had time to heal. She's still pretty broken up about the fact that the object of her affection was unable or unwilling to return it."

"What does that prove?"

"You've always said yourself that passion is a strong motive for murder," said Ransom, a mischievous glint in his eye.

He started down the stairs again, but Gerald stopped him. "But wait. Liddle *gave* us Sands's name and address. Why would he do that if he knew he was dead?"

"I can think of a few reasons," said Ransom, leaning against the dusty wooden bannister.

"One," Gerald prompted.

"He didn't know."

"Oh come on!"

Ransom shrugged. "It's the most obvious answer. If he didn't know Sands was dead, he wouldn't have given a second thought to providing the name and address."

Gerald considered his partner for a moment, searching his face for some indication of whether or not he actually believed this, but Ransom did not betray his thoughts.

"All right," said Gerald, deciding to hear the rest, "two."

"He might have been afraid that Gail would remember that Sands was there when we questioned her, so he *had* to tell us. I'd already accused him of lying once. He knew if he didn't give us the name himself, he'd be implicated."

"But then he would've known we'd find the body."

"So what?" said Ransom, grinning shyly. "It rounds out the audience members. Sands was the first of many; it would be my guess that they died to cover his murder."

"All right," said Gerald, unconvinced, "is there a three?"

"We caught him off guard. He didn't have time to think of anything else. Lies, lies, lies, Gerald. So hard to keep track of everything. Presence of mind, just like I always said. Of course, the most obvious explanation is that he didn't know Sands was dead. If that's true, then the pathetic woman we left crying upstairs is a cold-blooded killer."

He started down the stairs again, followed by his partner. Bright sunlight streamed through the front door to the building, illuminating the tile floor at the bottom of the stairs. When he reached the door, Ransom stopped again.

"Damn!"

"What is it?" said Gerald.

Ransom explained, his face reflecting that he was thoroughly disgusted at the thought of being bested. "I just realized that the bloated idiot of a lawyer—Virgil Danners—he was right. Lawrence Watson was just in the wrong place at the wrong time. He should have stuck with going to the movies."

FOURTEEN

RANSOM GLANCED OUT through the curtains of the living room window of Emily's little wood-frame house. If the situation were not so serious, the sight would be almost comical. Gerald sat in the car directly outside the house waiting for him to reappear, and three doors down Sanders sat in her car waiting for something, whatever it might be—to happen.

"You were saying, Jeremy?" said Emily, straightening her light blue skirt as she sat in a high-backed, cushioned chair.

Ransom turned from the window and smiled warmly at the old woman. She looked up at him through her clear, gray eyes, a perfect picture of trust. It had always been his policy not to become emotionally involved with the women in the cases he investigated, but he found to his dismay that the policy only extended to young women who were possible lifetime partners—or at least, nighttime partners. It did not extend to little old ladies who reminded him of his grandmother, like Emily, with her trusting eyes and clearheaded logic.

"I was just thinking that this is a lovely neighborhood."

"Oh yes, isn't it?" said Emily, almost twittering. "My late husband chose the neighborhood, this house. He thought it was the ideal place to raise children. Unfortunately, as it turned out we never had any."

A shame, he thought: He was sure she would have made a wonderful mother and grandmother.

"He—my husband, that is—thought this neighborhood was safe."

"He was right, you know. This is a safe neighborhood."

"Then why have the police started visiting me on a daily basis?" she said with a twinkle in her eye.

"Right," he said, smiling ruefully. He turned his gaze back out to the street as if he couldn't bear to look into her eyes knowing what his presence would mean to her, and knowing what he had to say.

"You must have a purpose in visiting me this morning," she said, sensing that he had unpleasant business to attend to and was stalling before beginning.

"Yes, I do," he said quietly. He came away from the window and sat on the couch, facing her. "Emily, things are about to come to a head."

"Really? That's good, isn't it?" she said brightly.

He looked at her appraisingly. It was difficult to te' with Emily how well or how badly she took anything. He was sure that any other old person—well, *anyone*, young or old—who was involved in the type of murder investigation that she was would be at wit's end. But Emily seemed to almost take it all in stride.

"Aren't you afraid of anything?"

Emily was surprised by the question. "Well, I suppose I'm not afraid of very many things—no," she said, shaking her head quickly so that the little wisps of gray hair that framed her head danced. "I think fear comes from uncertainty—because you don't know exactly what's going to happen. That's why you young people are so seldom afraid—you're always so sure about everything."

He laughed lightly.

"But as you get older," she continued, "things get more and more uncertain—which I must admit is odd, because you would think it would be the other way around, but it's not. Things get more and more uncertain. You simply can't spend your life being afraid of that."

"And yet, so many people do."

"You're quite right about that," she said, shaking her head sadly, looking as if she were remembering the names of all the fear-ridden people she'd known. She suddenly realized that they had gotten off the track again and decided to steer the conversation back on course.

"What are you doing to solve our case?"

He paused for a moment, dreading the thought of endangering this woman. Then, realizing he couldn't put it off any longer, he began. "I have it narrowed down to two people. I'm sure one or the other of them did it. One is the young man who sold you your tickets, and the other is the young woman who worked props for the play—the one who came into the lobby briefly during the intermission. I am certain that one of them has killed off the audience one by one because of something you saw during the intermission."

"But I told you—"

"I know what you told me," he said, cutting her off. He was not being rude, but now that he had started he felt the pressing need to go on. "But it doesn't matter. You *did* notice something, something very important, and I know what it was, but it's not important now. I'm not sure which one it is, although I have my suspicions. But the biggest problem is the burden of proof. We have nothing to tie either of them to any of the murders—with one possible exception. And for my money, both of them had a good reason for that one."

"If," she said, raising her index finger in a gesture of correction, "there *can* be a good reason for committing murder."

He smiled at her warmly. "Quite right. I meant a *plausible* reason."

She nodded her head in approval at his choice of words. He drew a chair up beside her and sat down, lightly laying his right hand on hers.

"I think I know how to prove who the murderer is."

"Then I think you should do it."

"My primary concern right now is your safety. I haven't wanted to alarm you in the past, but there's no way around it now, the danger is very real." He looked directly into her eyes, as if the directness would accentuate the importance of the statement he was about to make. "Emily, you are the only one left alive from that audience."

"What about the young man—the one you didn't know about?"

"The man you saw leave at intermission is dead, too. That leaves only you. You are the last one. You are the only witness we've got, and it is of the utmost importance that you stay alive!"

Though her eyes had grown considerably wider as he had spoken, she managed to smile up at him.

"I shall do everything in my power to oblige you!"

"THIS IS IT!" said Damien with a flourish as he swung open the door to the dingy storefront. He held the door open as Ransom and Gerald entered, then followed them in. Immediately inside was the small area that served as the lobby. The remnants of the box office still lay scattered on the floor.

"That's where the answering machine was," said Damien, indicating the wreckage.

The detectives gave it only a cursory glance, then turned back to Damien.

"And the theater?"

"Through there."

The "theater" was separated by a wall made of pressboard that had been painted black. A cheap black curtain covered the doorway. They passed through it into the theater. The stage was small and at floor level, which was two steps down from the lobby level, and located directly to the left of the doorway. The seating area consisted of several rows of cheap folding chairs. Ransom knew immediately that he wouldn't need to be Emily's age to have very quickly grown uncomfortable sitting here. They all proceeded down the two steps to the stage. When Ransom reached center stage, he turned suddenly and confronted Damien.

"You wouldn't happen to recall where the audience members were sitting, would you?"

"No...no," said Damien, startled.

"Hmmm." Ransom stared out at the chairs as if he could conjure up the audience by sheer force of will, then turned back to Damien. "And through there?" He motioned to the area on the opposite side of the theater from the lobby, what would be the back of the store.

"That's backstage, what there is of it. Everyone in our plays had to exit, stage left," said Damien in a failed attempt at joviality.

The backstage area was separated from the theater by flat bedsheets that had been dyed black and strung from ceiling to floor from one wall to the other so that they bordered both the stage and the audience. Ransom pulled aside the ersatz curtain and stepped backstage, closely followed by Gerald. Damien stood in the opening, holding the curtain back.

One thing was certain, the actors had not lied about the backstage area. The close proximity of the actors to the audience and the thin sheets separating them would have made it impossible for anyone to speak backstage without being heard in the audience. The space was smaller than Ransom had pictured it, and it was difficult to imagine that ten people had successfully managed to do anything there, let alone change costumes, makeup, and so on. A small, filthy bathroom no bigger than a broom closet was located just inside the back door. The bathroom consisted of a toilet that he would have been loathe to use, a sink smeared with dirt and makeup, and a bare bulb hanging from the ceiling that made the whole thing look dingy and glaring at the same time. Ransom switched off the light just as Gail's voice was heard in the theater.

"Are you here?" she called as she walked through the lobby. She stopped when she saw Damien holding open the curtain. They stared at each other, but neither spoke.

"We're here," said Ransom, stepping past Damien. Gerald followed him and Damien let go of the curtain.

"Thanks for coming," said Ransom graciously.

"I'm sorry I'm late," she said nervously, averting her eyes from Damien. "A call came in just as I was about to leave and I had to take it. It was for my boss and I had to take a very long message for him."

"That's quite all right," said Ransom, taking her arm lightly and leading her to center stage. "There was one thing Mr. Liddle wasn't able to help us with. Maybe you can."

"I'll...I'll try."

Standing behind her, he turned her toward the audience and rested his hands on her shoulders. Damien watched the detective curiously, and Gerald stood off to the side watching, his notebook poised.

"Do you think you can remember where everyone was sitting?" Ransom said rather quietly over her left shoulder. Gail closed her eyes for a moment as if trying to remember, then opened them again, and pointed to the left end of the second row. As she continued, she pointed to each member's seat in succession.

"There was a man about middle age sitting over there. The young woman was sitting there, in the middle of the same row. Two old ladies were sitting at the right end of...the third row. And there was a couple sitting behind them a little to the left."

"And Eric Sands?"

"He was...sitting in the last row, I think."

"Thank you. Thank you very much." Gail's shoulders relaxed.

He continued to look at the empty seats. Gail wandered away in her usual nondescript manner, stopping at the edge of the first row.

Ransom addressed the assembly in the tone of an instructor speaking to a rather dense class. "All of these people are now dead...except one."

There was a shocked silence. Gail looked dumbfounded, her face drained of color.

"Even..." Gail started anxiously, then glanced at Damien. "Even Eric?"

Ransom studied her face carefully. "We haven't been able to speak to him yet."

Gail looked away, concerned. Damien's expression didn't change.

"Do you have any idea who did it?" he asked.

"At the moment? I have ideas, yes. I think it's only a matter of time. You see, we were very fortunate in that there was a very sharp old lady in the audience that night—Emily Charters. The only audience member we know to be alive. She is an amazing woman. She saw everything."

Gail stared at him blankly, Damien said nothing.

"It's really rather ironic," Ransom continued. "Whoever has been killing your audience was *fairly* clever, but not clever enough. The killer has been outsmarted by an old lady."

"How so?" asked Damien with a quick smile.

"Well, because we wouldn't have connected the murders to each other or to the theater without her help. The killer apparently underestimated the old girl—didn't think she'd be a problem. After all, she hasn't been killed yet. Either that, or the killer simply wasn't clever enough to find out who she was. Her name, you see, wasn't on the answering machine that was so conveniently stolen from your theater."

Gail looked as if she was going to be ill.

"The funny thing is, here's this little old lady, whom the killer hasn't given a second thought to—but she's smart, she's observant, she's got a good memory—and she reads the papers. She saw pictures of the murder victims in the paper, put the whole thing together, walked into my office, and gave it to me on a silver platter. She's made the killer look like a fool!"

He paused dramatically, letting the words hang in the silence for effect, then moved away from center stage. He stopped beside Gail and said quietly over his shoulder, "It would be best if the two of you remained available for questioning."

He motioned to Gerald to follow him, and the detective left the two suspects in silence. Damien glanced at Gail, who averted her eyes. She walked out of the theater without saying a word, leaving Damien alone.

LATE MONDAY NIGHT dozens of deepening shadows played across the lawn beneath the marred oak tree with its off-center bird feeder: shadows of solid things standing or swaying in the waning moonlight. One shadow stood alone by the tree, a lone mass in a field of reflection. This shadow stood gazing up at the second-floor window of the gray wood-frame house, where the final light had been extinguished some twenty minutes earlier. It wavered on the lawn, experiencing an indecision that was by now uncommon to it. The Shadow's ego was such that it didn't believe it could be fooled or tricked. It didn't believe it could be outsmarted. And yet...it *had* been outsmarted already—by the occupant of the room above. The other crimes had been discovered. What if this were a final attempt to outsmart this wavering Shadow? What if it were a trap? It was a thought that could not be dismissed.

At the same time, the task was now set, there was really no choice. There was only this one person who could tie the elusive Shadow to the crimes, and that danger must be disposed of, whatever the risk might be. There was no choice, or was there? The Shadow trembled, half in fear and half in anger.

The Shadow stepped away from the tree but quickly darted back to its shelter. Why the hesitation? Oh Lord, there are so many strands...the whole thing is slipping away from me. The Shadow leaned back against the tree and closed its eyes, conjuring up visions of other grisly tasks it had performed. It called to mind the elation it had felt as it wrested the life from its other victims—and it recalled the feeling of power it had realized, knowing that life and death, who should live or die, was in his hands. It was successful, unstoppable. It couldn't be caught. No, not outsmarted yet. The Shadow held within itself the necessary power and skill to eliminate this last problem.

With a cool resolve, the Shadow swept across the lawn to the rear of the house, pulling from its dark pockets two sharp metal objects that it inserted into the keyhole of the back door. The Shadow worked quickly, having by now become accustomed to this form of entry, and opened the lock and door, passing through the door with an alacrity that would have been startling in anything but a shadow.

The Shadow paused in the kitchen, just long enough to allow itself to adjust to the darkness. This shadow did not fade without the moonlight to give it substance. It paused and listened for sounds of movement more closely than it had ever listened before. The silence of the house seemed to crackle in its ears.

Hearing nothing, she shadow glided quietly down the hallway, stopping at the foot of the stairs. It was unnecessary at this point for the Shadow to screw up its courage to proceed, the deeds it had already performed making this night's task second nature.

The Shadow slid silently up the staircase, watching and listening intently. At the top of the staircase, it paused. Directly ahead was a bedroom, its door standing open. Inside the room, in full view, was the old lady, sleeping, bathed in shadow.

The watching Shadow continued on its path into the bedroom: a remorseless entity, bent on its own end, not to be turned aside. The shadows mingled and danced on the bed. The one solid Shadow gently lifted the old lady's head and slid the pillow out from beneath it. It lifted the pillow in its shadowy hand, and pressed it down on the old lady's face.

Suddenly, all shadows were obliterated by the glare of a ceiling light. All of the shadows but the one that held the pillow, its now clearly visible features distorted with shock and hatred.

"Good evening, Mr. Liddle," said Ransom, who was

standing to the left of the open door, his left hand still on the light switch, his right hand holding a gun.

Damien stood frozen in place, still poised over Emily, his face more than a study in shock and terror.

"No! No! You can't!" he screamed.

Gerald appeared from behind the bedroom door with a pair of handcuffs and pulled Damien away from the bed, handing the pillow to Emily. He pulled Damien's hands behind his back and cuffed them.

"Are you all right, Emily?" said Ransom, approaching the foot of the bed.

"Yes, yes!" Emily sputtered. She looked a trifle dazed but unharmed.

The sound of her voice seemed to waken in Damien a full realization of his situation. He wheeled around upon her and tried to pull away from Gerald, his face seething with rage.

"Bitch! You bitch! You bitch! You've ruined me!"

Ransom, a personally nonviolent man, could not stand idly by during the verbal assault of this distinguished old woman. He took one strong swing at Liddle, his fist connecting with Damien's face with a loud snap that indicated he'd broken his nose. The force of the blow hurled the actor back against a closet door, and he then sank to his knees, sobbing.

Emily looked up at Ransom, her dusty eyes so wide that the pupils seemed to be floating in a white sea. He was shaking his hand to relieve the pain of the blow.

"I can't say that was entirely necessary," she said, "but I do appreciate the gesture."

EPILOGUE

EMILY TOOK A sip of her tea, smiled at Ransom, and wordlessly offered him another cookie, pushing the plate across the table to him.

"You are a very brave woman."

Emily coughed lightly into her hand as her cheeks turned a bright pink. "Thank you. But it's rather easy to be brave when flanked by two able detectives."

Ransom sat back on the kitchen chair, its metal legs creaking slightly under the shifted weight. The kitchen was so bright and cheerful this morning, it was hard to believe that any unpleasantness had ever taken place here, let alone that barely two nights ago the lady of the house had been stalked by a murderer.

"How did you know he was the killer?" asked Emily with polite curiosity.

Ransom, although fully aware of his powers as a detective, was also fairly honest about his own accomplishments.

"I didn't exactly *know*," he said, setting his cup down to give her his full attention while explaining. "Once it was established that the audience was being killed off..."

"I told you that right from the start," she said with a smile.

He blushed and rephrased, contritely, "When we *accepted* that the audience was being killed off, we naturally suspected that for whatever reason it was either Damien Liddle or Gail Shelly, since they were the only ones that came in contact with the audience. They were also the only ones that had had access to the names of most of the audience. Of course, Liddle had the presence of mind to fake a break-in at the theater and steal the phone-answering machine, so that if the murders were ever traced to the theater, it would look as if someone from outside had broken in to get the names of the audience. He was counting on many things—like, for example, that if we ever traced one of the murders to the theater, we wouldn't be able to locate the rest of the audience members. But Gail was too sharp: She always secretly copied down the names of the audience immediately upon listening to the tape."

"Why would she do a thing like that?"

"She was building a mailing list for the theater as a gift for Damien."

"Funny gift."

"I assure you, she is not a funny girl," he said ruefully. "She is very sad."

He took a sip of tea before continuing. "Anyway, both of them had access to the names, and both of them were lying about that night, so we didn't know which one had done it."

"But why was he killing the audience?" Emily asked, setting her cup down in its saucer emphatically. Her tone suggested the demand for an answer not simply because she'd been involved, but because she very much wanted to get a difficult situation straight in her mind.

"As we thought, he was killing you off because of what you'd seen."

"But I didn't see anything."

"But you *did*," he said with a hint of pride in his voice betraying a certain admiration for her powers of observation. "You saw Eric Sands. Worse yet, you saw him arguing with Damien. Once we found he had been murdered, we knew for certain that one of the two of them was the murderer. We, of course, thought it was passion, because both of them had a motive of sorts for killing Sands out of passion: Damien because they were former lovers, and Gail because she was infatuated with Damien and had discovered his sexual proclivities. We thought maybe she'd decided to kill his lover. As it turned out, it was money after all—or maybe both money and passion, I'm not sure. It's funny, there was a bit from Dickens that kept going through my head: I read it in *Bleak House* the other night and didn't understand its importance. I do now."

He stopped and took a sip of his tea. Emily pulled the plate of cookies back to her side of the table and selected a butter cookie with a solitary chocolate deep in the middle to nibble as Ransom continued his story.

"In *Bleak House*, Lady Dedlock had been sexually indiscreet," he said, choosing his words carefully so as not to offend Emily, "and the result was a daughter whose mere existence was a constant danger to her."

"Yes?" said Emily eagerly.

"Damien Liddle had also been sexually indiscreet. He had a long-term relationship with Eric Sands, who was proving to be a constant danger to him. Mr. Sands had threatened him."

Emily looked quite perplexed. "With what?"

"As you know, Mr. Liddle was on the brink of 'making it' as they say in show business. Possible stardom. Certainly money. From what Mr. Liddle has now admitted to us, Eric Sands tried to extort money from him. Sands was a greedy, grasping sort of person who couldn't hold a job and lived off the kindness of strangers, as the saying goes. You heard him mention money to Liddle on the fateful night. It wasn't a loan, it was blackmail."

"He had to have something to threaten Mr. Liddle with, then."

"He did. Himself."

"What?" she asked, her eyebrows raised.

"Sands was quite clever. He told Damien that if he didn't start paying him off the moment he started making big money, he would tell the world about Damien's sexual preferences."

"But what possible difference could that make? Rumors of that sort of thing come out of Hollywood all the time."

"That's what I thought at first," said Ransom thoughtfully, staring down at his teacup. "But Eric threatened him with more than rumors. The night of the performance he cornered Liddle and said the one word that could strike fear into his heart."

"What was that?"

"Palimony. Liddle had made no secret of the fact that he thought he was about to make it big, and although he professed an undying love for Shakespeare, I think he had quite a taste for money. But Eric threatened to ruin him if he didn't start regular payments the moment he started making big money—not by rumors, but by naming him in a palimony suit."

"Oh dear," said Emily softly.

"And he would have been able to prove it, too. Everyone at the theater knew about the two of them—apparently even Gail. You know, I almost felt sorry for Liddle when he told us about it. He was really just starting out and could already see his career crumbling at his feet."

"It's very difficult for me to feel sorry for him after he has murdered so many people."

"Yes, I suppose so," said Ransom, sitting up straight and clearing his throat. "Anyway, Liddle, afraid that the audience would overhear them, got Sands to leave the theater by promising to go to his apartment after the show and talk to him. I don't think he planned to kill him, I think he really believed that he could reason with Sands—by way of his superior intelligence—and make Sands realize that his plan was futile. But the opposite was the case.

"Sands taunted him, pointing out how handsome Liddle is (a fact of which Liddle seems greatly aware) and that he was only fit for romantic leads. Sands asked him how many parts he thought he'd get when everyone knew the truth. How many people could stomach seeing him play opposite beautiful women. Liddle quoted Sands as saying, 'You'll be laughed off the screen.'"

"He doesn't sound like a very pleasant person," said Emily, clucking her tongue.

"It was at this point that Liddle lost himself. He knew it was true: Rumors he could withstand—they all do—but a palimony suit would destroy his career. Even in this day and age, he knew the public would never accept him once it happened." Ransom paused for a moment as the memory of the amused deprecation in his partner's voice when discussing male couples, and the sneering reference Lorrie Reed had made about Damien's sexuality flashed through his mind. "It remains a sad fact in this country that one's sexuality can still be subject to blackmail.

"Anyway, he completely lost control and grabbed the nearest thing at hand—a lamp—and bludgeoned Eric to death. When he realized what he'd done, he was terrified—he knew the murder would eventually be discovered, and he was afraid that once that happened, you—the people in the audience, that is—might possibly read about it or see Sands's picture in the paper or on the news and remember that you'd seen them arguing at the theater.

So he set off to kill you one by one, hoping that by the time Eric's body was discovered, everyone that could connect the two of them on the night would be dead, and he would be safely in Los Angeles, not having run away from town, but having simply left on schedule. Sands doesn't seem to have been exactly the nicest character in the world—many other people might have had reason to kill him. Liddle did have the presence of mind to kill each audience member in a different manner so that the murders might not be connected."

"Why didn't he simply leave after killing Mr. Sands?"

Ransom sighed thoughtfully. "It's hard to say. I think it was a combination of panic and pride. In his panic, I don't think he realized how difficult it would be to pin Sands's murder on him; in his pride, I think he believed himself clever enough to eliminate all the potential witnesses without any trouble. What he hadn't counted on was you." That same hint of pride for her crept back into his voice.

"He didn't know who I was," said Emily proudly, sounding as if she meant that the actor didn't know who he was dealing with rather than that he simply didn't know her name.

Ransom hated to deflate her, but he couldn't resist the further explanation. He did, however, have the grace to blush as he said it: "I suspect he thought—because of your age—that even if he couldn't discover your identity, you wouldn't pose a threat. Possibly he thought you'd never put any of it together."

"Well," she said with a trace of haughtiness, "that will teach him." She took a sip of her tea as if to punctuate her sentence. Ransom suppressed a laugh but couldn't suppress the broad smile that swept across his face as he watched her.

"Oh!" she said suddenly. "There's one thing I don't understand. Why did the girl—Gail Shelly—why did she lie about having been in the lobby during intermission?"

Ransom set down his now-empty tea cup, a cloud passing across his face.

"Ah...poor, sad Gail. As it turns out, she was always in the lobby during intermission. She had so hopelessly fallen for Liddle—I don't think he led her on at all, I think she'd built it up in her mind—that she was near him whenever possible. Her pretense was that she helped with the coffee when the audience was large, which it never was. And she lied about it because she's one of those poor, desperate creatures—she didn't want anyone to know how attracted to him she was. The awful thing is that, as always happens, *everybody* knew. It was the big joke around the theater."

Emily set her cup down, shaking her head. "Loneliness is a terrible thing."

"It may be fortunate for her in this case that she was so insignificant. If Liddle had noticed her that night—if he'd seen her come into the lobby—she would be dead now."

They sat silently for a moment, reflecting. The stillness of the house on this mild morning was only interrupted occasionally by the sounds of children playing on the sidewalks out front. Emily sighed.

"You know, it's all a great shame."

"Yes, none of these people should be dead."

"Oh, I didn't mean that!"

He looked at her quizzically.

"I mean we should have suspected Mr. Liddle much earlier. It's clear he didn't know Shakespeare at all, otherwise he'd never had gotten himself into this mess."

"How do you mean?"

"Just that he should have known right from the start that he couldn't secure his future by killing people. It says right in *King John*, Act Four: 'There is no sure foundation set on blood, no certain life achieved by others' death.'"

She folded her hands and looked at him across the table, smiling with the knowledge that Shakespeare had bested Dickens, and that she'd had the last word.

And Ransom conceded.

MURDER & SULLIVAN

by Sara Hoskinson Frommer

A JOAN SPENCER MYSTERY

OPENING NIGHT IS MURDER

The town of Oliver, Indiana, is ready for opening night of Gilbert & Sullivan's *Ruddigore*. Joan Spencer, flexing her bow arm in the orchestra pit, doesn't see a thing. The victim, Judge David Putnam, was awaiting his cue, before he became too dead to hear it.

Who wanted the good judge dead? Local detective Fred Lundquist and his lady love, Joan, discover that the sparse trail has a surprise twist—with a vengeful killer waiting at the end.

Available at your favorite retail outlet in September 1998.

WORLDWIDE LIBRARY®

Look us up on-line at: http://www.romance.net

WSHF285

Looking For More Romance?

Visit Romance.net

Look us up on-line at: http://www.romance.net

Check in daily for these and other exciting features:

Hot off the press — View all current titles, and purchase them on-line.

What do the stars have in store for you?

Horoscope

Hot deals — Exclusive offers available only at Romance.net

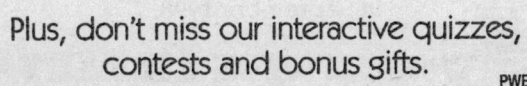

Plus, don't miss our interactive quizzes, contests and bonus gifts.

PWEB

September 1998
A Lieutenant Marian Larch Mystery

No Quarter

Four-year-old Bobby Galloway is a trophy, victim in a vicious child-custody battle made all the more savage because of the enormous wealth involved. The case moves from disturbing to deadly with a string of coldly casual murders.

The killer's brilliant insanity has rendered him nearly untouchable—until he violates Marian's world in a bold, obscene gambit that puts her skills as a police officer and her own inner strength to the ultimate test.

Don't miss

Full Frontal MURDER
by Barbara Paul

Available at your favorite retail outlet.

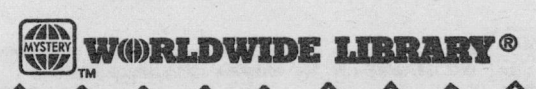

WORLDWIDE LIBRARY®

Look us up on-line at: http://www.romance.net

WBP284

In September 1998 watch for

BURIED IN STONE

by ERIC WRIGHT

Retired Toronto detective Mel Pickett is intrigued by the body discovered near his cabin in the woods. The corpse is that of a local lothario, and Larch River folks are busy guessing who might be the culprit: a jealous husband or a jilted lover.

Someone is arrested, but Mel, with instincts honed by years as a big-city cop, suspects there's more to the case than meets the eye. His probe reveals secrets buried in stone...and a clever, nearly perfect crime and a devious killer.

Available at your favorite retail outlet only from

WORLDWIDE LIBRARY®

Look us up on-line at: http://www.romance.net

WEW286

FREE BOOK OFFER!

Dear Reader,

Thank you for reading this Worldwide Mystery™ title! Please take a few moments to tell us about your reading preferences. When you have finished answering the survey, please mail it to the appropriate address listed below and we'll send you a free mystery novel as a token of our appreciation! Thank you for sharing your opinions!

1. How would you rate this particular mystery book?
   - 1.1 ❑ Excellent
   - .2 ❑ Good
   - .3 ❑ Satisfactory
   - .4 ❑ Fair
   - .5 ❑ Poor

2. Please indicate your satisfaction with The Mystery Library™ in terms of the editorial content we deliver to you every month:
   - 2.1 ❑ Very satisfied with editorial choice
   - .2 ❑ Somewhat satisfied with editorial choice
   - .3 ❑ Somewhat dissatisfied with editorial choice
   - .4 ❑ Very dissatisfied with editorial choice

   Comments _____
   _____(3, 8)

3. What are the most important elements of a mystery fiction book to you?

   _____
   _____(9, 14)

4. Which of the following types of mystery fiction do you enjoy reading? (check all that apply)
   - 15 ❑ American Cozy (e.g. Joan Hess)
   - 16 ❑ British Cozy (e.g. Jill Paton Walsh)
   - 17 ❑ Noire (e.g. James Ellroy, Loren D. Estleman)
   - 18 ❑ Hard-boiled (male or female private eye) (e.g. Robert Parker)
   - 19 ❑ American Police Procedural (e.g. Ed McBain)
   - 20 ❑ British Police Procedural (e.g. Ian Rankin, P. D. James)

5. Which of the following other types of paperback books have you read in the past 12 months? (check all that apply)
   - 21 ❑ Espionage/Spy (e.g. Tom Clancy, Robert Ludlum)
   - 22 ❑ Mainstream Contemporary Fiction (e.g. Patricia Cornwell)
   - 23 ❑ Occult/Horror (e.g. Stephen King, Anne Rice)
   - 24 ❑ Popular Women's Fiction (e.g. Danielle Steel, Nora Roberts)

WWWD98H1

25 ❏ Fantasy (e.g. Terry Brooks)
26 ❏ Science Fiction (e.g. Isaac Asimov)
27 ❏ Series Romance Fiction (e.g. Harlequin Romance®)
28 ❏ Action Adventure paperbacks (e.g. Mack Bolan)
29 ❏ Paperback Biographies
30 ❏ Paperback Humor
31 ❏ Self-help paperbacks

6. How do you usually obtain your mystery paperbacks? (check all that apply)

32 ❏ National chain bookstore (e.g. Waldenbooks, Borders)
33 ❏ Supermarket
34 ❏ General or discount merchandise store (e.g. Kmart, Target)
35 ❏ Specialty mystery bookstore
36 ❏ Borrow or trade with family members or friends
37 ❏ By mail
38 ❏ Secondhand bookstore
39 ❏ Library
40 ❏ Other _____ (41, 46)

7. How many mystery novels have you read in the past 6 months?

Paperback _____ (47, 48)   Hardcover _____ (49, 50)

8. Please indicate your gender:

51.1 ❏ female   .2 ❏ male

9. Into which of the following age groups do you fall?

52.1 ❏ Under 18 years   .4 ❏ 35 to 49 years
  .2 ❏ 18 to 24 years   .5 ❏ 50 to 64 years
  .3 ❏ 25 to 34 years   .6 ❏ 65 years or older

Thank you very much for your cooperation! To receive your free mystery novel, please print your name and address clearly and return the survey to the appropriate address listed below.

Name: _____

Address: _____ City: _____

State/Province: _____ Zip/Postal Code: _____

In U.S.: Worldwide Mystery Survey, 3010 Walden Avenue, P.O. Box 9057, Buffalo, NY 14269-9057
In Canada: Worldwide Mystery Survey, P.O. Box 622, Fort Erie, Ontario L2A 5X3